"Are you sure you want to take on another full-time job on top of the ranch? With a new baby?"

"That's the question, isn't it?"

"That's part of what brought me here, Halle."

She grabbed a napkin from the acrylic holder on the table and wiped her eyes, then blew her nose. Alastair made a note to order the finest linen handkerchiefs for her, with the Scottish thistle embroidered on them. Her hands were long, her fingers graceful. Would their child have her hands?

Her long, shuddering breath emphasized her ramrod-straight posture. He was certain she was made of steel. She rested her sharp whiskey eyes on him.

"Go on."

"Marry me, Halle. For the sake of our child, marry me."

* * *

The Coltons of Shadow Creek:
Only family can keep you safe...

THE BILLIONAIRE'S COLTON THREAT

BY
GERI KROTOW

First Published in Great Britain 2017
By Mills & Boon, an imprint of HarperCollins*Publishers*
1 London Bridge Street, London, SE1 9GF

© 2017 Harlequin Books S.A.

Special thanks and acknowledgement are given to Geri Krotow for her contribution to *The Coltons of Shadow Creek* series.

ISBN: 978-0-263-93050-4

18-1117

Former naval intelligence officer and US Naval Academy graduate **Geri Krotow** draws inspiration from the global situations she's experienced. Geri loves to hear from her readers. You can email her via her website and blog, www.gerikrotow.com.

To my fearless agent,
Emily Sylvan Kim—thank you
for your belief in me.

Chapter 1

Halle Ford allowed her gaze to soak in the hill country that surrounded her family ranch. She'd been fortunate to travel around the country and world, but her heart always remained in Shadow Creek, Texas. Bluewood Ranch appealed to her inner cowgirl more than her slick corporate CPA job in Austin ever had. She leaned on the fence and sipped her morning cup of coffee, relishing this private time, her version of meditation. The split cedar logs that circled the paddock were as familiar as her father's hug had been. As long as she didn't think about how much he'd spent on the fancy fencing before he'd died. An eastern spotted lizard was on the top of the fence, sunning himself in the late summer sunshine. "Hey, little guy." He ignored her, stretching his neck and displaying his brilliant green skin covered with flamboyant spots to his advantage.

Running her father's ranch had always been a far-off dream, but Chancellor Ford's sudden death in a horrific car crash six months ago had turned her dream into a nightmare. Besides facing the fact that Dad was gone forever, she'd had to come to terms with how he'd been killed. He'd been taken away by a hit-and-run driver, the same woman who'd terrorized Shadow Creek for decades until her imprisonment. Her terror had continued after her escape from prison and until her presumed death six months ago. Thanks to cop-bribing prison-escapee Livia Colton, Halle's life had been shattered and she had inherited Bluewood Ranch. At present, Bluewood wasn't faring well financially, much to her heartbreak. Even with her accounting and business acumen that she'd sharpened at that high-powered marketing firm in Austin, she'd been unable to bring the ranch back to life.

Yet. It had only been a little over six months, and the first six weeks or so after the accident didn't count as far as she was concerned. The shock of Daddy's death and her transition from an office career to running Bluewood had been tough. The move back to rugged, beautiful Shadow Creek from her well-appointed Austin condominium had been an adjustment in and of itself.

A soft whinny floated on the chilly morning breeze and she smiled as she recognized Elvis. The gelding was a gift from her dear friend Jade Colton. Jade ran Hill Country Farms, an off-track Thoroughbred rehab center. Jade had also sold Halle's mare Buttercup to her after Chancellor Ford's sudden death. Jade had known what a new horse would mean to Halle. Buttercup, along with Elvis and the other horses, had kept her from going over the edge after Daddy's death. *Murder* was more like it.

Not for the first time she wanted to hurl the blue stone-fired mug at one of the boulders that sat in the makeshift rock garden between the ranch house and paddock. To smash the ceramic into lethal shards, as her heart had been when evil Livia Colton had killed her father. Even after being apparently killed in a freak flash flood right after the accident, Livia still haunted Halle. She wasn't one for superstition but it was hard to remain practical in the face of such tragedy. More than once Halle wished she could bring Livia back from the dead so that she could confront the murderer. She had destroyed so many dreams in Shadow Creek.

The reminder that she wasn't the only one who'd had her life torn apart by Livia Colton was little consolation but it did shake her out of the pity party she was brewing. She needed to focus on what she could change and at the moment that meant getting new tours scheduled. Horseback riding classes and pony rides brought in steady income, but nothing increased Bluewood's revenue as quickly as the overnight tours. Halle loved showing her guests the best trails that wound through Texas Hill Country. Most of her groups were families, and as summer ended, kids were back in school. Her group tours dwindled, making her cash flow as spotty as her lizard buddy.

Her phone vibrated in her back pocket and she ignored it. The house phone was the main business line so she only answered her cell at her convenience. This was her rare quiet time in the day, the one part she kept sacred to herself unless she was on the trail with a ranch guest. After the vibration stopped, a second, shorter vibration informed her there was a voice mail.

"Dang it." She pulled out the phone and saw that the message was from Jeremy Kincaid, her neighbor and friend. Halle pressed the callback button. Jeremy picked up immediately.

"Good morning, Jeremy."

"Halle, how's it going?"

"Right now, out here next to the stables? Great."

Jeremy chuckled, low and deep. "That's why we live here, right? Hey, I'm sorry to bug you so early but I've got an offer for you."

"Okay." She straightened from the fence and turned around, leaning her back against it. It wasn't a secret that she was having trouble keeping Bluewood afloat, but Jeremy wasn't about to offer her a pity job, was he?

"Don't sound so grim. It's a good thing. I have a friend in town who's investing in the Austin tech scene, but he knows nothing about the area or Texas. I thought that if he booked a trail ride with you, it would be a perfect immersion experience for him."

Relief thrummed through her. Jeremy was offering her a new client!

"Of course. When is he thinking of coming to Bluewood? And do you have any idea how long he wants to stay?" She figured a full-day ride would be what a techie business friend of Jeremy Kincaid's would desire. Since Jeremy was a millionaire and famous in his field, chances were his friend would be successful, too. Longer than a day away from business would be unbearable to a type A techie, no matter how rich. And there wasn't Wi-Fi on the trail.

"That's the hitch. He'd like to start tomorrow, and he agreed to three nights, the better part of four days."

She put her mug of coffee on the fence post and the spotted lizard darted away. "Three nights? Is it just him?" She'd taken out individual clients before, but she made sure they were safe with an indiscreet background check courtesy of Shadow Creek's local PI, Adeline Kincaid, Jeremy's new wife. She wasn't sure one could be done on such short notice, but if anyone could do it for her, especially in these unusual circumstances, it would be Adeline.

"He's looking at a sizable investment in our area, maybe involving virtual reality. It's something Shadow Creek and Austin would benefit greatly from. Since we've been friends for so long, I suggested he immerse himself in the local culture and start with you."

Relief that Jeremy knew the man so well allowed for a glimmer of hope. "A four-day trail ride isn't going to tell him much about Austin."

"No, but he'll understand what makes a Texan tick. And I can vouch for him, Halle. He's safe, the real deal. You don't have to take an extra ranch hand with you." Jeremy must have heard the trepidation in her voice. And he knew that paying an extra man to go on the trail would hurt her bottom line.

"You're not playing matchmaker here, are you, Jeremy?" She kept her tone light.

"Well, you are both around the same age, and both single, but what you do with that is your business."

They both laughed. Halle had missed the easygoing friendships of the countryside. Austin was a friendly city, but it was still a city. She hadn't felt as much a part of a community as she did in Shadow Creek.

"There's one more thing, Halle." Jeremy sounded pleased, the way he did when he'd introduced Adeline as his wife. As if he'd discovered the secret to happiness and wanted to share it with the world.

"Go ahead."

"He's offered to pay extra for the late notice and one-on-one trail time." Jeremy named a figure that made Halle glad she'd put her coffee mug down or she would have spilled it.

"That's not necessary."

"Rule one of business, Halle, is to never undersell your product. Since your expertise and knowledge are the product, one could argue that a place on a Bluewood ride is priceless."

He was right. Of course he was—he was a millionaire. He hadn't earned his money because he didn't understand the basics of business. "Thanks, Jeremy. I'll expect him tomorrow morning. Better yet, have him call me before sundown so that I can figure out what his riding experience is."

"He's not going to have time to call, as we're heading into Austin for a full day of meetings. He says he's ridden on and off since he was a kid, and he's about my size, same age, so you can plan for the camp food and equipment."

"So he's never really been on a horse for longer than an hour or two at birthday parties."

Jeremy's pause confirmed her suspicions. "He'll take whatever direction you give him, Halle."

"Okay, that's all I need to know. He can sign the injury liability waiver when he shows up. And, Jeremy—thanks for this." She knew there were other trails and ranch businesses that catered to tourists and Jeremy probably knew all of them. He was doing her a huge favor.

"Hey, it's the neighborly thing to do. Besides, I wouldn't trust him with anyone else."

She wondered what he meant but wasn't going to pose any questions that could rock this lucrative boat. "I appreciate your confidence in me, Jeremy. Tell Adeline I said 'hi.'"

"Will do. She's packing right now or I'd put her on."

"Taking the family to Disney?" She knew Jeremy loved nothing more than spoiling Adeline and their child.

Jeremy chuckled. "No, but we are going out of the country for a much-needed break. You can always reach me on my cell phone, no matter where I am."

"Thanks." She didn't say it but she'd never bother them while they were on vacation, unless it was life or death.

"And by the way, Halle? Your guest's name is Alastair Buchanan. Adeline says to tell you he's safe." Jeremy ended the call.

Halle shoved the phone into her rear pocket, heat hitting her cheeks as she realized she hadn't asked the client's name. Jeremy knew her, so he didn't think she was careless, but she'd come off exactly how she never wanted to. Desperate. But if Adeline Kincaid said he was safe, he was. The Kincaids were a family of their word. And Adeline knew more than anyone the importance of personal security, after all she'd been through with the son she'd carried for Jeremy and his first wife, Tess, now deceased.

The sad memory of Tess's death, and the initial suspicion that Livia Colton had been involved, threatened to sabotage the good news Jeremy had just given her. Bluewood had a new client.

Halle grabbed her mug and rolled her shoulders back as she headed toward the ranch house. The best way for her to stop obsessing over her own tragic loss was work, and she had a three-day trail ride to prepare for. She'd be grateful for this, no matter her grief.

* * *

The next morning Halle sprang out of bed an hour before dawn, unable to sleep with the anticipation of a full four-day trail ride galloping through her mind all night. She took her time with her shower and watched the sky start to lighten as her coffee brewed. With a full, hot mug, she headed for the paddock fence to greet the day.

Leaning against it, she wondered if her father had done this, too, after her mother had died when she was a toddler. Soothed his broken heart with the beauty of a Texas sunrise.

"Good morning."

"Whoa!" Halle startled, spilling some of her coffee on her bare hand. She spun around from her morning meditation spot on the fence.

"Mr. Buchanan!" Her sole guest stood in front of her, dressed to ride in a combination of what she considered very high-end outdoor clothing and more practical items, like blue jeans. His height was impressive, as was his physical bearing. This wasn't a man tied to a desk all day, not with those broad shoulders that filled out his Western snap-front shirt and olive pullover. His tapered waist was that of a man with abs of steel, and a vision of her fingers touching said stomach made them tingle. He was the full package, but that wasn't what drew her, pulled her to look up into his eyes, brilliant flashes of the North Sea reflecting back at her. It was his essence. Alastair Buchanan had a spirit about him that intrigued her. It wasn't anything she could chalk up to his ability to afford the top-end cowboy boots or hat he wore with the ease of the financially sound.

The expensive accessories were nothing she'd afford for a long while. She'd donated all but two of her busi-

ness suits to the battered women's shelter in Austin, so
determined was she to make a go of the ranch and leave
her old life behind. Because the property was so deep in
debt she'd only been able to put together her newer clothing from the big box superstore nearest to Shadow Creek,
on the way to Austin. Would someone like Alastair Buchanan know from how she was dressed that she was
barely keeping her business afloat?

More important, why did she care?

"I wasn't expecting you for another hour." She struggled to shove down her self-consciousness.

"I'm sorry, I didn't mean to startle you." His Scottish
accent was at odds with their surroundings and yet he
looked comfortable as he watched her, one side of his
mouth lifted as if he was holding back a smile. As if he
belonged in Shadow Creek, fancy clothes excused. Her
quick internet search hadn't told her a lot, except that
Alastair was one of the most eligible bachelors in the
UK. He owned a whiskey business that had been in his
family for generations, and invested all over the globe
in other ventures. Clyde Whiskey remained its core, but
Clyde Whiskey had morphed into a global conglomerate, including tech. "I can sit on the porch until you're
ready to start the tour."

"We'll start in a bit." She sized him up but hoped
she came off as a caring hostess. Ready? Alastair Buchanan would find out soon enough how "ready" she,
and Bluewood, were. "Can I get you a cup of coffee, Mr.
Buchanan?"

"No, thanks, but I'd appreciate a cup of tea if you
have it."

"Sure thing. Follow me." She held her breath until he

fell in next to her. "I'm not used to my trail guests being ready to go so early."

"I've always been up with the sun." The words rolled from his mouth like music and she had to force herself to stop staring at his lips. Well-formed, sensual, male lips. And that voice—she hadn't realized how much she'd missed hearing that brogue until now. As a junior in college, she'd spent a year abroad in Scotland and loved every minute of it. But she hadn't met men like Alastair when she was at university.

What the heck was going on with her? Clearly she'd been holed up at Bluewood for too long, not seeing the usual bevy of attractive men she'd gotten used to at her job in Austin. She couldn't help her primal physical response to him or any man, but clients were out of bounds. She didn't go there. But if she could, Alastair would be a temptation.

"Getting up early will serve you well. We'll get to cover more land the sooner we're on the trail each day. And other than tonight, it's supposed to stay clear and dry."

"Rain isn't an issue for me. I'm from a land of rain." Alastair's lilt made her want to sit down and listen to him tell his life story. But this wasn't a pub in Edinburgh and he wasn't Robert Burns. He was her client; this trail ride was her job.

Get it together, girl.

"We'll get going as soon as we have our teatime." She opened the door to the ranch house and motioned for him to enter, shushing the barking Australian shepherd dogs. "Guests first. Don't worry about the pups—they think it's their job to herd ranch guests, but they don't bite." He looked a little put off at going in before her, underscoring his so far impeccable manners. He walked across the threshold and she caught a whiff of his soap. The sexy combination of sheets dried in the sun with Buchanan musk had to be some super expensive cologne, because no scent had ever made her skin tingle. She held back a groan as she watched his impeccably shaped ass in his jeans. This was going to be one heck of a ride.

Alastair shrugged out of his thin over-layer as he followed Halle Ford to her house. He appreciated the brief respite from her penetrating gaze and obvious appraisal of him. Normally he enjoyed the sexual tension of a female's assessment, but his blood had rushed so quickly to his dick he'd gotten flustered.

He, Alastair, the family rock who kept their business afloat and globe-trotted with the best of them, felt like an adolescent at Eton who'd snuck his first glance at a naked woman.

"Once I have the ranch fully up and operational, we'll have a full guest building with at least four or six rooms and a total of twelve bunks. For now, the guest room is the house. While you won't be staying here as we're heading out today, feel free to leave any luggage or extras you don't want to bother with on the trail." She glanced up at him and he was jolted by her no-holds-barred beauty. Unlike the women he was used to in Glasgow and even here since his arrival in Texas, Halle showed no signs of wearing makeup. She didn't need it, not with that peachy cream skin and blinding smile. Her dimples projected an innocence her body and expression were in direct conflict with. And her lips… *Hell.*

He fought to keep his erection at bay but it was futile.

His body was reacting to something beyond him, something intangible. The Halle effect.

"I didn't realize your business was new." He took off his cowboy hat and removed his boots, shadowing her movements as they entered the small house. Three herding dogs swarmed around them and he smiled.

"Sorry about the doggies." She offered a half grin.

"Are you kidding? I adore dogs." He crouched down and held his hands out for sniffing. It took a few minutes but eventually all three allowed him to scratch behind their ears.

"They don't usually warm up this quickly to strangers." At the hoarseness of her voice, he looked up. Were those tears in her liquid brown eyes?

Halle cleared her throat and motioned for him to stand. "Bathroom's on the right. I'll be in the kitchen making tea."

"Thank you." Alastair didn't really need to use the loo, but again found himself needing a bit of a buffer between Halle and himself. Or was it more that he needed space from the sexual awareness arcing between them? As certain as he was that it was mutual, he'd only just met the woman. So why did he feel as though he'd known her his entire life?

After she had another fortifying cup of coffee and made her Scottish client tea, she gathered what she'd packed last night for the ride and escorted Alastair Buchanan back outside, nearer the stables.

"Let me start over the right way, Mr. Buchanan. Welcome to Bluewood Ranch in Shadow Creek, Texas. We're an authentic cattle operation with two herds of cattle. A herd of cattle for our ranch is approximately one hundred steer and our product is longhorn steer." Halle smiled and opened her mouth to continue her usual opening remarks, words she shared with every tourist group she hosted on her ranch. With perfect timing, a bug flew into her mouth. Halle's throat squeezed into a spasm and she started to cough uncontrollably. She stomped the dirt in front of the broken corral fence and clutched a weathered post for balance as her body rejected the horsefly that had obviously been aiming for her tonsils. Alastair gracefully took her mug out of her hand, allowing her to cough more forcefully.

Her momentary hacking fit wouldn't have been so bad if she were addressing a group of local elementary school students, or tourists who simply wanted a taste of the Wild West by working a cattle drive. But her audience was none other than a tall, incredibly hot man whose left hand was bare. And he had a delicious Scottish brogue. Halle's love life had been dry for so long she might have thought any single man looked good, but this Scot in fancy cowboy clothes was looking mighty tasty to her.

Unlike the flavor of Texas dirt the fly put in her mouth.

"Excuse me." Halle held up her index finger, hoping her mascara wasn't smudged by her streaming tears.

Alastair didn't seem to notice that she was choking to death. In fact, the VIP whiskey billionaire for whom Jeremy requested she provide a "special" no-notice tour was decidedly bored.

"You can skip the touristy chitchat, Ms. Ford. Call me Alastair, and save the riding lesson, as well. Once you catch your breath, feel free to give me the basic overview of the land. Keep it simple. I'm not asking for anything more than you usually do." He flicked his North Sea–

blue gaze from her to the countryside, as if measuring her against the rugged backdrop. The outskirts of Austin, Texas—and Shadow Creek in particular—weren't noted for appearing anything but the wild countryside it was. In his quick glance she felt measured against her native surroundings. His stern stance made her feel as though she hadn't measured up to whatever his yardstick was. Did he think she was in over her head?

"If you're sure about ignoring the riding safety review..." She'd had him sign the appropriate paperwork. He couldn't sue her if he fell off his horse.

"Certain." His voice was sexy even when he was being a typical successful businessman—emotionally detached and certain his way was the only way. Halle had handled tourists of all ilk on her ranch and it took a lot to rattle her. Alastair Buchanan's know-it-all air shook her usually relaxed demeanor and it annoyed her. "Can we get moving, Ms. Ford?"

Well, all righty, then. "Sure thing. If you're Alastair, I'm Halle. You did say you're an experienced rider and camper, and you're a party of one, so I'll forgo the preliminaries. Are you interested in Central Texas history at all?"

The man had offered to pay five times her usual fee for a group of up to twelve people. All she had to do was promise it would be an exclusive, private tour. With the ranch's accounting books decidedly in the red this past quarter, she couldn't afford to not please her client. Her horses needed to eat. At his stiff silence, she belatedly added a smile to her query. "I was a history minor in college."

"History always interests me. I'm here to try to absorb the lay of the land, to get a feel for its appeal." His blue gaze steadied on her again with laser accuracy. His eyes had been the first things she'd noticed about him after his ruggedly tall frame. His mouth twisted. "I know I sound like an ass. I apologize. I've been distracted with business issues. Thank you for agreeing to take me on such short notice. Jeremy told me it was pure luck that you had the next few days open. And while I appreciate you rolling out the red carpet, the next seventy-two hours are my only chance to see the countryside surrounding Austin before I fly back to Glasgow. I hope I can put you at ease by assuring you that I'm adept on a horse and I've done my share of roughing it." He offered her a lopsided grin, which she much preferred. "And I've swallowed a mosquito or two myself."

Halle sucked down half the contents of her refillable water bottle, watching Alastair as she did so. She wanted to inform him that she wasn't merely a local bumpkin, that she'd in fact spent her junior year of college in Glasgow. But it wasn't her job to tell a client off. This was Jeremy and Adeline's friend, so ending the tour here and now was out of the question. And her overdue utility bills demanded she complete the job and get the paycheck. But while she'd play the gracious hostess as best she could, she didn't have to take Alastair's attitude. He was on her turf. This was Texas, and she was born and bred by one of the most outstanding Texans ever to live in these parts. Stinging tears tore at her already wet eyeballs at the reminder of her father. She drew in a shaky breath and steeled her spine.

"Excuse me, Alastair. We grow our bugs a bit bigger in Austin than you do in Glasgow. Same for our countryside—it's easy to think you know where you are, that you're on the path you started out on, and that you're safe. But the hills and desert can turn life threatening in a blink."

"I'm sure they can." Spoken like the wealthy man he was. Her internet search last night had yielded that Alastair had surpassed "wealthy" a decade ago. He was indeed one of the richest men in the UK. Halle didn't give an armadillo's ass. Rich or destitute, all men put their Wranglers on the same way. Although not all fit as well as Alastair's jeans.

Another reminder that since her father's death she'd been too busy to date, to contemplate being in a man's arms. The thrum that Alastair's good looks spiked in her core underscored her unwitting sexual fast.

"The best equipment in the world, the finest trail horse, the most proficient riding technique—none of them matter if you get lost in the desert, or stranded by a lame animal. It always boils down to wit and humility." She didn't mean to sound so bossy but something about the tall Scottish dude and his burr was making her crazy. He looked at her as if she was irking him, too.

"Got it." His gaze flickered to his mount. "And your best horses are these two? Won't we need a third for the camping gear?"

Heat rushed her face. "All of the horses at Bluewood are exceptional. I rotate the workload amongst them, and several are in need of a rest. Buster and Buttercup will serve us well. I've packed as lightly as possible, with enough for the two of us for four days and three nights. I always take a little extra in case of an unexpected event. I can guarantee you that we'll be hungry when we get back at the end of that last day, and we'll have a hearty meal here." Her other horses were having annual checkups while they were out. Even though her veterinarian gave her a huge discount, it was going to be another costly bill. She'd had the lousiest luck with the timing of ranch and animal maintenance expenses lately. As if someone or something was trying to tell her that she'd never get Bluewood Ranch up and running at a profit again. She shook off the shudder that raced down her spine. Superstitions were nonsense. Not something she was going to share with this billionaire bronco rider wannabe, though. "You'll have a great ride with Buster."

"How do you know these two won't fall ill?"

"They're perfectly healthy. My vet checked them over last week." She patted Buttercup's side and watched Alastair as he smoothed his large hand over Buster's spotted neck. The pinto was still a bit of a handful but Alastair had insisted on him over Buttercup. Elvis was behind her in the paddock, where Charlie, her ranch hand, had put him as she'd spoken to Alastair. While she would have loved to take Elvis today, he'd just finished up two daylong trail rides in a row. And Buttercup was in need of exercise.

"You're anxious to let off some steam, aren't you?" Alastair's brogue was low and sexy as he spoke to Buster. Something shifted in Halle's defenses. A man who cared about a horse he'd only just met couldn't be all bad.

He's a client. Nothing more. It was sad that she had to talk her hormones down from the ledge that would have her jumping on Alastair in an Austin minute.

Client. He's a client. It could be her new mantra.

"How long have you known Jeremy, Alastair?"

"Long enough to trust his business judgment. He says Austin is the new Silicon Valley—the place for tech."

"Yes, but you're smart to check out the rest of Austin." The *real* Austin, as far as she was concerned. Away from the congested city and ever-expanding suburbs.

"Am I?" His patronizing expression galled her. Again she wanted so badly to set him straight, tell him that she knew a hell of a lot more about the socio-economic status of a city in which she'd held down a high-level corporate job, but she shoved it down. With what she earned this trail ride, she might be able to pay off the remaining bills for the cedar rail fencing and the latest round of vet expenses.

"Well, then, let's get moving."

"After you." He took his cowboy hat off and used it to emphasize the sweep of his arm toward the start of the trail. A trail etched on Halle's heart long ago, worn smooth by rides with her father. She looked at the sky to confirm what she already knew—the weather wasn't on their side today.

"Thank you, Alastair. Normally I'd spend a little more time going over our itinerary with you before we set off, but with the cold front coming in I think it's best we get a move on. We want to pitch our camp ahead of the rain." She waved toward the thin silver line visible across the mostly flat parcels of land. Before they made camp the clouds would grow, the wind increase. Winter was coming in its usual, no-nonsense Texas manner.

"A gal after my own heart—I wouldn't mind making camp sooner, either, as I have some work to do. On my phone, of course."

"I can guarantee you there won't be any Wi-Fi where we're headed, and cellular signal strength isn't dependable."

"Ah, ye of little faith, Ms. Ford. I have magic in my pocket that will take care of that."

"Halle. Call me Halle." She choked on her words as she really, really wanted to add a playful comment about what exactly the sexy Scotsman had in his pocket but didn't want to risk that he'd think she was coming on to him. Or that her tourist business offered anything more than a foray into Texas Hill Country. She almost laughed out loud at the thought of her company becoming an escort service.

The morning sun cast long shadows of their figures upon the rolling hills outside the corral. Since Alastair said he knew how to ride, she'd given in to allowing him to ride Buster, her tallest horse by far at seventeen hands. She hated to admit it but his tall, lanky frame fit Buster's muscular structure perfectly. Alastair Buchanan looked like every woman's dream of a sexy, chiseled cowboy.

Not *her* dream, of course. She didn't care whether her client was attractive or not.

"Jeremy mentioned you're here to scout out Austin. Are you planning to start a business here?"

"Yeah. Maybe. Something like that."

She hadn't meant to sound nosy. "What kind of horse do you ride in Scotland?"

"A big one."

Halle couldn't help the glare she knew she shot him when she glanced his way. The crinkles around his eyes made her want to dig her heels into her mount and take off for the hills—the hell with impressing Jeremy's important friend.

Alastair let out a short laugh. "I'm sorry, Halle, but you're so serious. I understand that you probably deal with a lot of beginner riders out here as well as wilderness newbies. I'm not that person. I meant it when I told you that I'm interested in seeing as much of the countryside as three days allow me to. There's no need to put on your regular show for me, or to be so polite with the cocktail banter. Please, can we be a bit less formal?"

"Sure. For the record, though? I don't put on a 'show.' What you see is what you get. I'm interested in anyone who's thinking of adding to our area. I love this land and make no apologies for it."

"I'd expect no less." There he was again, being all polite and sensible, almost gallant. She snorted. Alastair's voice might sound like she imagined a knight's would have five centuries ago, but he had very modern sensibilities. Billionaire instincts.

They rode for a few minutes, silent save for the creak of their saddles. Alastair kept looking at his cell phone, which he'd rested on the front of his saddle in some kind of contraption that she'd seen a few clients bring along. She'd required them to put their phones away, for safety. But since Alastair claimed he was an expert rider, she said nothing. If he ended up on his butt because he missed a rough spot in the trail, so be it. As long as he didn't injure her horse. Or blame her for the fall.

Halle cleared her throat. "So what do you want to know about Austin?"

He switched off his screen and she found herself the sole object of his attention. It was at once intimidating and stimulating. "What brought you here, Halle? To Bluewood, Shadow Creek?"

"That has nothing to do with your exploration of the area, Alastair."

"It does. You're young and can manage a ranch. Why not use your talents in another business, something more lucrative?" So he had noticed the worn-down ranch, her inexpensive riding gear.

"I grew up on this ranch. The only time I left was for college, after which I worked for several years in the city. I returned here to run the ranch for personal reasons."

"What did you do in the city?"

She paused. Alastair was a client, period. She owed him no explanation for who she was, why she was doing this. Working the ranch that had been her father's heartbeat.

"I'm a CPA. Corporate business." She looked at her interrogator. "If it's all right with you, since you're an experienced horseman, I'm going to take the lead. The horses will appreciate a good workout."

"Lead on." Again, the gentlemanly nod. It would look ridiculous if it were any other man doing it, but Alastair Buchanan didn't strike her as any other man.

Alastair didn't mind the rear view he had of his fearless tour guide as he and Halle trotted, galloped and strode over mile upon mile of rough, Central Texas ranch land. It seemed he didn't mind any view he'd had of her since they'd met. How was it that this woman, a complete stranger to him before this morning, was absorbing all of his attention? He was single and enjoyed dating as much as he could while running the family whiskey and investment business. This had to be a result of knowing he was going to be alone with her for several days, with no interruption. He trusted Jeremy implicitly—his friend wouldn't steer him wrong as far as suggesting he get to know more about the Texas countryside with Halle. And Jeremy had encouraged him to flirt with her.

It wasn't Jeremy's fault that Alastair had fought against his boner since meeting Halle.

Telling himself to get a grip, Alastair forced himself

to concentrate on the countryside instead of Halle's ass. If only for a minute. Or thirty seconds.

It was different from any other kind he'd seen before. Flatter and far less green than his family properties in Scotland, but stunning in its plain ruggedness. And the unexpected copses of trees in Texas—they were unique, as were the several creeks and rivers they'd rode around and through all day. The sun was warm and the breeze almost crisp. He had a hard time believing it was due to storm anytime soon, as the skies were bluer than Loch Ness in September. Save for the line of clouds at the very edge of the northwestern horizon. He already felt connected to this land, something he didn't experience with every business deal, to be sure. Alastair enjoyed travel and prided himself on learning about local cultures wherever Clyde Whiskey had interests. But Texas already felt far more important, far more significant to him than a place to invest in tech. His gut told him his fearless tour guide might have something to do with it, but it wasn't just about sexual attraction.

Used to trusting his intuition in business, he was thrown off balance by how strongly he felt about Halle and Texas. It was more than a good hunch; it was more like a soul moment.

The jet lag must have caught up to him. He'd faired fine over his first week, but now, in the Texas wilds, his circadian rhythm was doing a quick two-step.

"Let's stop over there for lunch." He heard her suggestion with great relief. Food, that was what he needed. Sustenance. Halle's profile was partially hidden under her cowboy hat as she spoke over her shoulder. He tore his gaze from her body, a body that filled out weathered blue jeans in a way that made it easy for him to imagine her naked. Halle sat in the leather saddle as if it were a part of her. He reluctantly looked at the trees she pointed to.

"Looks like the perfect spot." He guided Buster to the shady area under several willows. They dismounted and he followed Halle and Buttercup. In the few short hours they'd been riding, he learned that in Texas, where there were trees, there'd be some water nearby. Unlike his native Scotland, where lochs and rivers were liable to spring up without any surrounding forest. Sure enough, a small creek gurgled just past the slight rise of mossy ground, beyond the willows.

"We'll let them get their fill first." Halle's voice was quiet, almost contemplative. Alastair stood next to her, their horses providing a sense of privacy on either side.

"It's amazing how a ride in which your animal does most of the work has the same effect as several hours in the gym."

Her sharp amber gaze raked his face as if surprised. "Yes. When I lived downtown, I belonged to a gym and hated it."

"You prefer the outdoors?"

Her eyes widened and he wanted to check himself. Why did everything he said to her sound like a cheap come-on?

"I don't mind a fun class with lots of loud music, but when the day's done, I'm most at home here." Her guard was back up. What made her so wary, so suspicious?

"Do you ever feel threatened out here? With your clients?"

"I have Adeline run a background check whenever I get a request for a private tour. As for you? I trust Jeremy and Adeline. The Kincaids are good people. They

wouldn't send me anyone who I needed to be afraid of."
Her tongue flicked out and licked her lip right before
she bit into the plump skin. Instant erection. Holy hell,
what was he, a teenager? He tried to recall his most recent dates. He'd only left Scotland a little over a week
ago. That meant he'd been away from a woman's company for what, ten days, a fortnight? Not enough to be
losing his cool in front of a sexy Texas babe.

"Er, no, I'm certain they wouldn't, either. About where
we're spending the night—will there be a shelter of some
sort?"

Halle snorted. "I've brought two quick-setup tents, one
for each of us. This isn't the Appalachian Trail, Alastair.
We don't have lean-tos out here, if that's what you're
getting at."

"I assure you I can manage. And I'd prefer to sleep
under the stars sans any tent or structure. I asked about
the shelter to offer it to you." And to see if they'd be alone
the entire four days. He was finding he rather enjoyed
the prospect of alone time with Halle Ford.

Save for his work. It seemed he was never without
work, never had a break from worrying about his investments. Hiking in the wilderness had always been his
way to let go of his responsibilities. He'd camped often
as a boy, and enjoyed it through university. When Jeremy had suggested he do this with Halle, Alastair had
relished the idea of sleeping on the ground again. What
he hadn't anticipated was such an attractive companion.
He'd mistakenly thought he'd regret that anyone was with
him, as Alastair's solitude was his most precious pos-
session. Somehow, Halle didn't intrude on that for him.

"I'm sure you're quite the camper, from what you've
said." Her tone indicated she didn't believe it in the least.

"Before you judge me, I have to tell you that there are some business items I still have to take care of, even out here. Is this a good time for me to send off a few emails?"

"Suit yourself."

He walked to the far side of the shady area and pulled his phone off his saddle. He felt guilty, as if he were infringing on the serenity of their surroundings, on the delightful companionship he was finding with Halle. His gut kept tugging at him, telling him that for some inexplicable reason his time with Halle Ford was precious.

He sighed and started to take care of business. The sooner he was done, the sooner he'd be able to fully enjoy Halle's company.

More than for calls or texts, his phone was a mini-satellite reception tower, all in one unit that fit in his pocket. Being a billionaire had its perks, one of which included solid Wi-Fi in the middle of Nowhere, Texas. He'd lied to Halle, too. He wasn't checking email—he was checking the London Exchange, and the New York Stock Exchange. One thing that he'd inherited from the long line of Buchanan men who'd turned a farm distillery into a single malt Scotch global empire was his killer business instinct.

And right now, someone was trying to kill his life's work, his legacy. Someone, either an entity or group of investors, was attempting a hostile takeover of Clyde Whiskey. It was strange, as it had popped up only since he'd arrived at Bluewood. He didn't have the solid proof yet to alert his team, but he knew it the same way he knew why his family's Scotch recipe was singularly the best of the best.

A crisp dry beating sound drew his gaze from his phone screen to the brush under his feet, next to the clay of the riverbank. He'd seen enough nature programs to recognize the copper-skinned reptile as a rattlesnake. It sported a black diamond pattern and was no farther than three feet from him. As thick as his wrist and coiled into a tight ball, its rattles shook inside the tail, indicating it was a highly agitated snake. He'd watched enough BBC nature programs to know that much.

Alastair also knew he had no defense against the deadly creature. He was rooted to the spot, afraid a sudden movement would force the snake to strike. No way would he be able to outrun its deadly speed, either. And if he got struck, he wouldn't be able to warn Halle. Was this how he and Halle were going to meet their end? In the backwoods of Texas?

An unstoppable wave of primal emotion propelled him to raise his arm and throw his phone at the snake. Before his phone made it airborne, the snake struck.

Chapter 2

"Back toward my voice, slowly." Alastair would feel like a damned fool if he wasn't certain he was near death. He held on to Halle's voice. The snake's head had hit the ground not two inches from the toes of his too-shiny, too-new cowboy boots as it had struck out at Alastair. The boots had seemed a more practical, if impulsive, buy when he was in Austin. He thanked God he was wearing them and not sneakers.

Halle's voice gave him courage, not something he usually drew on from others. Even with a close family, Alastair considered himself a loner. His strength came from within. Not now. Halle was his rock as he complied, moving backward until he bumped into her. To his visceral relief, the snake slithered back underneath the rock it had been sunning on before he'd disturbed it.

He turned and found Halle's eyes watching him, her

luscious lips curved in a small smile. "Was that your first rattlesnake?"

"Yes." But not the only threat out here in the Texas wilderness. Halle held a revolver in her hand. "Tell me, Halle. Do you always carry weapons on family trail rides?"

"Yes. For rattlesnakes and to warn off coyotes." He suspected it was also in case she ran into criminals.

"Have you ever had to use it against a human being?"

"Not yet, but there've been a few scrapes."

He was looking down at her, close enough to see that her eyes weren't brown or even amber but the perfect shade of Clyde Whiskey. Single malt, the premium drink that enjoyed worldwide acclaim. But her eyes were just the start of a beautiful face, her nose small and classical, her lips full and incredibly erotic.

"Thank you for saving me, Halle."

Her eyes looked at his mouth for a full heartbeat before she stepped away.

"You were fine. Rattlers don't strike unless they feel cornered. You startled him off his sunning spot, that's all. He would have backed off as long as you didn't go after him." Her speech was increasing in velocity. "Your boots helped, too—if he hit your leg you would have been safe. Although you wouldn't need thousand-dollar boots for that. And for the record, you would have never hit him with your phone."

"You really know how to make a man feel like John Wayne."

"It's all part of your special tour, Alastair. Are you hungry yet?" Her grin was genuine, a flash of inviting white. "We've got the best trail food in Texas. I cheated and used my two horseback coolers so that you could enjoy some real food out here. Of course, if you'd caught your friend, barbecued rattlesnake is tasty."

"Like chicken, I take it?"

She laughed. "You might just survive out here, after all. Let's eat."

She spoke as they walked to the horses, and put the gun away in one of her saddlebags. "Sliced Texas brisket or egg salad sandwich?" She pulled out a small bag and held up two wax-paper wrapped bundles.

"Beef."

They ate in relative silence, for which Alastair was grateful. He needed time to process what he'd just done for the first time in his life. He'd relied on someone other than himself or family to help him out of a life-threatening situation. Gratitude, sexual attraction and downright affection fought for first place in his heart as he took a full account of his feelings since he'd met her. Although a sexual relationship with Halle or any woman was never a sure thing, he knew one thing for certain. Halle made the best kind of friend. She was trustworthy and true to her word. Not boastful but sure of her capabilities and not afraid to use them, as she had been to scare the snake away.

Halle Ford was a woman that Alastair suspected would be difficult to say goodbye to, whether she ended up being his friend or lover.

What he'd really like best would be for her to be both.

Halle used the lunch break to get her imagination under control. Because it was a total nightmare to even contemplate a sexual rodeo with Alastair, but contemplate she had as she'd been up close and personal with him. When his hard body had backed away from the rattler and into hers, she couldn't help but wonder how all of that hard muscle would feel, naked under her hands.

Her unintentional vow of chastity to Bluewood was making her crazy. Maybe she needed to start dating again, once she had the ranch running at a profit, or enough of a cash flow for nicer groceries, anyway. Halle wasn't a food snob by any means but she enjoyed sushi and other less economical treats as much as the next millennial.

"You're worried about the rain. Is it supposed to flood?" His Adam's apple moved under his skin as he finished the last of his bottle of sparkling water. Halle noted that he hadn't spoken as he ate. More like wolfed down his meal—the man might be a gazillionaire but money didn't take away his basic makeup.

He was incredibly attractive. The man was a sex swizzle stick, for God's sake. Yet he didn't act like a jerk, didn't make a play for her. He treated her like a professional.

Which of course made him even more attractive. Not only for how the integrity that simmered underneath his all-business, all-the-time demeanor. He was a true gentleman in that he hadn't flung a crude come-on at her or tried to flirt with her in a creepy way. His good manners reminded her of her father's. Although she had to admit she'd love it if he decided to make any kind of romantic move. Client and all. She'd always enjoyed the challenge, the push and pull, the delicate balance of tension that surrounded a full flirtation. She was her father's daughter, for sure. Chancellor Ford had never backed away from any challenge.

White-hot anger seared her heart. Her father's life had ended horribly, in a car accident he'd had no warning was coming. He'd been murdered in cold blood by a hit-and-run driver, a woman Halle would never forgive. She had to physically shake her head to break free of the grief that threatened to swamp her.

"Halle? The rain—is it going to be that bad?" Alastair's concern was in the lines around his mouth, the intensity of his stare. The words were about weather but the subtext was clear. *Are you okay? Are you nuts or something?*

Halle wrapped her waxed paper and napkin into a ball. "*Worried* is a strong word. I'm concerned that we'll get caught in the downpour and get soaked. Hypothermia would be a quick end to our adventure."

"The rattlesnake could have ended it, too. And while I still hope that I can sleep directly under the stars tonight, I'll take you up on the spare tent if you think it's best. But only after we get yours set up, and you convince me you'll be safe. You're my trusted tour guide, after all. It wouldn't be prudent to have you hurt this early in the adventure."

Halle's heart warmed. It had to be a major concession for such a worldly man, even though he'd couched it as her decision, to sleep in the tent instead of under the stars directly. His manner of trying to disguise his concern for her as selfishness on his part was downright adorable. And sexy as all get-out.

"All of the riders I bring out here dream of sleeping under the stars, but I have to say that rattlesnakes and scorpions can ruin a perfectly good night's sleep. The tent is the easiest solution. We'll set them both up. You can see the stars best before sunup, anyhow. We'll have our coffee with the dawn."

Alastair laughed and with growing dread Halle realized it was a sound she could get used to. *Too fast, too deep.*

wouldn't want to meet our friend from earlier in
bedroll. Or make you have to shoot it in the middle
of the night."

"Trust me, if there's a snake in your bed, you're on
your own."

"Really?" The gray-blue gaze, the relaxed mouth,
the day's rough growth of stubble. Her face heated at
Alastair's innuendo. A normal reaction, but the heat that
entered farther down her belly and into her female core
went too far for her sense of professionalism.

"Since neither of us wants that, let's get going. We've
got a couple of hours till we're at the first night's campsite." She couldn't get astride Buttercup fast enough.

"You don't have to keep running away from me. Unlike the rattlesnakes and scorpions, I don't bite." He'd
maneuvered Buster up next to her and Buttercup with the
ease of a skilled horseman. She had to give him credit—
he may not appreciate just how brutal "roughing it" could
be in Texas, but he knew his way around a horse.

"I'm sorry to give you the impression that I'm avoiding you. I'm used to leading a dozen folks at a time,
many beginner riders. They usually like to be together
with someone they know, to keep their conversation easy.
Even when I take out single guests, I'm not used to making more than small talk on the trail."

"Our conversation can be easy. And I'll follow you
wherever you want to go."

Zing. Her attraction to him lit up like a Christmas tree.
The way it made her body feel was like a special gift.
She knew her face was flushed and hoped he couldn't see
her hardened nipples under her shirt. Because as much
as she loved Christmas and the live tree she continued
to cut down, drag in and set up each year in Bluewood

Ranch's modest living room, she didn't need her sexual desires on full display in front of a business client.

"You don't strike me as the easy-talking type, Alastair. You don't run a successful business like Clyde Whiskey without being very exacting."

"True, but that's work. Which I can't seem to get away from these days." He lifted his hat and let the breeze lift his short locks before replacing it. "It's never done, never secure. Not in the age of HFT."

"HFT?"

"High-frequency trading. Have you thought of investing your profits from the ranch into the market, when you're ready?" He was so sincere, so earnest in his concern for her financial well-being.

Halle couldn't have stopped the laugh if she'd wanted to. "I'm lucky to be able to invest in groceries at the end of a month."

Alastair's eyes filled with compassion. "Getting a business up and running is difficult, but continuing to successfully run one year after year can prove just as challenging, if not more so. We're two of a kind, Halle Ford. I suspect we both have a passion for our businesses, and that's why we do what we do. All the sacrifice. Tell me about your business, Halle."

To her surprise, she did.

Alastair kept his eyes on Halle the entire time she confided in him. He was so touched, so damn honored that she trusted him enough to tell him what she'd been through. His concern over her welfare spiked as he listened. Halle spoke as if the tragic death of her father, which she clearly blamed a dead woman named Livia Colton for, had happened in another family, not hers.

She was *too* detached. He wondered if she'd properly processed the ordeal, and worried for her when she did, when it would all hit her. He hoped he'd be around to help her through it, as ridiculous as it seemed on paper, since they'd known one another for such a short time. Alastair got Halle's dilemma—he knew what it meant to have to shove down pain that would otherwise choke the last gasp of joy out of him.

"I've gone through similar trials. We've almost lost our business half a dozen times over the past decade. It's so hard at times. If it weren't for my family and the fact that Clyde Whiskey is a family business, I'd have hung it up on more than one occasion." As he spoke he felt tremendous relief. As if he were the one unburdening to her. Maybe he was.

She nodded.

"It's important to me to keep Bluewood Ranch running. I know that the tourist business isn't going to keep it alive forever, but I haven't figured out what else I want to do, what would be financially feasible, for the ranch." She spoke with the weight of an executive CEO, which he found admirable, since Bluewood seemed like a relatively small operation. Halle took her responsibilities seriously, her experience with larger corporate concerns evident. It was another reason she was unlike any other person he'd ever known, and why he desperately wanted to know her better. So much better. Halle did nothing halfway. She was the epitome of "go big or go home."

"Have you thought about attracting outside investors?" He thought he'd asked it innocently enough, not mentioning Jeremy outright.

"A pity handout? Never. The big money around these parts is the Colton family and I will never take a penny from them. Even in the wrongful death of my father, I never sought restitution. The only payback would have been to put Livia Colton behind bars. Since she's dead, it's a moot point."

"Understood. But Jeremy's not a Colton."

"No, but he's my friend, as is Adeline. I don't want to mix friendship and business. Not when investing in the ranch is such a risk. For the moment." A cloud ran across the sky, putting them in shadow. Halle's face was guarded.

"And yet you allowed Jeremy to send me here. Is there something you aren't telling me about the risk at Bluewood?"

"No, not at all." She let out a soft sigh as she looked at the horizon. "I always planned to take over Bluewood from my dad. Looked forward to it. I knew that someday I'd be running it."

"But?"

"It's happened too quickly. I've had to learn my way around ranching and the tourism industry while still booking clients. I never feel as if I'm one hundred percent in either role—apprentice or ranch expert."

"Do you have any staff to help out?" He'd only noticed one ranch hand tending to the barn and stables before they set out.

Halle laughed. "No, that takes time and money." Neither of which she would have yet since her schedule was full taking people on tours like this one and pouring the revenue into repairs. "My full-time ranch hand, Charlie, hasn't had a raise in two years. He's loyal but he could decide today to move on and I'd have no recourse. And frankly, I wouldn't blame him. I hire other ranch hands as needed."

"I hear you on feeling as though you're never doing enough. It's part of being in business for yourself. That's what I've learned, anyhow. I give you credit, Halle. You're remarkable. I inherited a solid business and grew it. You're taking something with a lot of challenges and turning it around. I wish I had as much courage as you." He meant the words and could feel his heart beat with each one uttered. Halle had a way of forcing him to dig deeper, to find the best way possible to let her know how incredible she was. He'd been under his own work stress lately, but it didn't compare to Halle's. Except that they shared indefatigable work ethics. His work was never done, and with his current situation the anxiety of an unforeseen buyout made it so much worse. Nothing he could tell Halle, nothing he'd want anyone in Shadow Creek to know about, no matter how much he trusted them. Not yet. They'd know soon enough if he decided to not invest in tech in the Austin area. Because if he lacked the funds, he wouldn't invest or ask others to. Alastair might be a billionaire but to him his word was worth more than any commodity, cash included.

They pulled the horses up to a wide leg that offered a breathtaking view of the countryside below and in front of them. They sat in companionable silence as they watched the sun start its descent. Streaks of peach, apricot and purple hues soared over the Texas sky. Even Buttercup and Buster were still, as if showing reverence for nature's spectacle.

"Let's dismount and set up camp. We're over there, near the grove of willows." She nodded toward their night camp. Halle's eyes reflected the fiery shades of the beginning sunset. It didn't escape Alastair that if they'd met anywhere else in time, or on earth, they might be together tonight in the best of ways.

But Halle had made her boundaries clear. This was solely a business excursion. He understood and in fact admired her for her professionalism. Even if it meant losing out on an opportunity to explore the undeniable attraction that arced between them. How could he consider campsite extracurriculars with Halle when his entire livelihood could be at risk?

Chapter 3

The second day and evening went as the first. They spent the morning and afternoon meandering through the Texas countryside and the evening in front of the campfire sipping the wine Halle had brought. The first night Alastair had used the single-person tent Halle gave him and stayed dry under the brief rain showers they'd endured, but the next night he'd been granted his wish and slept under the stars. Nothing but an armadillo crossed near his bedroll, for which he was grateful. He'd had a hard time falling asleep, knowing Halle was in her own tent. He heard her soft rustles in her sleeping bag as she turned, imagined how warm and soft she'd feel against his body. Did she have as hard a time as he did in not crossing the unseen line between them? The hired tour guide—client line? He admired Halle's dedication to duty and obvious professionalism, but sincerely hoped she'd ease up and consider allowing them to fully enjoy each other's company.

By the third morning, Alastair expected he'd wake up ready to finish the journey. Instead, as he looked at Halle packing and loading up their horses, he felt a twinge of regret.

"Where to today?"

"Does it matter?" She faced him as they stood in between the horses. "You've had your head in your phone all morning. Is there some international news I need to be aware of?"

"No, nothing earth-shattering. And that's not completely true. I've checked in to see what I can do to help." More like he'd wanted to check on her, make sure she was safe. Aw, hell, he'd wanted to check her out, look at her up close, see if her body, her smile, still made him hard. And then he'd distracted himself with work, so that he didn't push her too far too soon. Even though they only had one more night and two days together. Even business, bad business—it appeared his stocks were being gobbled up again, and he had no idea by whom—wasn't enough to take his thoughts off Halle.

Halle grunted. Even that was sexy. "Don't ever play poker, Alastair."

He didn't answer her. He couldn't. Because as she spoke, he watched her expression and her body language, and realized they'd become ingrained in his memory. It wasn't just the close quarters or long days together. It was Halle.

No, it's you and Halle. He'd never felt so in tune with another person this early in a relationship before. And they weren't in a relationship—she considered herself his tour guide. Period. She'd made that clear more than once. And he hated it. He'd finally met a woman who made him come off the hamster wheel of his business and he wanted to enjoy her more than as his trail guide. Halle was one of a kind—a skilled horsewoman, intelligent business owner and a compassionate, loyal human being. He loved how she was so dedicated to her family, as small as it'd been, and how she'd given up everything she'd worked for to honor her father's legacy. How she accepted his legacy as her own without blinking. This was the kind of woman a man could take as a life partner. As a best friend. As a lover.

Yet he was only a client to her.

But he'd cease being a client once they were back at the ranch house tomorrow evening. Would she ever consider making an exception for him and let him take her out for dinner?

He snorted as hard as either of the horses. Dinner was the least of things he wanted from Halle. He suspected she knew it, too.

"What can I do to help you this last full day and night, Halle? I feel like I've been a bit of a lug, going along for the ride without doing any of the muscle work."

"That's what you've paid for. It's not a big deal to me. I've done this dozens upon dozens of times. You feel more relaxed than you did when you arrived, don't you?" Her head was cocked to the side, allowing him to see her creamy skin under the brim of her white cowboy hat. The stylish, top brand hat appeared to be her one concession to her femininity and perhaps her former corporate life. It accentuated her chestnut hair and highlighted the whiskey hue of her eyes.

"As long as I'm not looking at my stock portfolio, yes."

She laughed and swung up onto Buttercup. God, his

fingers itched to grasp her waist and spin her around, their bodies touching—

"Let's get a move on, cowboy. We've got a river to ford." Her lighthearted prompt shattered what would have become a very naughty cowboy daydream. Usually he'd think about a previous woman he'd dated when he was getting randy. Or the next one he'd ask out on a date. Alastair was an expert at fine dining, precious wine and pleasing the women he took to bed.

Halle was different. She was the kind of woman who put an end to a man's casual dating life. Because she would be the one he'd always compare anyone else to.

Halle had to ignore the lump in her throat. Being alone with any off-limits single man she was attracted to, day and night for four days, would have been difficult. Make it a male like Alastair Buchanan and it was downright excruciating to be so near yet unable to even pretend there could be any hanky-panky. And they still had one more night to get through. *Of course* her hormones were humming. At least that's what she told herself. It wasn't that he was special. A man she could sink her teeth into, have a real relationship with.

Besides, even if he wasn't a client, he lived the better part of five thousand miles away. She hadn't been able to maintain a romance with a man she'd been dating in Austin once she moved to Shadow Creek, only thirty miles apart.

"Not happening," she muttered to herself and Buttercup as they wound through a field of dead sunflowers on a narrow clay path.

"What was that?" Alastair's brogue was lovely, even

when he showed flashes of the vigilant CEO he must be to run such a lucrative business.

"I said we're getting closer to the fun part of the day." The low rumble they'd had in front of them for the past mile or so had turned into a loud roar. The river crossing was going to be interesting, but nothing she couldn't manage. She navigated the narrow trail, passed through a field and onto a rise with the river in sight, where she waited for Alastair to fall in next to her.

"That looks no wider than a creek. It's shallow, I take it?"

"Not sure, and make no mistake, this is a river. Shadow Creek River. With all the rain, it might be higher than usual. One thing about flowing water in the Western US is that it's very deceptive. I've waded in my bare feet through it when I was a kid, and ridden across it on several different horses. But each time it's different. I've had to turn around and come back before, when it was too deep or the current too strong."

"Our lochs, or lakes, as you say—" he put emphasis on the vowels in "lake" and "say," making them rhyme, "—are the same. They drop off with no warning to unfathomable depths."

"Well, you won't see Nessie here, but we have to take our time crossing." She hoped to relax him with the Loch Ness Monster reference. Halle wondered how much of a challenge the crossing would be but didn't see a need to alarm him about it.

"I'm game for whatever." The statement was bold and she thought his profile was a little stiff with arrogance.

"I know you're a good horseman, Alastair, but you have to trust my judgment about the river. It's not like a still loch in Scotland."

"And you know so much about lochs?" The sun caught the flash of his grin and her gut tightened. He was so damned handsome. Too much.

"Haven't I told you yet? I spent my junior year abroad in Glasgow. I traveled all over Scotland and the UK." It had felt like a second home and she'd always wanted to return. But then life after college had her deep into her career, and then her father's death, and now her life's work at Bluewood got in the way.

"I'd love for you to see Scotland now, as an adult, without the baggage of a student budget." His insight stilled her. It sounded as if he had a normal upbringing, not one of privilege.

"You sound as if you backpacked across Europe on a budget, too."

"I did, in a sense. My father was very strict with my spending until I graduated and became fully employed with the company. Sure, I knew I had a fallback if I needed it, but I kept my spending to what he gave me. It taught me how to budget and where to save money." He laughed and she loved the rolling sound. Easy and strong, like a Highland brook. "It's crazy, I know, coming from someone like me, but I do appreciate frugality. Easy to say when I've never had to do without anything." She liked how he was self-deprecating when it came to money. Alastair was in touch with how regular people lived, even though he had a billionaire's life and all the sparkly things to go with it.

"Someday I'll see Scotland again, and a lot of the rest of the world. For now, running Bluewood is enough for me." She allowed herself to share his glance for a heart-stopping moment before refocusing on the river. "At the moment I'd say we've got a tough crossing on our hands."

"No worries, Halle. Your word is my command."

"Good. As I said, it's important that you rely on my commands as we cross. I need you to stay right alongside me as we approach the water and hopefully get across without issue. Let's see how deep it is." When there were younger children on the tour she liked to ham it up a bit here, emphasizing how the personality of the river could change on a dime. With Alastair the last thing she wanted to do was add any drama to their time together. She had to focus on keeping any hormonal chaos she had going on to herself.

The horses' hooves were leaving prints in the clay bank of the river, the water lapping impatiently at their powerful legs. Halle took it all in, but not before checking out Alastair's profile. Satisfaction unfurled in her rib cage, knowing he was moved by the scenery. In this fleeting moment she knew she'd done her job. The strong breeze, the white rapids where the water raced around the bend, the quieter area farther downstream that would be too deep to cross—all played their part to showcase the spectrum of the river's strength. "We're going to have to cross here, where it's still shallow enough. See that part, where it looks like it's not moving?" She waited for him to nod. "That's most likely a deep ditch from the current. We want to steer clear of it. The horses know what to do but we need to stay steady and confident as we guide them."

"Yes, ma'am." His smile was almost a smirk, but not quite. Part of her wished he'd fall off his damned high perch, but a bigger part wouldn't ever want to put Buster at risk of rolling over or breaking a leg.

She answered his grin with her own. "Ready?"

"By your side, yes."

Damn it, he took her breath away. She couldn't blame it on the Scottish accent any longer. She had a major crush on her sexy billionaire cowboy. It was going to remain a *secret* crush.

"Let's do it. And please put your phone away, Alastair. You don't want to become another tourist who loses their device because of a lack of judgment."

"Okay, you're the river crossing expert but I'm the tech expert. My phone is in a LifeProof case and will survive any submersion in water. It also floats. And it's quite secure in the saddle, where it'll stay while we get our horses across safely." He pointed at the phone nestled in the holder he'd brought with him. The contraption fit perfectly around his saddle horn, and while she admired its convenience she preferred to keep her phone in her wraparound thigh pocket when riding. Her mobile was for emergencies only out here on the trail.

Alastair didn't move.

"Good to hear. We don't need any distractions. Paying attention is key." She wasn't in the mood to fish him out of the river if he went in.

"I've got this, Halle. Trust me." He patted Buster's neck as he spoke, his focus clearly on his mount and not the phone he'd tucked back into its holder.

"Whatever. I warned you." She urged Buttercup into the river and waited for Alastair to do the same with Buster. Just as he promised, Alastair took Buster into the river without hesitation. He stayed with her, following every suggestion to maneuver Buster as she gave them. Until a loud *ding* sounded over the gushing water. To her horror, Alastair looked at the phone. Her gut twisted, cutting off her air.

"Pay attention. Your horse needs you." Her voice

sounded weak over the roar of the river and the gusty wind that blew her hair from its ponytail.

"I just need a minute, Halle." Alastair's face was grim, his mouth pulled down. He'd pulled the phone out and scrolled through some message or other. After he finished whatever he was reading he shot her a huge grin and placed the phone back in its makeshift saddle holder. "Just teasing you, Halle. I wouldn't be so stupid as to risk Bust—whoa!"

Buster's manners, decent until now, fled as a large, fallen tree that had been swept into the river came into view not more than one hundred yards away. It appeared to be aimed straight at them. The large horse bucked and bolted across the river, as if reaching the other shore in record time meant life or death.

Alastair, unfortunately, didn't make it to the bank with Buster. As soon as Buster bolted, Alastair flew through the air and landed with a large splash in the middle of the river. When he disappeared under the water Halle panicked. If he hit his head and was unconscious, he'd drown in minutes. She slid off Buttercup and slapped her rump. "Go, girl!"

She waded to where she'd watched Alastair's body submerge. There was no sign of him. She stood on solid ground, able to withstand the force of the river but unable to see one flash of his clothing. Nothing but the froth of the water from the sudden uptick in current. And then his head popped up, his arms working around him in the water. Did he think he could outswim a swollen Texas river?

"Alastair!" He turned toward her and grinned. They were moments from a cold death and he was grinning like a fool. Or someone whose brain was operating in a fog. Panic rose as she realized he might already be hypothermic.

Her boots filled with water and her soles slipped on the rocky river bottom as she reached for Alastair, her fingers desperate to reach his shirt or jeans and haul him up. Instead the current knocked her against him, her entire body plastered against his in the freezing water.

Blue eyes with no evidence of the danger they were in sparkled at her. "Now th-th-this is what I c-c-call a T-Texas adventure!"

"Look at me, Alastair. Can you walk?"

"Of course." Alastair stood up. Dripping wet, he started to shiver. Violently. "D-d-don't b-b-be m-m-mad at m-m-me." In spite of his body's immediate reaction to the frigid water, his eyes were alight with genuine contrition. If she weren't so afraid for his life, she'd find the situation comic.

"We need to get to the other side. Now!" At which point she was going to strip the wet clothes off of him, wrap him in a first aid space blanket, start a warm campfire and then kill him for his ignorance.

"D-d-don't w-w-worry." He leaned heavily against her and she braced her boots in the silty bottom of the river. They made their way, one step at a time. As they neared the bank where Buster and Buttercup patiently waited, the river stilled. "L-l-look, it-t-t's all b-b-better."

"Shut up, Alastair."

Halle Ford had saved his life. Alastair prided himself on his inner strength, the core of his being that had gotten him through the bullying he'd endured as a grade schooler. His entire school career, actually, until he'd grown taller and his shoulders wider than those of his mean classmates. The same financial status that had blessed him with such a protected life in many ways had been his enemy then, as jealous classmates went after him with a vengeance. He'd never told his parents; he'd used his brains to outwit his adversaries and taken the punches he'd had to.

Until the school psychologist had called him in and insisted he confess to the beatings, the terrorizing episodes of being dragged out of bed in the wee hours and hung by his ankles outside of his dormitory window. His enemies had been expelled and he'd faced another uphill battle, working with the counselor to undo the years of abuse and anxiety.

He'd thought he'd survive anything after that. Scaled mountains, in fact. Yet a river in Texas had almost done him in. Without Halle, he'd never have waded out of that cold water.

"You're okay, Alastair." She placed her hand on his shoulder for a brief moment as she rubbed his legs. The pins and needles sensation hurt like hell, but somewhere in the icy sludge of his brain he recognized she was preventing hypothermia.

"Th-th-thanks." The word barely made it out around his chattering teeth.

"Don't talk. Save your energy to heat back up." Her massage continued, and he knew that when he felt himself again he'd regret that he'd been naked under the space blanket and unable to act on the fantasies he'd had of Halle for the past couple of days.

"Here are some dry socks." She expertly unrolled heavy hiking socks onto his feet. Wool had never felt so good against his skin. Almost as good as her warm hands, hands that had moved on to his thighs.

"I'm aiming at your larger muscle groups to get your circulation going and warm you up quicker." Her eyes were warm chocolate as she met his gaze. The smile in them reached her lips and she winked. "Don't worry, Alastair. You're not the first person to underestimate that river, and you won't be the last. We'll have you feeling yourself in no time."

He wondered if she knew that when he was feeling himself again it could be awkward, as he had no doubt his erection would make a prominent teepee in the aluminum fabric blanket.

Problem was, as much as wanted to make love to this woman who was rubbing him back to life, he didn't want her to think it was all about the sex. There was something stronger, deeper here. The kind of connection that could go the distance.

Alastair let out a groan as pain shot up his leg and into his groin. He'd worry about his dick after he got all of his feeling back.

"Here, drink this." Halle handed Alastair a tin mug of hot tea. "Take little sips."

"L-l-l-like I c-c-c-can m-m-m-manage more." He was still visibly shaking, his body in all-out warm-up mode.

"If you hadn't refused to strip down and get wrapped in the blanket for so long, you wouldn't be so miserable now." She'd pulled him out of the water almost an hour ago. He'd all but made her wrestle him to get him to take the wet clothes off and get in the blanket. She knew he was hurting when he made no quips about her seeing him naked or about her getting undressed with him. It had been awkward for a millisecond when her skin came into contact with his, but since his was alarmingly cold, she'd switched into first aid mode. They'd lain together on top of the bedrolls, and she'd wished she could will Alastair's body back to normal temperature.

"I can't believe it. You could have died out there." She allowed the heat of her tea to warm her, ignoring the urge to return to the cocoon of heat she and Alastair had enjoyed until she sensed he was out of danger. More like his erection had clued her in. It would have been too easy to make a joke about it, to ease his obvious discomfort. But she didn't know him well enough yet. At least not chronologically. Her soul felt as though she'd known him her whole life.

"I'm better." His eyes were half-hooded, his expression predatory. Pretty fast recovery for a man she'd thought was going to freeze to death a half hour earlier.

As he sat and sipped his tea, she set up camp. Her tent popped up and she cast a look at Alastair, next to the fire. The sun was a distant memory and the navy sky began to sparkle with countless stars. Hypothermia was a real risk. His shivering was a good sign, but he'd been in those wet clothes for too long. She'd gotten out of their embrace and put on sweatpants and socks while he'd procrastinated at putting on dry clothing.

"I think you'd better let me help you." She sat next to him and started to rub his arms through the crinkly metallic blanket. As she worked over him, praying his blood would start warming up and that he'd be more of the Alastair she'd spent the last three days with, a terrifying thought occurred to her.

You care about him.

Impossible. She barely knew the man. And while their physical chemistry had been often palpable over their trail ride, it wasn't enough to ensure a promise of deeper feelings. Was it?

"Thanks. That feels good." His teeth weren't chattering anymore; a very good sign.

"Are you getting warmer?"

"A bit, but I'm afraid you're right. I may have waited too long to get naked." His expression was unreadable as she stood between the fire and him, massaging his legs. Very muscular legs that no longer felt clammy. Before her hands betrayed her and moved up under the blanket to the tops of his legs, or more accurately, between them, Halle leaned back on her heels, her hands on her thighs.

"Now's not the time to flirt, Alastair. You could have died in the river. And all for what? Your stupid cell phone?"

"While it's my brain trust, most of the time, I wasn't as worried about it as I let you think. I was trying to push your buttons. It was poor flirting style on my part." His voice had lowered, returning to its usual pitch. Halle grasped his left foot and rubbed briskly at it, then massaged his arch, his toes. He groaned with relief once the initial stiffness melted away.

"It wasn't the flirting that was off, it was your timing." She didn't want to reveal too much, but after seeing him so close to hypothermia it seemed silly to play coy. "Are your muscles cramping up at all?" She was on her knees, looking up at him. If the blanket moved one inch she was going to be treated to a lot more of Alastair than she'd bargained for. She'd seen his backside as she'd stripped him, had felt his erection as he'd warmed up, but had successfully kept her gaze off any private parts. The parts that she'd see if he wore a kilt.

The vision of Alastair in a kilt was a bad idea. Now

all she wanted was to touch him, everywhere. More like *taste* him everywhere.

"Halle." His hands were on her wrists and he pulled her off balance, forcing her up against him. They were chest to chest, the blanket the only barrier to his bare skin. Her shirt and sweatpants felt too bulky, in the way.

"You're feeling better, I take it." Her voice was breathy, and she didn't care about his risk of hypothermia any longer. Not with his eyes sparking in the firelight, her insides quaking not with cold but insane desire. Shock. She had to be going into shock over the ordeal. It wasn't every day she came close to losing a client.

"Warm me up, Halle." His words tugged at her resolve and she swallowed, refusing to make any move.

"No. Listen, Alastair—you, me, we're in shock. That was a close call out there. I know you think you feel better, but believe me, you need a good night's rest and a chance to recover from your body's temperature drop."

"You'll warm me up better than anything. As a matter of fact, that's the best way to make sure I stay warm. You get naked again, and we lie next to one another. Skin on skin."

Her desire was at a fever pitch but she was reminded of her place. And the kind of business she did not operate. She walked a few steps away and stirred the soup she'd heated over the fire. Her hands were shaking with want. Want for him.

"Drink some more of the hot tea, Alastair. It'll raise your internal temperature." Her voice was as shaky as her insides. Damn it. There was no way she was going to touch him, no way she could justify—

His lips touched her throat, his blanket-wrapped front up against her back as she stirred.

"Alastair, I—"

"It's okay to have needs other than running Blue-wood, Halle." Why couldn't he sound like he was sick, or still chilled, or unable to think straight? Why did he have to sound so sane, so steady, so sure of what would be best for her?

Alastair knew he was coming off a bit too heavy-handed, especially for a man who'd been totally at Halle's mercy only an hour earlier. He took a step backward, gave Halle room as he stepped to her side, in front of the small fire.

"I'm sorry—that was presumptive. I wish I could blame it on the cold water but I have a bad habit of telling others what's best for them."

Halle stirred the dirt with a stick she'd picked up off the ground. "I get that. When you have to rely on your instincts for so long, it's easy to think your way is the right way."

"I don't know you well, Halle, not as well as I'd like to. But is it fair to say that you've done little, probably nothing, for yourself since your father died?"

Her lids lifted and revealed the depths of pain she'd walked through. "At first I didn't want to do anything. I think I stayed in pajamas for the first two days after the funeral. But then, then I knew I owed him more. Daddy didn't raise me to be a slacker, and this land was every-thing to him."

"You need a break. We all do. Sometimes when I'm travelling for weeks on end I plan a quick trip to a resort or island to escape. Believe it or not, I go completely off the grid from time to time."

That got a grin out of her. And a beautiful grin it was.

He loved how her entire expression lit up like the Highlands did when the heather bloomed.

"That might have been a good decision today."

"Although, if I had, you may have never had the privilege of seeing my bum."

"Never, Alastair?"

Halle wasn't flirting or teasing. The heat in her eyes wasn't a reflection of the fire, either. She was a woman boldly expressing her want, and Alastair had never been more turned on.

Halle turned toward him and didn't know who moved first, but the tiny space between them disappeared and Alastair's lips were on hers. He stamped her mouth with his, and her senses were on overload with his musk and the coolness of his tongue. The pent-up sexual attraction they'd fought against each and every hour on the trail had won. Halle surrendered to her desire and the relief was as sharp as her sexual response to him. When his tongue licked around her lips and insisted entry, she opened her mouth fully and took him in. He tasted as good as she'd imagined. Tea, honey and Alastair. Tea she'd given him to warm up. She pushed against his chest, breaking their contact, their gasps loud and harsh in the still Texas night.

"You could have died. Are you up for this?" They both laughed at her question. His erection, which he ground against her pulsating center, answered it.

"Outside or in your tent?" He growled the words as he sucked gently at the skin on her throat, his hands moving up and under her shirt, on her waist, cupping her breasts through her sports bra. When he tweaked her nipples Halle groaned.

"Tent. You're still at risk from the cold."

They half walked, half stumbled into her tent. Alastair was definitely feeling better as he pressed her shoulders onto the sleeping bag and rose above her. "I want to make love to you in so many ways, Halle. But later. This time I don't want to wait or draw it out. I need you now. Pure and simple."

"Yes." Amazing she could force the word out, as turned on as she was.

"Condoms?" His Scottish accent made the request seem as gentlemanly as it was.

"In the zipper bag, here—" She reached to the small pouch in the tiny tent where she kept first aid items and condoms. She'd had clients request them, clients she'd envied who'd decided to take her trip as a honeymoon or lovers' vacation. But she'd put them there as an afterthought, after she'd made him tea at the house. Somewhere inside of her she'd hoped this might happen. Alastair and her, together in the most basic way.

Alastair grasped the wrapper as soon as she plucked the small packet from the bag. "You're moving awfully well for a man who was just on the brink of hypothermia." She tried to think, tried to focus but the way he so quickly donned the protection and then lifted her head to deeply kiss her again allowed her to only think of the incredible sensations his touch brought.

"Halle." He said her name as if she were the Holy Grail. Dispensing with any illusion of a romantic buildup, Alastair entered her in one powerful thrust and Halle met him, eager to match him, their need mutual. As they moved together it occurred to her that it had never been this natural, this raw, this perfect the first time with any other man. Not just the first time—any time with another man.

Then the delicious sensations that pushed her over the edge of her most satisfying climax ever blew any vestige of rational thought out of her brain. Alastair's matching release, punctuated by his deep shout, was all she needed.

Chapter 4

Three months later

"Thanks for taking them in, Charlie." Halle handed off the leather lead shanks to her ranch hand, hoping he didn't notice her excessive sweat. She had to make it back to the house before she threw up in front of him.

"No problem, Boss." Charlie walked toward the stables with Elvis and Buttercup. She'd already worked Buster and two other geldings. It lifted her mood to see how well cared for her mounts were. As much as Bluewood was in the red, she'd managed to squeeze out enough to keep the horses healthy.

Unlike the majority of her cattle, which she'd had to sell off to keep things running. That had hurt, but not as much as she knew the next few minutes would. Going into the house, she made straight for the bathroom as her loyal herding dogs followed her. She looked at the stick she'd peed on before her anxiety got any worse.

The plus sign stared accusingly at her. Her weight loss from the constant worry over Bluewood's survival hadn't left her body fat too low to warrant missing menstrual cycles. That had been her excuse the first month she'd skipped her period.

Her attempts to deny a second month without a period, however, were met with her swollen, tender breasts and her constant exhaustion. The last few days the nausea had caught up to her. So she'd done what millions of women did every year. Last night she'd purchased a home pregnancy test at the Shadow Creek drugstore. She'd left it in the bathroom overnight, in case her cycle started by morning. She'd taken the test first thing upon waking.

Somehow, the protection she and Alastair had used had failed. She was single, near bankruptcy and pregnant. No time to process it all right now, though, as her stomach did what it was becoming too good at doing.

Halle threw up.

It was time to tell the father, but she felt horrible even thinking about calling Alastair. She'd ignored his persistent attempts to contact her the first few weeks after he'd left Texas. It was a nonstarter, any kind of relationship with the sexy billionaire. Halle was a native of Shadow Creek, Texas—fun for a diversion or maybe even some real dating. Until Alastair realized his jet-set lifestyle wasn't enough to get her out of Texas. And Halle was as dedicated as ever to Bluewood. It'd have to be as a single mom now, was all.

Wrapping a towel she'd soaked in cold water around her neck, she went to find her phone.

* * *

Alastair Buchanan frowned at his cell phone. Halle Ford had called three times in the past two days, but never left a message. Desire startled him as it slammed into his gut and made a direct line to his crotch. *Halle.*

It'd been such an incredible time with her in the Texas Hill Country. The sex, yes, but so much more. Her. The way she listened. He'd really thought more might come of it. He'd been ready to convince her more *should* come of it, that with his resources that included a private jet they'd make the miles and hours between them manageable.

But she'd never taken any of his calls, and while he was persistent, he wasn't a stalker.

After never hearing from her for three months, the three attempts so close together seemed urgent. And they painfully reminded him of the countless messages he'd left her in the first few weeks after their time together.

Maybe she'd reconsidered dropping him like a hot jacket potato. When they'd hooked up he didn't imagine she'd want more than their brief liaison. Not that Halle wasn't his type, or the most beautiful woman he'd ever been with. He wasn't in a place to commit to any woman. Long-distance relationships could work, but so many thousands of miles apart made for a lot more effort on both their parts. And mostly on his company jet's dime. The deeper, more pressing reason to stay away from any kind of relationship was that Clyde Whiskey was in peril.

He tried to refocus on his computer screen, to put Halle out of his mind. It was probably good that they lived so far apart, and if he went back to Texas it would only be to set up his investment business. Short-term. He wondered if she'd be open to seeing him when he went back, if he did. For old times' sake. They'd been exceptionally compatible, once they'd given in to their attraction.

Halle's incredibly sensual body and throaty moans had underscored the once-in-a-lifetime night they'd shared on the banks of Shadow Creek River, at Halle's ranch outside of Austin, Texas. It was odd, in a way, that he'd found his thoughts drifting to the Texas land whenever the pressure of work had gotten to him these last months. And at night, when his head hit the pillow, he felt as if he missed Halle lying next to him. Which was absolutely ridiculous. He'd known her, really known her, one night. They'd spent a total of three nights and four days together. How was it possible that she'd made such an impression on him?

"Alastair, Jeremy Kincaid's on line one." His receptionist's voice buzzed in his wireless earbud. Alastair tapped the accept button on his phone.

"Jeremy, just the man I need to hear from."

"Hey, Alastair. Returning your call. What's the holdup on the tech investment?"

His friend's words socked him in the gut. Like him, Jeremy was never one for small talk. He didn't want to admit what was happening with Clyde Whiskey but he wouldn't lie to Jeremy, either. "I'm having a major problem. Someone—an unknown—is trying to gobble up shares of Clyde Whiskey."

"Hostile takeover?"

"More like apocalyptic takeover." Alastair let out a growl of frustration. "It's been insane since I got back from visiting you and Adeline." *And Halle.* "It's all I can do to shore up the business. I keep putting out fires that pop up elsewhere."

"I've been there, man, more than once. You'll get

through this, and trust me, no one is going to take Clyde Whiskey from you. Tell me what I can do to help."

"Nothing, not yet. I have a team on it. I hope to have answers soon. The one weird thing is that it all started while I was in Texas." As if someone hadn't liked the thought of him investing in tech in the area.

"You wouldn't be the first person to have bad luck while in Shadow Creek."

"If you're referring to the havoc caused by that woman Livia Colton, she's dead. She'd have no reason to come after me if she were alive."

"Sounds like you and Halle talked about more than indigenous history of Texas out on the trail."

Alastair remained silent. He wasn't going to share what had happened on the trail with Halle. It was too personal.

"I'm here if you need me, Alastair. So are your investment opportunities in Austin. And let me put it out there for you—our house in Shadow Creek is always open to you. Maybe time away from your home turf would help. Clear the mind."

"Thanks, Jeremy." As he disconnected he couldn't ignore the tug in his gut at the mention of Shadow Creek. If he were to stay with anyone, he'd want to be with Halle. He grinned at the realization that he'd prefer the cozy ranch house at Bluewood over Jeremy's spectacular contemporary mansion. In a rare moment of deep reflection he admitted that he hadn't been himself, hadn't felt grounded in Glasgow since he'd departed Austin. When he'd left Halle Ford and his adventure on Bluewood Ranch behind.

You haven't left it behind.

Maybe it was time to return some calls.

* * *

Halle held her phone over her head as she lay on her back on the living room sofa. It was ringing, buzzing, breaking into the quiet zone she'd tried to establish for herself. Lying flat was the only thing that kept her from getting sick. The phone buzzed again and she peered from beneath the cold cloth she had on her forehead.

Alastair Buchanan. A jolt of awareness forced her into a seated position.

Dang. Hell. Crap.

"Halle here."

"Is it a Texas custom to wait three months to return a call from a paramour?" Alastair's rich Scottish brogue made tingles shoot straight to her center, as if they'd made love last night and not fourteen weeks ago. As if they were more than a one-night stand.

Yeah. As if.

"Halle?"

"I—I'm here. And any rudeness is on me. Just, just my bad manners. I'm sorry I didn't reply sooner. Thanks for returning my call." Nausea rolled over her and she groaned as she lay back down, groping for the lost cold cloth.

"Are you all right, Halle? Have I caught you at a bad time—coming out of the shower, perhaps?" God bless the man, he was flirting. She almost laughed at the ridiculousness of it. His playful tone was going to flatten out pronto. As soon as he found out why she'd called.

"Look, Alastair, this isn't a fun call. I mean, not a social call—"

"It's perfectly fine to admit you missed me. I was just thinking about you, remembering how your breasts feel in my hands." Her body reacted so quickly she couldn't keep up with it, from her nipples puckering to the tingles of want that ran down her midsection to between her legs.

"I'm pregnant. It's yours. No doubt."

Palpable silence blew the sexual tension into sharp shards of shock. Not one iota of static sounded to break the heavy quiet. There wasn't much that could take away the physical pull Alastair had on her, but telling the billionaire bachelor that his fun had resulted in a lifetime commitment did. Halle sucked in a breath, hoping she didn't puke while he was on the line.

"Well." A whole lifetime in his one-word reply. Yeah, no more sexy talk.

"I'm sorry to tell you on the phone, but a trip to Glasgow isn't practical for me at the moment." Did he even know how difficult it could be for the average person to travel? Without a private jet at her disposal, not to mention the unlimited funds a billionaire like Alastair had.

"I don't suppose the fact that you found out what I'm worth motivated you to reach out?" His tone carried the full body of a Highland Scotch but had the venom of a Texas rattlesnake laced through it. Smooth, silky, sexy as sin and deadly.

"No offense, Alastair, but I don't give a flying fig what you think about me. For the record, I'd looked you up before we went on the trail and while I knew you were a wealthy investor, I didn't know the extent of your fortune until after you left." When she'd spent hours poring through the web searches, wondering what kind of father her baby had. "What you need to be thinking about is that I'm three months pregnant and the kid is yours." Agitated past her nausea, her hands shaking, Halle pushed herself up and leaned against her sofa's deep cushions.

The old worn leather still smelled like her dad, Chancellor "Chance" Ford, the man who'd been taken from the world, from her, too soon. It was the closest she could come to a much-needed hug from him, save a walk out to the paddock fence, where she had so many memories of standing next to him, watching the horses.

"What do you want from me, Halle?" Cold, ruthless, pure business-deal negotiator. Let him be whatever he needed to be. She didn't need him or anything else from him.

"Nothing, Alastair. Absolutely nothing. As far as I'm concerned I've fulfilled my obligation to tell you of your baby. I certainly don't need your help raising a child." Strong words when she didn't know what the hell she was doing, didn't know how she was going to afford to buy groceries for herself, let alone diapers for a newborn. And running the trail business was exponentially trickier when battling morning sickness, let alone trying to find a babysitter for the overnight rides in the future.

Halle didn't dislike children but she'd never been one to dream of having her own someday. And certainly not without a grandfather around. Her grief welled up and tears flowed. Damn her hormones.

"Halle, wait. You've caught me off guard." She heard the clink of what could be ice into a glass. Was Alastair sampling some of the family brew? It made her stomach turn to think of drinking anything but ginger ale, but if pregnancy didn't preclude alcohol consumption, she'd join Alastair in a shot of something.

"Better?" She kept the sniffs out of her voice.

"You can see me across the pond?" A peek at the man who'd made love to her all night under the Texas deep sky, strewn with stars and full of the orchestra of the country.

"Is it Scotch? If I could join you I would. Although I would have thought you'd take it neat."

His laughter rumbled over the connection. "I am an anomaly in that I do like my whiskey on the rocks."

A long pause. An inhalation. "Yes, the baby. You say you're sure it's mine, Halle, but as I recall, we used protection. Each and every time."

Grateful he couldn't see the blush flaming her cheeks, she gritted her teeth. So he remembered it had been more than once. "Nothing is one hundred percent. They have basic biology in Scottish schools, don't they?"

His laughter wound around her and she actually felt the heavy burden she'd carried since she'd used the home pregnancy kit last week lift off her. It had taken a couple days to let it sink in, and a few more expensive tests from the local drugstore, before she made an appointment with her general practitioner, who confirmed that yes, she was indeed pregnant. Thirteen weeks, almost fourteen today.

"I imagine nothing is foolproof, you're right. And we were rather vigorous, especially when we…" The sexy vibration of his voice in her ear trailed off and an image of them making love against a willow tree flashed in her mind. Had that been when the condom had failed them? Or had it been the time next to the slow-moving creek, where they heard beavers building a dam as they reveled in each other's caress?

"As I've said, I don't expect anything from you, Alastair. But you have a right to know."

"So you're keeping the child."

"Yes." She'd been over every option with her good

friend Maggie Colton ad infinitum. Drawing a deep breath, she blew it out before continuing. "I know being a single parent is difficult, and it would be a much more celebratory situation if my father was still alive." Tears threatened at the reminder her baby would never know his or her grandfather. "I'm not getting any younger, and with the responsibilities of the ranch, it's feasible I'd never meet someone in time to have a family. The timing sucks but it's possible this is the best thing ever to happen to me."

His silence spoke volumes. She imagined him, saw his face and all its expressions as clearly as if he sat next to her on the sofa.

"I'm fully capable of raising a child, Alastair."

"What about your livelihood, Halle? How are you going to support a child? Bluewood Ranch was barely above drowning when I visited. Has something unforeseen happened in the last three months to make it soluble?"

As soon as the harsh words left his mouth, Alastair wanted to reach across the Atlantic and grab them back.

"Other than me getting knocked up?" Anger spiked Halle's tone, and rightfully so. "I have a college degree and several skill sets. I can go back to my job in Austin. The child will survive. We live in a wonderful school district. My friends are all very supportive and are raising young kids of their own. I'm far from alone or destitute, Alastair."

This was the Halle he remembered. Strong, beautiful, willing to fight to the death for what she believed in. She'd pulled him out of that deathtrap of a river, for heaven's sake.

"I didn't mean to imply that you were. You're highly capable. But Bluewood may not be as viable, and in the short time we were together, it was clear it's very important to you." How could he get through to her? He didn't see her as just another woman he'd slept with.

Her silence stretched into a full moment and frustration that he wasn't there in person to comfort her made him pace.

"I'm coming out to Texas. I'll be there within a day."

"No, no! I didn't call you to have you come here. There's nothing you can do, nothing for you to do." Panic assuaged her and she felt the nausea return. "Listen, Alastair, don't come here. We'll talk again. I won't keep you from your child. I promise to work out some kind of custody agreement with you, if that's what you want." She'd already thought it out, without a sliver of him in the picture. He had made that good of an impression—*not*.

"But you're going to hang up, aren't you?" He didn't care if he sounded like he was pleading, groveling. Whatever it took to let her know he was going to be there for her. For their baby. He was going to be a father! "Why, Halle? Why are you hanging up?"

"Because I'm going to throw up."

Chapter 5

Shadow Creek appealed more to Alastair now than it had three months ago. The silhouettes of the houses, barn and stables became larger and he had a sense of comfort he hadn't felt since…he'd left Bluewood. He took it all in as the Uber driver drove up to Halle's house and again reviewed how he planned to convince her to marry him. She hadn't sounded impressed with anything he'd had to say on the phone yesterday. And showing up without her invitation—only twenty-four hours after he'd found out he was going to be a father—ranked as his most impulsive decision yet.

Marriage wasn't the option he came to most easily but it was the best solution to their issue at hand. It was the only way he'd guarantee that the child would be his legal heir, and provided a way for Halle to benefit, as well. He would help Halle out with Bluewood, make certain it would be around for a long while—long enough for his future child to know this part of his or her heritage. He only had to convince Halle to enter into a temporary marriage of convenience, which he considered his most challenging business deal to date. Halle was as smart and stubborn as his fiercest competitors.

The front door was closed, the screen door in front of it hanging on its hinge. Paint on the once-red house flaked and the shingles were a faded gray, from what he surmised had originally been black. Cosmetic upkeep on a building went by the wayside when the funds weren't available. He understood that as a businessman. From all appearances nothing had changed—Halle was still struggling to keep the ranch afloat. It was good to know, an asset to take into his negotiations with her. Unlike regular business, though, he felt a tug in his chest that he never felt when anticipating a merger. Maybe expectant fathers had their own kind of morning sickness, some kind of paternal anxiety. It couldn't be anything else. He hadn't known Halle that long. Yet the anticipation of becoming a parent, a father, a dad kept inserting itself in all his thoughts. His life as he'd known it was about to change, and he found he welcomed it.

Now to convince Halle he was sincere about his offer of assistance. He wanted nothing less than to be a full parent to his child. Their child.

Alastair drew in a deep breath and knocked on her door. He heard several loud barks as her three dogs sounded the alert, followed by the sounds of someone hushing them, and then the woman he'd made love to a million times in his mind since he'd actually taken her on the Texas trail opened the door and stood in front of him.

"Alastair."

"Halle." Words refused to form, to squeeze past the jolt of seeing her again. Her amber eyes were a balm to his soul and her face reflected complete surprise and maybe even a little bit of joy. As if she were sizing him up and thinking the same thing. He offered a smile.

The blank look on her expression turned hard, but it didn't diminish her beauty. Nothing could. "I told you not to bother."

"I know." He held up what he now realized was a ridiculously huge bouquet of pink roses. "A peace offering."

She pushed back the broken screen door and reached for the flowers. He honest-to-God expected her to toss them to the ground, or better, feed them to her dogs, who all stood around her, staring at Alastair. They didn't yip at him; there was that. At least the dogs were willing to give him a chance. Maybe they remembered him?

Halle looked at the pink blooms in her hands and bent her face to them, audibly inhaling the scent. "Mmm. I love roses." The lines around her eyes and mouth softened, and he saw the shadow of her smile but she didn't waste it on him. It was gone as soon as she looked back up. "You can go now." She swung the door to close it.

"No, wait." He put his foot on the threshold, preventing her from closing the door. Two dogs barked and one growled. "Easy, boys."

"They're all girls."

"Right. Okay, easy, ladies. Is that better?" Now all three growled.

Halle showed no sign of relenting, either. "There's nothing to 'wait' for, Alastair. I don't need or want anything from you. This was a sweet gesture and I do adore roses. Thank you. We're good. I'll let you know what I name the baby when it's time."

"I'm not leaving, Halle." Not until she heard him out. Not until she agreed to his proposal.

"Please tell me you didn't fly from Scotland to make a florist delivery. Certainly you can afford an overnight express shipment."

This was the Halle he'd missed. The strength that allowed her humor to come through in the midst of what had to be a tough time for her. He felt the warmth emanating from inside the house and saw the way she held her long cardigan wrapped around her body, still not showing any obvious sign of a baby bump.

"It's cold out here, Halle."

Whiskey eyes flickered to the retreating Uber car and back to him. "I'm sure there's a heater in your ride. You should call them back before they get too far away." She moved again to shut the door. Two dogs barked and one growled. Four sets of female eyes on him.

"No, don't! I want, I hope—bloody hell, Halle! Will you please let me in? I'd like to have a reasonable conversation without the hounds of hell at my feet."

She surprised him again and laughed. Did she have any idea how pretty she looked in her crumpled white blouse, blue jeans and pink sweater? Bare feet with pale blue polish? Her hair mussed as if he'd waken her up from—

"How do you feel?"

She stopped smiling. "Awful. I was just lying flat again—it seems to be the only solution to it. My worst times are now, late afternoon."

"I'm sorry."

Their gazes met and connected this time. Wariness and a deep sadness reflected in their bourbon depths. And maybe, just maybe—a flicker of hope?

She sighed, loud and long, her shoulders drooped in resignation. "Come on in. Girls, settle down and be quiet!" The Australian shepherds circled around them both, herding Alastair into a clump with Halle. It was his turn to laugh.

"They really think we're sheep they have to manage?"

"Pretty much, yes. You've seen herding dogs in Scotland, I'm sure. I'd hoped to have sheep and alpaca on the ranch by now, something to keep them busy, but, well, I've got more work to do before that happens." Money to earn was what she really meant, he'd bet. He didn't know a whole lot about her yet but he knew she'd never admit she was worried about her finances, or lack thereof.

She led him through the small yet cozy house to a narrow kitchen in the back. "Have a seat." He complied, easily settling at her maple wood table set.

"This is a comfortable chair." He ran his hands over the wide arms of the wooden barrel seat.

A shadow flickered over her features, barely a whisper of yearning. "Yes, it was built for my father. He was tall, like you."

Watching her as she chose a vase, filled it with water from the tap and trimmed the rose stems was oddly soothing. Homey.

Careful. Keep it strictly business.

"Here. We can enjoy them more." She placed the arrangement on the table between them, against the window that overlooked her fields. The barn and corral were off to the right, decidedly empty.

"Where are the horses? Your steer?"

Halle lowered herself into the chair opposite his. Her figure was as sexy as ever, and while he couldn't detect a curve where the baby they'd conceived grew, he couldn't take his gaze off her smooth belly. An unfamiliar sense of protectiveness grabbed his heart—or was it possessiveness?

"It's too early for me to show, Alastair. Although I've noticed my clothes are getting very tight these days." Bam! She'd caught him. Instead of being embarrassed, he was intrigued. He'd actually helped make a baby that was in turn making Halle's body change. This was far more interesting than any high frequency stock trade.

"You were going to tell me about your livestock?"

"Yes. I've had all but six of the horses moved and stabled at friends' ranches until my profit margin increases, probably in the spring. I had to sell off some of my steer to pay bills. I can purchase more, one head at a time if necessary, as soon as things…settle down a bit."

"So. You're still having financial difficulty."

"The ranch is, yes." She spoke quietly, her face toward the window, her gaze far away. "I've had to depend totally on Charlie to take care of the horses while I get through this morning sickness. I'm lucky if I can manage to lead them through laps around the paddock. I've had to pay Charlie overtime. I'm not going to skimp on his paycheck. For now. And I'll get back on my feet soon and hopefully be able to run some more trail rides. I saw my doctor today and she gave me permission to ride, although it should be at a much slower pace or even a walk. I have three tours scheduled over the next two weeks, starting this weekend."

"How the hell are you going to do that when you feel so awful?"

"I'm pregnant, as eons of women before me have been. My doctor assures me that the nausea, while late-onset, will eventually pass. Or I'll learn to live with it. I already have. I mean, look, I feel green right now but I'm not throwing up on you. Trust me, it's progress compared to the last week or two." She did have a strong game face, he'd give her that.

"Will those tours be enough to get you through the next several months?" He knew the answer but wanted her to hear it. Feel it. She had to see that his answer was the best for her.

"Are you kidding? Of course not. The fee you paid me is the highest I've ever earned, and I've put that toward stabling the horses. I need to finish ten to twelve tours before the baby comes, then I'll be able to afford at least six weeks of not working much when he or she is a newborn."

"That sounds stressful." And her "not working much" comment meant that she'd be willing to work too soon after the baby was born, if necessary. That feeling of protectiveness toward Halle was getting too familiar. And it blew his mind that he was thinking of a child the size of a small plum as his son or daughter to forever protect. He'd done some internet searches on the stages of pregnancy and fetal development.

"You don't think I can do it?" Her chin jutted out and her lips were pouty. Not that he was thinking about kissing her at this particular time.

"I know you can do whatever you want to, Halle. You pulled me out of a raging river, for God's sake. That's not the question."

"The river was still by the time I got to you. Tell me, Alastair, what do you think is the issue? What's your point?"

"The concern I have is how you're going to make enough money to not only keep Bluewood running, but to invest in its future. I know you're fully capable of making it all work, but darn it, Halle, I don't want you running yourself into the ground. This should be a happy time for you, too."

Tears glistened in her eyes as she bit her trembling bottom lip. Not that he was looking at it for any particular reason. "I'll do whatever I have to, it's how my daddy raised me. Fords aren't quitters. Although Dad always found time for me, always let me know that I was first, the priority over the ranch. He was bringing in a lot more money when I was younger, though. I don't know if the ranch will ever get back to those days." She wiped tears off her cheeks.

"Are you sure you want to take on another full-time job on top of the ranch? With a new baby?"

"That's the question, isn't it?"

"*That*'s part of what brought me here, Halle. I want to help. To make this as easy a transition for you as possible. I'm hoping you'll trust me enough to allow me to help you financially with the business. I know how much it means to you."

"That…that's awfully generous of you, Alastair. Thank you."

She grabbed a napkin from the acrylic holder on the table and wiped her eyes, then blew her nose. He made a note to order the finest linen handkerchiefs for her, with the Scottish thistle embroidered on them. Her hands were long, her fingers graceful. Would their child have her hands?

"There's one more thing, Halle. I know it's going to sound absolutely crazy, so please hear me out."

Her long, shuddering breath emphasized her ramrod-straight posture. He was certain she was made of steel. She rested her sharp whiskey eyes on him.

"Go on."

"Marry me, Halle. For the sake of our child, marry me."

Chapter 6

Alastair's words "our child" had an unexpected effect on Halle. They calmed her. As ridiculous as the other part of his statement, a question that sounded more like a billionaire's demand to her. Because if she allowed herself to believe for one instant that Alastair was starting to have feelings for her, she'd misinterpret his proposal. She'd start to see a different slant to his insistent words. As if he meant it, as if he was really going to stay there and help her through the next six months and beyond. As if he…

No. Do not go there.

Halle channeled the Ford side of the family, the good judgment her father had left her. The business sense that had helped him make a nice tidy sum over the years with the ranch. A sum she'd gone through quicker than she'd ever expected. But the ranch had needed improvements.

Hell, it needed basic maintenance and she didn't even have the money for that. Yes, she had to draw upon her father's financial acumen. It was all she had left with the ranch failing and her bank accounts empty. Alastair wanted to literally bail Bluewood Ranch out of its financial straits, and set it up to thrive. With only one demand, apparently.

"You want to *marry* me? That's rich, Alastair. I mean, you have to wonder if you can trust me in the first place, don't you? Are you so certain that the baby is yours? I could be totally duping you! I can't figure out if you're crazy or, or…" She couldn't say it. Couldn't voice her dreams—that she'd fallen for a decent guy. Not that she was falling for Alastair. They shared potent chemistry, period.

"It's the right thing to do. It's not a real, romantic proposal, and I'm sorry for that. We can agree to divorce in a year, to prove to you my intentions are only to help the baby. But it's an opportunity for both of us to do the best thing for our baby." With his clipped Scottish brogue his words sounded like an edict from above. Not a statement from the man who'd made love to her like there was no tomorrow. Her inner thighs clenched at the memory, her lips throbbed with her attraction to him. Even in her throes of hormone-induced nausea, she remembered his kisses and longed for more.

Alastair didn't look like he was thinking along the same lines as he drummed his fingers on the table. She saw those fingers caressing her, sliding up her waist to her breast…

"Don't you agree, Halle?"

She looked away from his hands, from him. The pregnancy and recent vomiting made it difficult for her to keep her emotions locked down.

"It's the right thing if you're living in nineteenth-century Glasgow, maybe. But we don't have to run off to Gretna Green just because you got me knocked up. A lot of parents wait until after the baby is born to get married."

The drumming stopped. He raised his hand and ran it over his face, emphasizing the lines around the edges of his eyes. Even traveling in a private jet, he had to feel the effects of jet lag. Facing the consequences of fun he'd had three months ago couldn't be helping, either.

"Halle, I'm not some anonymous rancher that's gotten you pregnant. I'm a public figure, as much as I detest that part of my inheritance. Security is an everyday issue for me, and it's going to be for the baby, too. My child. Since you're the mother, you're already at risk. This is the most expedient way to handle this."

"At risk for what?"

"Kidnapping, extortion—God, Halle, please don't make me spell it all out for you."

"You already have. And for the record, I've already obsessed over the future threats to our baby. And I don't appreciate your slam against ranchers." She leaned on her elbows and rested her head in her hands. The stability of the kitchen table where her dad had helped her solve all of her adolescent problems comforted her. What would her father have thought about Alastair? After he'd locked and loaded his rifle, for demonstrative purposes?

"You're right. I realize I can come across way too intense. I have nothing against ranchers, you have to realize this." He ran his hands over his face. "I came here to help you take a load off, to ease the stress of finding out you're pregnant when you weren't planning it. I'm not doing a very good job of it, am I?" His expression softened, the light in his eyes making them appear silver. "Can I do something for you? Make you some tea? I've brought my favorite ginger tea. It's supposed to be an elixir for morning sickness."

"What would you know about being pregnant?"

"Not a lot, but I've seen enough of my friends and my siblings go through it." He stood up and walked to her counter. "Where's your kettle?"

"Kettle? Do you mean a pot to boil water? Or better, there's the microwave. That's how I made your tea when you were here before." She pointed to the appliance over the stove. "I usually heat up a measuring glass of water and then add enough tea bags to make a quart to pour over ice."

Alastair's blank stare was a first.

"I don't think I've ever made iced tea." He looked around. "I suppose an electric teakettle's out of the question, then." He sounded impatient and Halle couldn't hold back her giggles.

"What's so damned funny, Halle?"

"You. You have your own jet and you're upset because I don't have an electric kettle?"

"You're right. It's nothing to get worked up about." Aggravation was overridden by determination on his face, complete with a day-old beard, and if they were a real couple, a twosome who'd planned to have a baby together, Halle would get up and hug him. Lean into him. She was going to have to settle for his financial support. Which made her skin crawl. Handouts were never part of Bluewood's financial prospectus.

"About your proposal, Alastair, what exactly are you putting on the table?"

"Tea, Halle. Wait for the tea." He'd already filled a measuring glass with water and it was heating in the microwave. Without much fuss he'd found the mugs and put a tea bag in each. The clean cuts of his casual, outdoorsy wear screamed "expensive" and the tall Scot looked as polished as the granite countertops her father had installed mere weeks before his death. He'd been in the process of updating the ranch house, his skills as a carpenter budget-friendly. Unlike her need to hire an expert for the more laborious tasks. Her father had said he'd wanted the ranch house "ready for when you come back home." Of course she'd never planned on returning to Shadow Creek so quickly, and worse, to an empty house.

The microwave beeped. Alastair opened the door and reached for the measuring cup. Halle saw the water, still boiling. "Wait! There are pot holders in the drawer there, to the right of the stove."

"I've handled boiling water be— Oow!" Alastair muttered a few more words under his breath as some of the water splashed on his hand. He set the cup on the counter and ran his hand under the faucet for a few seconds.

Halle was in the kitchen next to him in no time. "Are you blistering?"

"No, no, nothing serious. I'm running the cold tap merely as a precaution."

"You're 'running the cold tap,' eh? We usually say 'running cold water,' plain and simple." She jokingly smirked.

"English is a vast language." He shut off the water and dried his hands with the floral dishcloth, the girly print emphasizing his masculinity. He ignored her as he poured the water over the tea bags and picked the mugs up with each hand. "Where shall we sit?"

"Um, the living room." Anywhere but where she'd have to look into his eyes so up close. The man didn't know how to be anything but intense.

Halle sat on the sofa and noted how easily her father's chair fit Alastair's athletic form. Long and lean as Chancellor had been, Alastair settled into the space as if he'd been living at Bluewood for years instead of on his second visit to her home.

He looked at her over the steaming liquid. "Sip it slowly. You can leave the bag to steep—it gets better as it cools." He took a drink and she wondered if his tongue was made of steel as he didn't even flinch at the heat.

You know his tongue is one hundred percent male flesh. And her memory of how he'd used it on her skin still made her shiver.

"Alastair, please don't take this wrong—and I don't want it lost in translation between Scottish and American English." Her soft teasing didn't seem to lighten his mood. "You say you want to marry me. While I appreciate your offer, it's not necessary. We can sign a custody agreement, and you can go back to Scotland until the baby comes. I'll keep you posted on the progress, and I understand that you'll want to meet him or her right away. You can be at the birth." He was a businessman; she was betting that he'd go for the optimal negotiation.

"Absolutely not." His immediate response reverberated in the small room. "I'm not going anywhere, Halle. You're going to marry me." The implications of his entrenched position echoed not only in the kitchen but her heart. She'd misjudged him. Apparently the ruthless billionaire had impeccable personal integrity.

"You may have spent four days with me on the trail, but you don't know me, Alastair. I'm not the marrying kind, and I'm definitely not going to agree to something so crazy when my hormones are trying to run the show." Heat rose from her chest, up her neck. But it wasn't the result of her pregnancy woes. He opened his mouth to speak and she held up her hand.

"No, let me finish. My life is Bluewood Ranch. And even though it looks like it's going to go belly-up, I know its potential. If I work with a couple of other independent ranches in the area to coordinate business and tours, I can be solvent within eighteen months. I don't need as much seed money as you might think."

"It doesn't matter how much you need, Halle."

"Oh sure, I get it. Several thousand dollars is pennies to you. But it's my entire future. The baby's future." She faltered. The baby was never going to solely rely on her, not financially. She'd never have to worry about a college fund. Alastair could pay for several lifetimes' worth of degrees. The power of his position began to sink in, and Halle wasn't feeling so spunky all of a sudden.

"Are you through?"

"For now."

"I'm not going to agree to a business contract, Halle. We must be married—it's the quickest way to ensure my child will be my direct heir and he or she will bear my name."

"What you're proposing is a business contract, Alastair. You plan for us to divorce in a year. Wait." Icy fear ran down her spine. "You're not planning on taking the baby from me, are you?"

"Of course not. As long as you agree to marry me. If you don't, we'll have a long, drawn-out custody battle before the baby is born. It'd undoubtedly bleed over into the first year after his or her birth. I don't think you want to put yourself or Bluewood through that."

Halle stared at him. His expression wasn't smug or patronizing. It could be, as he must know he had her right where he wanted. She'd never be able to afford the legal fees. Not with her current portfolio.

She wanted to damn the man and more, damn that night of passion with him. But she couldn't regret the actions that created the baby she was carrying. As much as it'd been a surprise, she was already thinking about how it would feel to hold him or her. She was looking forward to becoming a mother, less than ideal circumstances and all.

At her silence, Alastair leaned forward. "It's a marriage in name only as far as you and I are concerned, Halle. But it's everything for our child. This will eliminate any doubt about where they came from, who they belong to."

"They can have all of that without us being married. Marriage seems so important to you, but what do you know about divorce, Alastair? That's just as ugly."

"We'll be divorced within a year of the baby's birth. Too soon to affect them. They'll grow up knowing both of us and whomever we each choose to be with in the future. It'll seem normal to them."

"You have it all figured out, don't you?" She heard the fear in her voice, felt her gut tighten into a spasm. He was hitting her at her most tender place. She knew all too well what it was like to grow up with only one known parent, as her mom had died in a freak ranch accident when she was a child.

"I'm suggesting what's best for everyone involved,

Halle. It's what I do for my business every day." A flicker of an emotion she didn't associate with the billionaire crossed Alastair's face. Doubt?

"And you're sure this is best for all of us, Alastair?"

He stared at her. Had she mistaken the cause of his doubt? The niggling guilt that his status could disappear if he didn't get a handle on his bleeding stocks increased in urgency.

"I'm certain about this, yes. It's what's best for our child and in the long run, you and me as well, Halle. It's important that we're amicable as we raise this child together."

"We'd draw up a contract, sign it? Or maybe you've already done this?"

"Yes, and to make sure you don't feel as though I'm taking advantage of your situation, I'd want you to have your lawyer look it over, too."

Her face relaxed for a millisecond. "It's just so much, so soon." Her voice was but a whisper and he looked closer. Her skin was green and a sheen of sweat was reflected at the base of her throat.

"Excuse me." She bolted for the small loo off the kitchen and the door slammed shut. But she didn't take, or more likely have, the time to turn on the sink taps. He heard every wretch, each moan she made in between what sounded like three rounds of morning sickness. At three thirty in the afternoon.

Remorse sucker punched him. He should have continued to try to reach her after he'd left Bluewood three months ago, never given up. At the least he could have asked Jeremy or Adeline to find out how Halle was doing in a casual way. Although the chances of the Kincaids knowing about Halle's personal life were slim. From all he'd seen, Halle was a loner.

The bathroom door opened and a subdued version of Halle walked out, moving with slow deliberation. "Do you mind if we keep talking in the living room? I feel better when I lie flat."

Alastair was up and next to her. He reached for her but she brushed his arms away. "I'm fine." He watched her shuffle to the sofa and lower herself onto it, on her back, bending her knees and placing her arm over her eyes. "Please, take a seat. It's just what it is right now. My midwife says I need to ride it out. I saw her after my doctor's appointment."

He took the large easy chair, pushing aside the ottoman in front of it. "Shouldn't you be seeing a doctor exclusively?"

"The midwife is a nurse practitioner who works directly with my doctor. She knows her stuff, and I trust her. If she thought I needed a referral to an obstetrician, she wouldn't hesitate. I thought that the social medicine system in the UK utilized midwives, too?"

"I, I don't know. My mother's a surgeon, but we've never talked about it."

"Why should you have? You're a single, financially independent whiskey baron. But you did tell your mother about the baby? Or how would you have known about the ginger tea?"

"I didn't tell my mother, but I did tell my sister. I trust her most, we've always been tight since we're less than eighteen months apart."

"I've always wanted a mother to talk to. Mine died when I was very young." She sighed and peered at him from under her slim forearm. "I'm not myself. I'm being a bit of a bitch and I'm sorry."

"I understand. Well, of course I don't understand, but I can empathize. And you're not being a bitch." Later, after he'd solved it, he'd share with her the ordeal he was going through with the possible hostile takeover. Halle was a woman who invited openness, not something he was used to. The women he got involved with, no matter the length of time, were usually all about trying to stoke his ego, having a good roll in the sack and enjoying the perks of his financial status. If he was honest with himself, it had always been about the sex for him, too.

Not that he'd ever minded the latter but the inflating his ego part had grown old years ago. Alastair wanted to have a conversation with a woman where sex wasn't seen as a possible tool to get ahold of his fortune or to obtain the kind of lifestyle his money bought.

"Tell me about your family, Alastair."

Her polite demand startled him. "It's all available on the internet. I'm sure you've discovered more than I'd tell you in conversation."

"Maybe, but it doesn't matter to me what it says on Wikipedia. I want to know about your family and your life's story from you."

Impressive.

"I was born in Glasgow. My parents still live there. And my grandmother lives on the large estate with all of us, in her own cottage. It's what you call 'independent living for seniors' in the States, I think. She's totally on her own but with her family there for support."

"What a loving family."

"We've been blessed but we all have our foibles. Do you have any siblings, Halle?"

"No, none at all. My dad used to say that he and my mother planned to have a baseball team—nine kids. But since my mother died, that didn't happen. I barely remember her. My father raised me, and he never remarried. I used to dream he would find someone, a woman who was wonderful and had kids of her own so that I'd have brothers and sisters."

He looked at her as she shrugged off her childhood dream, something that hadn't come true for her, as if it was no big deal. Did she have any idea how strong she was?

"Well, now you're starting your own team."

"Perhaps."

She didn't have to say the rest. The baby was the only family Halle had. It might very well be the only child she ever had. The realization that she had no one besides the baby made his worries about Clyde Whiskey seem almost trivial.

"Halle, if we marry, you'll be ensuring the baby has the big family you never did." She'd be making sure she had one, too, including Alastair. On paper.

"You know how to maneuver your opponent into a place where there's no choice but to do your bidding, don't you?"

"You're not my opponent."

"Au contraire, Alastair. If I don't agree to marrying you, that's exactly how you'll treat me."

"You're reading me wrong again, Halle. There's no way to treat you but as the mother of my child. That will be the same no matter what you decide. But if you marry me, the child will be more secure, more protected. And the ranch will be secure." He knew he was repeating it but he wanted her to understand that his intent was to add to her life, in a good way. Not take away anything that mattered to her.

"Are there a lot of papers in your contract?" A gleam he hadn't seen in her eyes appeared. She was actually thinking about it. He was grateful he was sitting as he thought his legs would give out, he was so relieved. Not a usual feeling for him, not since maybe his first success- ful business deal after university—over a decade ago.

"No. Only a few."

"I'm totally willing to sign that I don't want any part of your fortune. This is only for the baby."

"Which is why I'm not having you sign any papers to that effect. I get it, Halle, and I—I trust you. Trust me that the marriage, the paperwork, is to make things most expedient for the baby. To give him or her their birth- right." Only after he said the words did he realize how much he did trust her. Stupid of him, perhaps, but he'd always trusted his gut. "My solicitors, however, do in- sist that there's a paternity test."

"I'd expect no less. I've already given my blood sam- ple for one—my midwife only needs your cheek swab to send in the kit. Wouldn't you like to wait until the re- sults are in to get married?"

"No. If the test proves I'm not the father, we'll divorce immediately. If I am, as both you and I know I must be, then we've done the right thing."

"Why are you trusting me, Alastair? You've known me for such a short time. I could have been to bed with countless cowboys, as you said."

"From all accounts, that's not who you are. And I have to confess something to you. I'm a bit superstitious when it comes to any dealings in life. I think it's important to leave some things to chance, in a good way."

"Please tell me that you don't think, by having faith that the baby is yours, that you believe it will somehow protect the baby, keep it safe from everything that could happen to it."

"Maybe not that far, but let me just say it's my way of acknowledging I don't have all the answers. In my line of business I have to be on top of everything, know all the answers. It's a relief and downright joy to be able to let go and trust whenever I can."

"And you've chosen me to trust."

"I have. And I trust the process of it all. Face it, Halle, this is bigger than both of us. We tried to prevent it but it happened anyway. Fate is involved." The golden gleam in her eyes turned into a full-fledged flame.

"How can I argue with that? I'll call the town hall as soon as they open in the morning."

Alastair was wrong about the relief he'd felt moments earlier. It wasn't relief—it was jubilation. Over a woman he barely knew agreeing to marry him with a ticking clock of one year.

"Allow me to do at least one thing right here, Halle." He got to his knee on her hardwood floor and grasped her hands in his. "Will you marry me, Halle Ford?"

His breathing and heartbeat stopped in unison as he waited for her response. To his immense satisfaction, a kind of joy he couldn't articulate, tears welled in her eyes. As if this meant something more to her, too.

"Yes, Alastair Buchanan. I'll marry you."

Chapter 7

"Here. Eat." Maggie Colton balanced a basket of laundry on one hip as she slid a plate of French toast toward Halle.

"You know, this is the first time I haven't wanted to throw up at the sight of food." And Maggie's original recipe had everything to do with it. "Being pregnant looked great on you. You have to tell me how to make this." Halle swirled the maple syrup in thin loops over the browned cinnamon roll bread, still amazed that her stomach wasn't revolting. Yet.

"It's all in the bread."

"Which you made from scratch as usual."

"Actually, no." Maggie lowered the basket to the floor. "I'll fold that later. How often do you and I get to talk? The last time I tried to make bread, my elbow hit the bowl with the rising dough and tipped it all over the floor.

I was hosting Easter brunch for Thorne's family the next day and had no time to start over, so I improvised with the bakery's cinnamon loaf. Thorne couldn't tell the difference, so it's my new recipe." Maggie's eyes remained trained on Halle, her speech casual but her laser-sharp awareness evident. Maggie topped off her coffee before sliding into the chair across from Halle's at the kitchen table. "You look pale, Halle."

"It's the not eating. My morning sickness has been awful. I wasn't kidding—this is the first full meal I've had since, since—" she counted back "—since he showed up at my door." She'd left Alastair at the ranch house, his nose buried in his computer. As much as it would have been nice to see what Maggie thought of him, Halle needed girl time.

Maggie nodded in sympathy. "You told me his reaction wasn't as bad as you expected. What exactly did he say?"

Halle put her fork down and took a gulp of water. "He wants to marry me."

To her credit, Maggie didn't react. Save for the flutter of her eyelashes. "Really? I have to say, that's not a bad response."

"Give me a break! You sound just like him."

"You've let Alastair in and he's doing the right thing, even if you don't want to take it to a legal level for your relationship with him. You do need to figure out what you want for the baby, however."

"I know. I know what I want for the baby, and that's to marry Alastair as soon as possible. The woman I was before this happened is screaming inside my head that I'm nuts." The delicious breakfast was starting to look not so good as thoughts of how much her life was going to change washed over her. "I've barely been able to land back on my feet since Dad died. And now this."

"You've had some awful breaks, true. But having a baby doesn't have to fall under the 'catastrophe' heading."

"I agree. as scared as I am, I'm also excited in a very basic way that I didn't expect."

"Primal?"

"Yes! That's it. But with all that's gone on, it's as if every good thing around Bluewood is destined to fail."

Maggie reached across the table and gave her hand a reassuring squeeze. "Nothing about you having a baby is going to fail. Your dad's passing was an awful tragedy caused by the wicked witch of Shadow Creek. I never thought I'd say it's a good thing that someone died, but when she was killed it confirmed my belief that good can come out of the worst things." Maggie had loved Chancellor Ford as much as her own family, as she and Halle had run around Bluewood together since the time they could walk.

"That means a lot to me, Maggie, especially since you married a Colton."

"Livia Colton shared only the surname with her family. Especially her children. They suffered so much at her hands, before and after her death. I'm proud to have taken the Colton name, and not just because my son's a Colton."

"How's Thorne doing?" Maggie hadn't said much about her new husband.

Maggie's eyes glazed over. "Wonderful."

Halle held up a hand. "Stop. Right. There. That's all I need to know. You have that starry-eyed look going on."

Maggie's smile turned into a Cheshire cat grin. "I'm very happy. Never more so."

"And I'm happy for you." It was her own life she was worried about. "Did you ever think something awful was going to happen—"

"Before I got to enjoy life to its fullest? Are you crazy?"

Halle put her fork down. "I'm sorry, Maggie, really I am. I don't deserve your friendship. Here I've been going on and on about two good things—being pregnant and getting married, even if it is out of convenience, as if it's the end of the world. I've been so totally self-centered, whining about my issues." And she had.

Maggie shrugged. "We're together the way we're supposed to be. Which brings me right back to my original point."

"Before you go any further, remember that you've known Thorne a heck of a lot longer than I have Alastair."

Maggie shook her head. "It's not the time. Seriously. It's how he makes you feel. And how you make him feel must be pretty darn fantastic if he's proposed to you."

"No, I mean, yes, we have amazing chemistry. There's that. But he's a billionaire with solid ethics. He has the ability to do what he feels is right while also affording a way out of it."

"Are you afraid he's going to bankrupt you for some reason?" Incredulity rang in Maggie's voice.

"Not exactly. He's promised to help me get Bluewood back in the black, and I'm sure he assumes I won't pay him back. But of course I will. I have to. For any of this to work, I can't feel as if he gave me a handout or bought his way to the altar."

"Well, he kind of is trying to buy your hand in marriage, but I can see his point of view. He's the outsider here. Not only is he from out of town, he's a different nationality than you and potentially his unborn child. He may be desperate to make sure he has a definite connection to the baby. And if your intention is to pay him back, why are you second guessing any of this? Just sign a prenup that's beneficial to both of you—it's done all the time."

Prenup. Not something she'd thought about, but Alastair would be insane to marry her without one. For some reason, while her head totally understood the need for a contract of sorts, a tiny part of her heart died at the thought of it. Not that she had ever been the romantic type, or anything close to it. "It's not a true prenup, and I've agreed to sign it. In fact, I already did. I guess it's hard to see that I haven't brought the ranch up to speed with my own resources. Add the fact that I allowed myself to get pregnant, and it's left me wondering why I even came back here."

"First off, what do you mean, 'allow' yourself to get pregnant? It can happen to anyone. No protection is one hundred percent. You've decided to keep the baby, so it's a moot point anyhow. Second, you know why you came back to Shadow Creek, Halle. We all knew you would, someday. And when Chance died so unexpectedly, you absolutely did the right thing. If you'd waited, there wouldn't have been a Bluewood to come back to."

Maggie's words were spot-on but more, her sentiment was in perfect harmony with Halle's thoughts. "I'm so lucky to have you and Thorne to help me through all of this."

"And now you have Alastair's helping hands, too." Maggie waggled her brows with innuendo. Halle couldn't stop the laughter from bubbling up if she wanted to.

"You're bad. You know that, right?" They laughed together and Halle wished she could freeze the moment. Her life was changing in ways she could have never imagined just a few months ago. Add in Chance Ford's death not so long ago, and her life had been turned completely upside down inside of a year.

Alastair Buchanan's involvement in her life was the last thing she needed, but that horse left the barn out on the trail when she'd given in to her desire and experienced the most erotic night of her life.

No matter how confused she was at the moment, she'd never felt more alive than she had in the hands of a near stranger. A man who was the father of her child and would in fact become her husband.

As Halle drove back to the ranch, she tried to see it all through Alastair's eyes. The dilapidated buildings, the weathered siding on the ranch house, the lack of livestock that once filled every pasture. She had to blink to keep tears from falling. It wasn't self-pity or despair at how far her father's property had fallen over the past few years. It was facing her failure to see further than her big-city career aspirations. Why hadn't she noticed that he hadn't been able to keep up with the regular maintenance? If that Livia Colton hadn't killed him, when would Halle have figured out that her father needed her help?

Guilt, familiar and deadly, pierced her as she recalled the years she'd spent at a high-powered yet meaningless job in the city. It wasn't that the position or the company she worked for had been superfluous, but knowing her destiny was at Bluewood had always been there, simmering, in her deepest being. Not unlike how she felt about the baby she carried. It was as if her body, her soul, had come home to their fate.

Chapter 8

Halle couldn't believe it. She'd agreed to Alastair's crazy plan. It made sense on paper; she was going to be able to keep the ranch, and the baby would have it, too. She'd marry him in an hour, at the Shadow Creek courthouse. It'd been too easy, too simple to plan her wedding. A call to the town secretary yesterday, a quick run into town for the license, making an appointment with the judge today. They could even bring in their own minister if they'd like. It was done every day. Well, at least a couple of times a month in the small enclave of Shadow Creek. That should reassure her. She wasn't nuts. This was best for the baby's future, and hers. Bluewood's.

So why did her hands shake so much? No matter how deeply she breathed, how slowly, her erratic fingers smeared her mascara and eyeliner. At least she'd managed to paint her nails a sheer shade of pink. She looked at her bare hands. Did Alastair have a wedding ring for her? She had nothing for him, as she didn't want to assume he'd want to wear a ring.

"Don't be ridiculous," she whispered in the privacy of her room. She'd spent last night alone, in her bed as usual. Alastair had been true to his word and slept in the tiny guest room.

A quick rap at her bedroom door increased the batting of angel wings in her stomach. "I'll be out in a minute, Alastair." She finished her makeup with a swipe of pale pink lipstick that matched her manicure. The corresponding blush made a good difference on her cheeks, pale from the morning sickness.

She left her room, ready to face her groom. Her *groom*.

Alastair stood in the family room, the sunlight illuminating him like some kind of Greek god as it spilled in from the skylights. He was taller, looking more powerful than ever in a close-tailored Italian suit of silver gray. She'd seen the tag when he'd unpacked, telling her about his trip here. The blue-gray tie matched his eyes and dark shadows under them. It appeared he hadn't slept well in the guest room, but she didn't have much compassion for him there. She hadn't slept well, either. The agreement they'd reached could be construed as a deal with the devil, if she allowed herself to obsess over all the awful things he could do to her and the baby with the power his money brought.

Focus on the man Alastair. Not the billionaire.

"You're lovely." His rich voice rolled over and around her and made what they were doing feel almost normal. Right, even.

"And you're quite handsome." If they were a real bride and groom, would they be talking like this to one another? "We're breaking a big American tradition. Normally the groom isn't allowed to see the bride before the ceremony."

"You don't strike me as the superstitious type, Halle."

"I'm not, not usually. It's just that this isn't about you and me, Alastair. It's about the baby. I want it to be right for him or her. And you said you were superstitious."

He walked to her and reached out his hands, palms up. And waited. She stared at his large hands, the deep lines in his palms—he wasn't a man who solely worked behind a desk, on his computer. He was who he'd said he was—an outdoorsman who needed to put in desk hours so that he could continue his passion to live a full life. To give back. He hadn't personally told her about all of the charities he not only financially supported but visited on a regular basis. It was all on his company's website—photos showing Alastair in famine-struck nations, making a difference. Doing what was right.

She decided to trust him that this big step of her own was the right thing to do.

Halle placed her hands in his, and allowed him to hold hers, his thumbs caressing her. "We are doing the right thing, Halle. This will secure our baby's future, and more important, his or her safety. And yours. You're important to me, too. I told you, you're the mother of my child." She looked up at him and wanted desperately to believe him.

"I don't doubt your intention, Alastair. But it's not fair to either of us to count on more than providing for our child at this point, is it? We barely know one another."

"Oh, but I think we're off to a good start, don't you?" His laugh rolled along her arms, up to her breasts, her heart. She felt him in the deepest parts of her, and couldn't deny the heat he ignited each time he looked at her. He gently tugged on her arms. "Let's put aside our concerns about not knowing each other too well, about what the next year will bring, about how we'll separate and divorce. Let's just enjoy today. Can you do that?"

"Agree to take today on today's terms?" She hadn't heard a better offer in a long while. "Sounds good to me." She winked, actually *winked*, at him as she let go of his hands, and then bent to retrieve her small pearl beaded clutch.

"I'm sorry, I didn't have a white dress, but I think this will do." She motioned at her pale pink sleeveless dress, the fit-and-flare cut perfect as it was loose in the right place—her lower abdomen. Under the skirt her belly was beginning to bulge ever-so-slightly, and she swore her rib cage had grown, too, as the fitted part of the dress was far snugger than it had been off the rack. Alastair had offered to buy her a new dress, an entire wardrobe, but she wasn't ready for that. There would be time enough for new clothes as her figure changed. "I bought it on sale, thinking it'd be great for a friend's wedding or such. I never imagined I'd wear it to mine."

"It'll do quite nicely." His voice was gruff, his expression enigmatic. God, Halle wondered if he felt the tension, too. She wrapped the sheer chiffon scarf around her shoulders and smiled at him. "Ready when you are."

They walked to the front door, her iridescent silver beaded high heel sandals clicking next to the strong tap of his leather soled shoes. Also from an Italian designer, she had no doubt. Alastair was a man of good taste and she didn't think it had so much to do with his fortune as with the man who'd shown her his most passionate side barely three months ago. She lifted her fluffy white winter coat and Alastair took it from her, helping her shrug into it.

Once in the drive he took the wheel of her pickup truck. "I take it you don't have anything a little fancier?" The skin around his eyes crinkled and she answered with her own laugh. She was touched by the fact he'd not flashed his wealth around with an expensive car but instead had paid for a lift from the Austin airport, where his jet waited for his next trip.

"Do you mean like a Jaguar? This is very fancy for these parts, Alastair. It's practical, and it even has Wi-Fi. I didn't want to use Uber, like you did when you came from the airport. And a limo would be a bit much, considering our circumstances. We belong in a family car today." She'd leased the truck as it was more affordable for her at the moment than purchasing a new or used vehicle. "There is my father's old Chrysler, but it drives like a boat and the battery is iffy. It's probably time I sold it, anyhow." Another change she had to deal with.

"This is perfect. I was only teasing you, you know. And keep your father's car—we'll have it serviced. They don't make classics like that anymore." He maneuvered the truck as if he drove it regularly. Until he got to the first intersection leading into Shadow Creek and turned into the oncoming traffic the wrong way.

"Right side! We drive on the right!" She screamed and clutched the ceiling handle as Alastair veered away from two sedans and a minivan onto the grassy median, barely avoiding a collision. He brought the car to a stop and turned toward her.

"I'm so sorry, Halle. It's wedding jitters." His eyes were wide, his face slack with concern.

"I'd say it's more like remembering you're in the States. Do you want me to drive?" She couldn't believe that was her shaky voice. Any other time she'd insist upon taking the wheel. Did she actually care about empowering Alastair's driving confidence?

"No, I've got it. Won't happen again." He took a visibly deep breath before putting the truck back into gear and edging onto the right side of the highway. True to his word, he didn't err again and they made it to the courthouse on time and in one piece.

"Wait for me to come around." He flashed her a smile before he slid out of the driver's seat. Halle watched his tall figure stride around the front of the truck, his shoulders broad in his perfectly tailored suit, hair ruffled by the Texas breeze. A swell of tenderness rose, a welcome change from the nausea of the past weeks. Alastair's physical attractiveness was unsurpassed, but her desire for him was based on far more than flat abs and his skilled lovemaking. Alastair listened to her and made her feel as if they were on the same team. A winning team.

He opened her door and reached up for her, his hands around her waist as he lifted her from the car.

"Whoa!" She laughed, her hands on his chest for balance. "That's a little more gallant that I expected."

"Anything for you on your wedding day, my lady." He theatrically drew out the words in his Scottish brogue. The pure masculine gesture had her thinking about the possibility of a real wedding night. Complete with being naked against Alastair, making love until dawn broke.

"Shall we?" He had one arm around her waist and motioned at the county courthouse steps. The white stone blazed in the Texas sun, a bright omen, as far as Halle was concerned. She relished their walk up the steps and into the small rotunda, the vastness of the building enveloping them. Even the security checkpoint didn't faze her as the guard searched her purse and had them each step through a metal detector.

As much as it seemed so sterile an environment compared to a lavish church or temple wedding, Halle found it no less sacred. She was making vows to her baby's father. That meant something.

Alastair loved the feel of Halle's hand in his. Holding hands was highly underrated as an erotic foreplay skill. Her palm was small compared to his, yet fit perfectly against his hand, her skin soft as a whisper.

"I should have insisted you come back to Scotland with me. My family would throw us a beautiful wedding. You deserve at least that much, Halle." She deserved more than he could ever give her.

"Shh. This is perfect for us, right now. What more could we ask for?" She smiled and gestured at the historic architecture, her eyes appreciative. "This is charming, Alastair."

"It is." He couldn't argue. The Southern charm mixed with Texas strength was reflected in each carved column, the rich wood paneling adding the gravitas necessary to emphasize that what happened in this building was significant. Life changing.

They waited no more than five minutes before being ushered into the judge's chambers. Two court-appointed witnesses stood on either side of them as the judge presided. They faced one another and held hands, as if they were a real couple getting married for a real, lifelong union, 'til death did they part.

Halle looked up at him with complete trust and respect, and Alastair wished these were real vows. And decided in the moment between Halle's blinks that for him, they were.

As Alastair vowed to take her as his wife, a tear slipped from her eye as she thought of the one person she wished were here. Her father. As much as the wedding wasn't traditional, the vows weren't meant for each other but for their baby, she longed for Chancellor Ford's bigger-than-life presence.

"Halle, your hand." Alastair's voice was low and an anchor for her grief. She looked at him, then the judge.

"I'm sorry, I wasn't paying attention. I mean, I am paying attention, it's just that—" She swiped at her tears with the lace handkerchief that had been her grandmother's. "We don't have rings."

"Indeed we do." Alastair held two simple rings in his outstretched, open hand. The justice of the peace waited patiently as Halle stared at the burnished gold bands.

She brushed away the last of her tears and held out her hand for Alastair to place her ring on. It was a Celtic knot wedding band—beautifully striking in its design—pale gold and definitely Scottish. Halle wondered if it were an antique. It had a heft to it that modern rings didn't. And it fit her perfectly. "How did you know my size?"

He gently smiled. "Your turn." He handed her the remaining ring, a more masculine version of hers, and she placed it on Alastair's strong, rugged yet elegant finger. On the hand that had stroked her to a fever pitch in the tent that night, more than once.

The judge pronounced them married and Alastair must have been thinking of what his hands and fingers could do to her, too, as he took her face in said hands and laid on a full-tongue kiss in view of the judge and court recorder. Not that Halle minded. Like the rest of the day, it felt right, destined. Her mind wanted to fight the euphoria she was experiencing and she shoved the buzzkill away. Maybe they weren't a "real" bride and groom, but they'd taken a big step for their baby. God willing they'd both be around to raise their child, and her baby would have a fuller family than she had. This was something to be celebrated.

"Come on, Mrs. Buchanan." He stood next to her, his hand palm up as he waited. Alastair's calculating nature was undeniable and an asset to his career, but at this moment she saw beneath her initial judgment of him to what motivated his deliberate manner. Sincerity. Integrity. A quest for justice, no matter how messy.

She took his hand and allowed his strength to flow through her as they left the courthouse hand in hand. As if they were starting the rest of their lives today.

"That was a crazy rush." She leaned up against him on the sidewalk and gave him a sound kiss on his cheek. "I've never been married before."

"Nor have I. Come on, I've got another surprise for you."

"The rings were enough of a surprise, Alastair. Are they family heirlooms?"

"Something like that." He used his favorite mysterious reply and she let it be. They had enough reality to deal with, having a baby on the way and being married after being intimate for such a short time in their lives.

Would Alastair want to keep their sleeping arrangements apart the entire year? Did she?

"And how did you know my ring size?" A much safer topic than her thoughts.

"I didn't. It seems you have the same size as Great-Grandmother Buchanan."

"Your great-grandmother? So you did have to tell someone in your family about us."

"No, as I said, only my sister. She had the family rings and I wanted them. My grandmother gave them to her when she got married and she never got around to giving them back to her. It's only fitting that you have this one." He fingered the ring with his thumb as they held hands, gave her hand a reassuring squeeze. "If we decide to divorce in a year, we'll save it for the baby's future."

He'd silenced her, and not with the thought of his concern for his child's future.

With one word.

If.

Alastair helped Halle climb up into the passenger seat of her truck, relishing his role as a new husband. He chalked it up to his success at convincing her to marry him. He slid into the driver's seat but instead of starting the vehicle right away he faced her. When their eyes met the now familiar sense of coming home hit him. Not ready to deal with that, he studied her features, and thought how Botticelli's Venus didn't come close to the beauty Halle radiated. Pleased that she was relaxed, he wanted to give her the moon. Until he noticed that she was starting to get that heathery-green tinge on her skin again.

"Halle, I'd planned to take you into Austin for dinner at Wink. But I want to make sure it's what you want to do. It's the bride's day, or so I'm told. As much as we're not traditional, I'd like to keep some things that way. How are you feeling? Are you up to a drive after the ceremony?"

"I'm so sorry, Alastair, but I'm not really up for a

big, fancy meal. I'd much rather be able to enjoy it, and right now, I know I won't. You have to be tired from the jet lag, too."

"I'm not growing our child in my belly. Is there any-place around here I can take you?" He tried not to gri-mace at the few choices he'd seen on the highway from Austin to Shadow Creek—all fast-food joints. As much as he enjoyed American drive-through fare, his bride de-served better today. His *bride*. He hoped she didn't see the stark awe he experienced toward this day. Toward Halle. All of it had thrown his carefully constructed plan to marry her for the sake of the baby on its rear end. He'd never expected the extreme depth of their bond. And he didn't think it was one-sided.

"Honestly?" She tilted her head, a tiny smile on her face. "I'm craving the chicken tortilla soup at El Torero's."

"Then chicken tortilla soup is what you'll have." He had no idea what that was, but he was about to find out.

Ten minutes later they sat together in a cracked red leather booth seat in front of a large side window. It looked nothing like the upscale Austin restaurant web-sites he'd browsed. In fact, it was definitely unroman-tic. Cars were lined up in a neat row on the other side of the glass and the low din of other diners made it all but impossible to clearly hear the strains of the background music. A tune that Alastair associated with sexy Latin dancing.

It wasn't how he'd ever thought his wedding day would be celebrated, in a restaurant in Shadow Creek, Texas. But as the sun streamed in and lit up Halle's face, and she put away a large bowl of soup along with a buttered tortilla, he knew this was the right place to be.

"Do you like it?" She held her tablespoon halfway between her bowl and lips, her steady gaze on him.

"It's very good. I wasn't sure what to expect—maybe a nacho-cheesy kind of soup."

"Um, no. That would be called 'fondue' and that's not very Tex-Mex." She nodded toward the cash register before sipping from her spoon. "They have the best tortillas in the entire area, not only Shadow Creek. Sometimes I come up here and get a bunch to take back for my ranch hands. I make my own fillings if I have time, but I could never duplicate the tortillas."

"I have to admit these don't even compare to what we pass as tortillas in the UK. I guess naan bread would come closest, and I do have a favorite place for that in Glasgow."

"We have a few really great Indian places in Austin if you're interested." She put her spoon down. "I'm sorry, Alastair. You wanted today to be a little fancier, and I made us come here."

"We'll make up for it." And they would. He'd take her to the best places in Glasgow—hell, the world. They had a year of being together. For the baby's sake, of course. "When you're feeling better."

"About that—the doctor said this could go on for the rest of the pregnancy. Usually most women are sick in the beginning, and the nausea wears off by this time. But mine started up only over the past month and it's not showing any signs of easing up."

"Whatever you need, I'll make it happen."

Her hand, soft and light on his, said more than her explanation. "I don't want you thinking you can throw money at everything to fix it, Alastair. This is just the way it is. The baby needs to throw out whatever hor-

mones to thrive, and they happen to make me very ill."
She slurped another spoonful of broth. "Except right now
I feel like I could eat a vat of this!"

He laughed and dug back into his. The broth provided
the best gastronomic vehicle for the roasted chicken,
fresh corn kernels and what he thought was some kind
of milder green jalapeño. Crisp fried tortilla strips, from
day-old tortillas, according to Halle, were generously
sprinkled atop the soup along with some kind of soft
white cheese. Manchego, Halle had said. The soup was
unlike anything he'd had before, and with his global
business travels he'd honestly thought there was little
he hadn't sampled.

He'd thought the same about women but Halle Ford
had come barreling out of nowhere three months ago.
And now she was bearing his child. Their son or daughter. The heir to the Clyde Whiskey fortune, the next in
the long line of Buchanans.

"You look so serious. Cold feet?" Halle giggled at
her own joke.

"A little late for that, isn't it?" As her expression
deflated, it was his turn to reach for her. He grasped
her forearm and gave what he hoped was a reassuring
squeeze. "No, not at all. Admittedly it's not the first option either of us considered for marriage, or a wedding,
but it's not so bad, is it?"

"No, it's not." She took her plastic glass of carbonated
water with a twist of lime and held it up to him. "Cheers."

"Cheers." He toasted with his sweetened iced tea.

"Well, look-y here. How the hell are you, Halle? I
haven't seen you since, well…" Lydia Wyatt, a grade
school classmate of Halle's and part-time waitress,
stopped at their table.

"Since my father died? It's okay. I haven't been out much. The ranch is taking up my time. You don't happen to know anyone who'd like a tour of Texas trail country, do you?" Halle's charm came through and Alastair's belief in her stamina increased.

Lydia looked at Halle, then Alastair. "No, I don't but you can bet I'll pass that on. Have you thought of advertising on the place mats?"

"That is a great idea!" Halle asked Lydia about herself and her family, and Alastair was content to observe his wife in her local town. One thing was clear, the town loved the Fords and had all suffered when Chancellor died at the hands of that madwoman named Livia Colton.

As he listened he absentmindedly noticed that there was an alert on his phone. A stock alert—he clicked on the notice and read that the concerns he'd had of a corporate buyout weren't only his imagination. Some unknown buyer named SullaXS had begun a hostile takeover of his company. It was too close to his arrival in Texas to be coincidence. Intuition came to Alastair by way of his neck, and at the moment the hairs on his nape were standing straight up. He immediately fired off a text to his chief corporate digital securities officer.

"How do you two know one another?" Lydia's bright smile belied the stormy clouds haunting his business.

He forced his attention away from his phone screen and onto Halle. Alastair's stomach stopped plummeting and he didn't have to force his smile quite so much. He'd deal with whomever SullaXS was later. Today was his wedding day.

"Halle?" Let Halle explain as much or little as she wanted.

His bride blushed. "Alastair's my husband. We were

just married in the courthouse. I'm sure you'll see it in *Everything's Blogger in Texas* before tomorrow."

"What's that?" Alastair was almost afraid to ask.

"The local gossip rag, except it's online and instant." Halle's meaningful look let him know all he needed. Their nuptials were as good as globally broadcasted.

"Oh my goodness, how wonderful! Congratulations. You aren't from here, are you?" Lydia's eyes narrowed and Alastair shifted in his seat.

"I'm from Scotland."

"How romantic!" Lydia appeared ready to stay and give them the Texan inquisition but to Alastair's relief one of her customers waved their hand at her.

"I'm so sorry, you two. I've got to take care of this. Enjoy your day and don't do anything I wouldn't!" She winked at them as if Halle and he were going to go back to Bluewood and spend the rest of the day in bed.

Something he'd love to do. Something his instant erection agreed with. Even the threat of a buyout that put his entire corporation at risk couldn't put a damper on his desire for Halle. Being married to her was a simple legal connection, minor compared to the invisible bonds he felt growing stronger each time he looked at her.

His heart was in danger of being bought out by Halle Ford.

Halle couldn't stop the traitorous sparks of attraction that arced over her arm and across her breasts when Alastair touched her after Lydia walked away.

"You okay?"

"Yes, but are you? Maybe you wanted to keep our arrangement quiet?"

"Not in the least. Nothing is private in the world of

digital commerce, including an elopement of sorts." He smiled and she loved the crinkles at his eyes. But did Alastair think this was nothing more than a contractual "elopement"? Of course he did. He was a billionaire CEO. Something she had to remind herself if she didn't want him to break her heart. This was a business arrangement between them, not a romantic ending or beginning.

It was her wedding day, however, and she couldn't squash the growing anticipation in her belly. It was enough to shove the nausea away, at least for now.

In broad daylight, during a Saturday lunch in the town's bustling restaurant, the man's pure ruggedness had her psychically keening for him to kiss her again. To do more than kiss her, to make love to her. The undeniable attraction she had to him wasn't going away anytime soon.

She focused on her meal to keep her mind's erotic wanderings at bay. The green gills she'd had earlier were at bay, thanks to the medicinal qualities of her favorite childhood soup. The sodium levels probably had a lot to do with it, too.

"Whenever I was sick my dad would order this exact soup, to-go. He'd get a quesadilla for us, too—that's our local Tex-Mex version of grilled cheese. Two tortillas melted together with cheese. It was so good. He said it used to be my mother's favorite."

"You don't talk about your mother much." Alastair's eyes were thoughtful, watching.

"She died when I was five. I remember a few things— her hugs, her laughter, her smell. She smelled like clean laundry drying in the sun, macaroni and cheese, and honeysuckle." Laughter bubbled over. "Crazy kid mash-up, I know. I'm sure I've blended them all together when in reality I associated those smells with different events. But I don't have the sadness over her dying that my dad carried. I was too young."

"What did she die of?"

Funny how an event she didn't remember still clawed at her heart. "It was a stupid ranching accident. She'd gone out to make sure the animals were safely put away in the barn when a storm was coming in. She slipped and hit her head on the corner of a paddock, right here." She held her hand to her temple. "You may have seen the reports in the news over the last few years about how it's the most dangerous spot for soccer players to get hit, on the goalposts. There's a lot of promotion about it, to make parents more aware. You call soccer 'football,' right?"

He nodded, quiet and unreadable.

"Yes, well, my father wasn't home—he'd gone out to repair the fences and was fighting against the storm himself. By the time he got home, when he found my mother, she was gone. I was at school."

"He found her dead?"

Halle nodded. "Yes, lying in the corral. He never forgave himself, even though the doctors told him that there was little he could have done. Now we have more advanced treatment, but she bled out from an internal brain injury on the spot. Nothing would have saved her."

"Were there any witnesses?"

Halle paused, a sick twist in her gut at his words. "Witnesses? It wasn't a murder, for God's sake, Alastair. Ranching, farming—it's all hard work. People get hurt and have freak accidents more often than you might expect." She pictured him living in some huge castle with a drawbridge, said contraption drawn and keeping his clan safe from marauders.

"I'm sorry, Halle. That's no way for a little girl to lose her mother."

"Yeah, well, like I said, I don't have any memory of it."

"Except for your father's reaction?" So soft, so tender, as if he expected her to shatter with his questioning.

"Yes, Dad's reaction. That was awful. At first I was surrounded by a lot of love from both sets of grandparents, and my father's sister, Aunt Betsy. My grandparents had all passed away by the time I hit high school, and that left Dad and Aunt Betsy. She is still a rock to me and in fact I was going to ask her to come with us today, but…"

"But?"

"I haven't told her I'm pregnant yet. She'll be concerned about me, too much so, and she's got her hands full with my cousins and her grandkids. I don't want her worrying about me."

"It seems to me she'd be thrilled to see your father's legacy continue."

"Yes. Did Jeremy tell you any more than I did, about my father's death?"

"No. Well, yes. The part about Livia Colton." He took on a pinched expression. Odd. "Only that you've been trying to keep the ranch going since and it hasn't been the best time, financially."

"No, it hasn't. I've invested all that Dad left me back into the ranch and it looks good on paper. The reality of it is a bit harsher, I'll admit. I just need a little more time to see the investments pay off." She fingered her paper place mat, the familiar printed advertisements promising the "best" salon, cemetery, dentist and more in Shadow Creek. Soon she'd have the Bluewood logo in one of the promotional boxes. "I suppose you don't allow yourself time to make good on your investments. You expect immediate positive payoff."

His laugh was short but powerful. "That would be ideal, but rarely happens. Not anymore." Something warm and soothing unfurled in her belly at the whiteness of his teeth against his skin. And his candidness with her.

"I thought it was an instant-gratification world?"

"In many businesses, yes, but I deal with a man-made, centuries-old recipe. That's what all of my business dealings and investments come down to. Whiskey is my core product. So no matter how modern technology or stock performance affects my industry, if my product isn't up to snuff it doesn't matter."

"So, even if all the modern trappings of business in the twenty-first century were to melt away, you'd still have your brew. Your whiskey."

"Yes. That's the secret to my success, to the sales margins of Clyde Whiskey."

"That's how I feel about Bluewood Ranch. It's an infinitesimal outfit compared to Clyde Whiskey, I get that. But it's just as important to me. And at its root I know it's a viable operation."

"It means everything to you, am I right?"

"Yes." She met his steel blue gaze. "It's my legacy. And now, our baby's."

Chapter 9

"Your carriage awaits, Madame." Alastair reached out to her with a small smile and his hand, which she grasped as she placed a foot on the truck's running board.

"Thank you." Before Halle could pull herself up onto the passenger seat, Alastair's hand was on her lower back, heat scorching through the thin dress fabric. She felt as if she'd see his handprint on her skin if she looked in a mirror, she was that tuned into him. Not to mention turned on by him. It had to be the wedding—it was natural for it to make her feel sexually needy, wasn't it? No matter the motivations, they were husband and wife.

His hand moved to her leg as soon as she was settled. He gave her thigh a squeeze just above her knee. "Okay?"

She looked down at his strong hand, only a portion of which was visible under the layers of her full tulle skirt. He hadn't meant it as a come-on, she was sure; it was a comforting gesture. But because of the slipperiness of the material his hand had slid to the top of her thigh, and as she looked at him she almost willed him to extend his glorious fingers up a bit higher, to find the lacy white slip of panties she'd worn to match the dress. *You didn't wear panties; you put on a thong.*

Yes, she'd put on a thong, and that was something she didn't do during the everyday work of running her ranch. She'd thought about Alastair's reaction, the familiar heat in his eyes, if he saw her sexy underwear. The heat that was radiating off him, fueled by the sparks in his blue eyes as they locked gazes over her frothy dress, could melt a snow cone in January. And he hadn't even seen her lingerie.

They were married—it wasn't illegal to have a midday sexual fantasy about her dearly beloved, was it?

"Okay." Her aroused state made her reply sound more like Marilyn Monroe about to sing "Happy Birthday" to her favorite president.

His eyes narrowed and an undeniable smoky want in their depths signaled that Alastair felt their chemistry, too. She offered him a smile. "We never said how long you'd be staying in the guest room."

His breath hissed in and he jerked his hand off her thigh. "No, we did not." He shut the passenger door and she watched him stride around the hood of the truck, his expression not as relaxed as it'd been in the diner. This was the look of Alastair on the prowl. Worked up, needing a toss in the hay.

Get a grip. This is a business arrangement. Her hormones disagreed.

The driver's side door opened and his scent preceded him. She loved the smell of Alastair—freshness and all-male sexy musk. Did Scotland smell like this? She didn't remember that from her year abroad. She laughed.

"What's so funny?" He didn't look at her as he spoke, shifting the gear into Drive and turning toward home.

"I'm thinking back to when I went to college in Glasgow for my junior year. It was so much fun, but now it's mostly a blur in my mind. I remember a lot of taverns, beer and The Mackintosh House." She was reluctant to tell him her more traitorous thoughts—ones that involved them both naked.

"And that's humorous why?"

"Um, private reason." She kept her gaze forward, hoping he'd let it go.

"How long ago, exactly, was that?" His words were clipped and sounded closer to a British accent than his usual Scottish brogue. This was professional, no-nonsense Alastair. The coolness in his tone didn't completely quench her desire for him but it helped.

"It was my junior year, so…twelve years ago." She looked out her window and watched Shadow Creek give way to the desolate countryside she so loved. Home.

"I daresay Glasgow would look the same to you as far as the city landmarks go, but it's expanding and modernizing at the most rapid rate since after the war."

"It's always been home to you, then? Your family, too?"

He shrugged. "All of Scotland is my home. With the family business headquartered in Glasgow, we've had to open offices in Edinburgh and London to facilitate distribution." He strummed his fingers on the steering wheel. "I live exclusively in Glasgow but my parents have semiretired and move to the Highlands come summer. I've purchased land not far from them and plan to build my own respite. Right now I have a smaller cottage on the property I use when I'm there. They live there along with my grandmother."

"Do you like city or country living better?"

"City living in Glasgow isn't the same as Dallas, or New York City, or even Austin. But yes, I prefer more activity."

"Then Shadow Creek must seem so boring to you."

"*Boring* isn't the adjective I'd use. To be honest I've never been uninterested in any part of the world—it's always about the people." Finally he blessed her again with his gaze. She'd never tire of it—as she'd never tire of watching the ocean when she stood on a beach. His eyes flicked to her belly, then back on the road. "My good friend Jeremy is here, of course, and now, I'll forever have a connection to Shadow Creek, won't I?"

Halle sure hoped the heat he was sending out was intentional, and that he wanted to celebrate their nuptial contract as much as she did. His signals were as mixed as her feelings—as if he, too, felt the need that thrummed between them but, like her, worried they were indulging where they shouldn't. It had been simpler on the trail, before their duty to the baby appeared.

"I never thought I'd get married." A lump grew in her throat, totally unexpected.

"Never? But all you speak about is your legacy. A legacy must be passed on."

"I know. And I never thought I'd be pregnant—it wasn't something I've ever longed for or felt was necessary for a complete life." She fiddled with the sheer overlay of her skirt. "Since my father was killed I've thought about it more, that if I didn't marry I'd eventually have my own child, either by in vitro or adoption."

"And now?"

"And now I'm driving home with my husband and I have a bun in the oven." Someone had to lighten the mood; it might as well be her.

"A 'bun in your oven'?" Alastair smiled. "Sounds like something my grandmother would say."

"The same one that lives near you?"

"Actually, yes, my only remaining grandparent. She's ninety-five and lives on the same property as my parents and I, but in her own small cottage. It's in between my small place that I mentioned and my folks'."

"She still lives by herself?"

"Yes. Of course, my father checks in on her each day, and my mother helps with any physical needs like bathing or lifting heavier items. Her shoulders are racked with arthritis from her years of working in the distillery. But she's very independent, and thank God has no symptoms of dementia. It's imperative she keep every last vestige of independence for as long as possible."

"She sounds like someone I'd get along well with."

"You're very much like her. And when she and my grandfather met, she was alone, too." He said no more and she didn't encourage him to open up. Their relationship wasn't like his grandparents' in one key aspect, she was certain. They hadn't signed a contract and agreed to divorce in one year.

"Tired?" His hand covered hers on the leather armrest between them. He must have heard her sigh, a breath she'd not been aware of.

"I'm fine. Although a nap might be in order."

"We're almost home."

Home. It wasn't hers alone anymore, no matter what Alastair promised about her keeping all of the assets she came into the marriage with. And hopefully left with, but in a much better financial state. She ignored any concern over what the state of her heart would be after they dissolved their union. Why borrow trouble?

Alastair didn't trust himself to speak as he drove up into Bluewood and headed straight for the ranch house. He'd been fighting a full erection since they'd left the diner, since after he'd kissed her so less-than-platonically at the courthouse. Probably since he'd landed in Shadow Creek, if he were to be brutally honest.

"Don't pull up at the door. Park the truck over there." She pointed to the grassy area alongside the corral and barn. "The truck blocks the view from the porch if we put it here. The sunsets are spectacular this time of year. You won't believe how it is next month, in December, as the air gets colder and the sky looks like an endless carpet sprinkled with stars."

He didn't reply but turned and stopped the truck where she'd asked. Halle's pale hand reached for her door and the click of the passenger door lock reverberated through the front seat as if it'd been a gunshot. Couldn't she wait to get away from him, out of his reach? Or was she as fired up as him? As confused?

"Halle, wait." He placed his hand on her shoulder. Her silky cover-up was the only thing between his palm and the creamy smoothness of her skin. The fabric bunched under his fingertips as he caressed her and he fought from ripping it away so that his tongue could taste that sweet spot between her nape and shoulder again.

She turned back, away from the door, and the smolder in her eyes slayed him. Her long locks had started to come loose from her sophisticated updo, framing her heart-shaped face. The auburn strands glinted copper in the afternoon sunlight. Her lips were full, her bottom lip more so, as if she'd been worrying them the entire drive home. Home. Whether he wanted it or not, he had another home where his child had been conceived.

"Before we go inside, I want to make sure we're on the same footing. It's not going to be easy this year, with all the changes." He ran his index finger down her creamy cheek.

Her eyes narrowed. "What do you mean by 'footing'?"

"I mean I don't want anything to happen that we'd both regret." Hell's bells, the tone of his voice was absolutely pleading. Definitely not a corporate boardroom manner.

"You mean we shouldn't partake in any connubial bliss?" Halle's sweet lips formed the words as sexily as if she'd uttered an erotic request. His gut tightened at the image of what that bliss would entail, while acknowledging the fresh, incredibly funny side of Halle he'd only just begun to discover. No woman had ever stoked him like this before.

"If we do, if we *did*, ah, go to bed, it has to be mutual and with no strings. I never want you to feel I'm pushing you into something."

"But I can push you into doing what I want?" Her dimples had teased him since they'd met and begged for his tongue to explore them and he allowed his fingers to stroke the side of her neck.

"Do you ever not joke about things, Halle? This isn't a comedy." He barely got the words out, so large was the rock in his throat. She had him tied in knots and he knew one sure way to get the tangles out. For both of them.

She continued to stare him down, and Alastair decided it was time to employ his most ingrained CEO leadership skills. Decisiveness. He moved his hand from her shoulder to her nape, and gently tugged. When she offered no resistance, but in fact leaned in toward him, Alastair imploded with his craving for Halle and hauled her to him, crushing his lips on hers.

Halle was as willing and as hungry as he, if the way she met his tongue with hers was any decent measure.

Her enthusiasm rocked his self-control. Her hands were cool on his nape, on his scalp. Her long fingers tugged on his short hair as her tongue dipped into his mouth and fought his. Her taste, so sweet, so hot.

"Halle." Her name came out on a groan, and he lifted his mouth from her lips only to suck teasingly at her throat. He needed the breasts he held to be free of her bra, out of the girly dress. Alastair wouldn't be satisfied until they were skin on skin. In broad daylight, across her bed or his or the damned truck bench seat, he didn't care. "I need to see you, all of you. Now, Halle."

Her gasps turned to soft pants as he touched her thigh, moved higher to her panties and stroked her heat. The thin fabric was wet from her arousal and he wanted to shout with relief at his discovery. "Let me see you, Halle."

She stilled and he froze. Regret started its freezing march across his heart. He'd pushed too far, too soon. He'd forgotten that at the center of it all, this was only a business negotiation. He braced for her rejection.

"Not here. Not in the truck, Alastair." She still wanted him!

Lust slammed into him again and he gave her a short, hard kiss, afraid to linger or he'd make love to her with no preliminaries in the damned vehicle. This was their wedding day, and he didn't want to treat her like a farm animal in heat.

"Wait here."

He was out of the cab and lifted her from her seat in record time. He grasped her hand and tugged her alongside him as they walked to the weathered front porch of her modest ranch home.

"Alastair, slow down. We have all day." He ignored her words and heard only the breathlessness with which she said them. He looked at her as he kept walking, taken in by the peachy rush of color on her cheeks and the deep red of her lips. She was as hot and ready for him as he was for her.

"Exactly. And I don't want to waste one minute, one second of it out here." He didn't stop, willing the hundred feet or so to close, seeing her splayed out on the bed, her dress hiked to her waist—

"Oh. My. God." Halle stopped dead in her tracks and he almost toppled over her before he let go of her hand. Absolute horror stamped her expression, obliterating the wanton aura of seconds ago. "Alastair, look." She pointed at the porch.

At first he saw nothing. The sun was still bright and the porch roofed, so all he made out was the dark area past the three steps to reach the door. And then, at the base of the door, he saw it. A severed cow's head, blood still fresh and dripping onto the wooden porch slats, leaned against Halle's front door.

Alastair immediately grabbed Halle to him, trying to shield her. "Don't look at it."

"Like hell I won't." The woman he barely knew, yet felt the deepest connection of his life with, shoved him away and strode up to the porch. "Oh God, it's Ernie."

She knelt next to the longhorn's head, placing her hand on the space between the dead steer's eyes. "He was the last steer that Daddy bought. I couldn't bear to sell him."

Alastair watched her, torn between wanting to rip her away from such horror, save her from any distress, and wanting to turn and go find whoever did this. Because the perpetrator would pay. Dearly.

Instead he knelt next to her and placed his arm around her shoulders. "I'm so sorry, lass. Who would have done this?"

She shook her head, her fancy chignon but a memory after their near-lovemaking in the truck and their hurried walk here. "No idea. Some sick, sick loser. What the hell is wrong with people?"

"Here." Alastair handed her the ivory handkerchief from his breast pocket. It somehow comforted him to see her use the same square of linen his great-grandmother had used to carry her wedding bouquet of Scottish heather and daisies. He'd tell her that detail later.

"Thanks." She gave her nose a hearty blow and crumpled the cloth in her hand, still staring at her beloved steer. The remains of him, at any rate. Crap. He was going to help her get rid of this, and then he'd go find the rest of the steer. His hands tightened into fists and he clenched his jaw. When he caught the criminal, they'd regret this for the rest of their life.

"I need to call the sheriff." His bride had an iron will.

"Here." He helped her stand before lowering both of them onto the porch swing not three feet away. A quiet, restful place on the ranch that some jerk had shattered with a gratuitous act of violence. Keeping his arm around her, he handed her his phone. "Call with my mobile."

Halle did so, and he noted her hands trembled but her

spine was steel-straight. He'd not married a shrinking violet, that was certain. As shaken as she was, her voice was steady and precise as she explained what was on her front porch in excruciating detail.

"The sheriff will be right out." Halle's eyes met his briefly before they moved back to the gruesome scene.

"Don't look at it, Halle."

"Ernie was mine. I owe it to him to see this through." She abruptly stood, leaving Alastair swinging. Before he could reach out to stop her, she leaned over the butchered animal, her hand grabbing what looked like a piece of paper that had been wedged into the screen door.

"A note. The bastard." Halle held up a business-sized envelope for him to see and he watched her tear it open and pull out a sheet of paper, along with a pink handkerchief.

"Halle, leave it—it could be evidence for the sheriff."

She paid no heed and stared at the letter, her expression grim and unyielding. She should have looked ridiculous, the infuriated ranch owner on whom someone played a vicious, awful prank. Her hair was a wild reddish mane about her, her crushed dress stained with blood on the hem, her dainty sandals standing in the blood that had started to congeal on the porch floor. Instead, Halle Ford was the embodiment of a Celtic warrior princess. His avenging angel.

Alastair knew in that moment that he was screwed. It wasn't the fact that he reacted so strongly to Halle's suffering. That he could chalk up to compassion, or even concern for the mother of his child. What clued him in that he'd passed the point of any possible emotional detachment from Halle was his heart's anguish.

Chapter 10

Halle stared at the blood note. Literally, a blood note, written in Ernie's, no doubt. She turned it around to show Alastair the one red word, "SELL."

"This wasn't just some kid's prank, Alastair. And this pink handkerchief? It's the type that Livia Colton uses. Except she's dead."

Alastair actually blanched, or was that a grimace? Her tough Scottish husband didn't strike her as squeamish. So was he holding back his deeper feelings about the slaughter? He hadn't balked at the grade-B horror movie scene on her front steps, but a word written in blood about a ranch that wasn't anything to him yet made him look as green as she'd felt these past weeks?

Halle couldn't stop the laughter if she wanted to. Alastair was immediately at her side, his hands on her shoulders. "Breathe, Halle. This is shock."

"No, no, it's not, Alastair. This is me laughing at the ridiculousness of this. This is the first time I haven't felt sick to my stomach and you're the one who looks like you're going to blow chunks at any moment!" She bent over with the giggles, hoping she didn't find herself needing to pee because getting to the bathroom with a dead steer's head in her way would be awkward at best.

Which only made her laugh more.

Alastair backed away but not before taking the note and handkerchief from her. He held both by their tippy-top corners and laid them on the porch swing. As soon as she could, she used the tissue he'd handed her to wipe the tears from her eyes, marveling that the lavender-scented object hadn't disintegrated after so much use. But it wasn't a paper tissue; it was a white linen handker-chief. Lace trimmed, with an elaborately embroidered *B* on one corner. It didn't feel starched but soft with wear, and the ivory shade indicated age. "Alastair, is this a family heirloom?"

A quick flash of the North Sea as he looked at her. "My great-grandmother's. My great-great-grandmother gave it to her in a set when she married into the Buchanan clan. The grandmother I told you about gave it to me, for my future bride. My sister has one, too." Thoughtful-ness, a softening of his features before he focused back on the creepy note.

"And you let me blow my nose in it?"

"Halle. You have a severed cow's head on your front door with a note from someone telling you to sell. My great-grandmother's handkerchief and how it will get laundered is the least of our problems. It's lasted over a century and a half, it'll last another day."

"I forgot about how Europeans take history for granted. And it's a steer. Not a cow."

"Come here, babe." He opened his arms and she went, telling herself it was for moral support and that her heart hadn't pulsed at his Scottish endearment. She wrapped her arms around his waist and rested her head on his chest, which was the perfect height for her. Strong arms held her close and when he started to caress between her shoulders she relaxed into him. "That's it, just let it all go. We're going to find out who did this and they'll get their comeuppance."

"You sound like Mary Poppins." She murmured into his ivory shirt, the silk tie smooth and cool against her cheeks. Grasping his lapels, she looked up at him as they stood on the battered porch, turned away from the grisly greeting that had welcomed them home. "I think I need more than a spoonful of sugar to get through this, Alastair."

He grinned and kissed her on the forehead. "You're not alone, Halle."

They were still standing in their embrace when the first sounds of the sheriff's vehicle reached Halle's ears. She lifted her head and saw the telltale plume of dust rising behind the car. In spite of the heavy rains of the last couple of weeks, the dirt had dried enough on the surface to allow brown clouds to form around his approach.

"I take it that's the sheriff?" Alastair's arms remained around her, as if he didn't want to let go any more than she did.

Reluctantly Halle pulled away. "Yes. It's Jimbo Mc-Croy. I went to high school with him."

"Is there anyone in Shadow Creek you don't know?"

"Actually, Jimbo is the Sheriff of Creek County, but

we're all a tight community. He works closely with the Shadow Creek Sheriff, Knox Colton, my friend Allison's husband. We're all very close in these parts. That's how I know word of our being married is going to get out quickly." And she had an awful feeling that their marriage had somehow set off this awful event.

The car turned on a dime and came to a halt perpendicular to the front porch. Halle thought the former high school athlete was overkilling it on the driving but kept it to herself. Right now, they needed help from the law.

Looking every bit the tall, studly Texan that he was, Jimbo got out and strolled over to them, his cowboy hat pulled low over his eyes. Halle suspected he was balding as she never saw him without the Stetson.

"Hey, Halle, honey. Bring it on in here." Jimbo held out his arms and Halle stepped off the porch to give him a friendly hug. Of course Jimbo had to show off his still fantastically built body and hugged her high, lifting her off her feet. Her breasts squashed against his chest and she looked at her former classmate with chagrin. "Really, Jimbo?"

White teeth flashed as he set her down and let out a laugh. "Halle, you haven't changed a bit. Don't ever, darlin'. Look at you—you're so pretty in that dress. Oh, sorry about the blood. I haven't seen you since your daddy passed. How you making out, other than today's fiasco?"

"I'm good, Jimbo." Alastair walked silently up next to her. She felt his heat shimmer off his body, and suspected it wasn't desire but something else aimed at Jimbo. Alastair wasn't jealous, why would he be? It had to be his anger at the situation.

"Jimbo McCroy." The former football star stuck out

his overdeveloped forearm and Alastair accepted the handshake.

"Alastair Buchanan."

"Alastair's my husband." Halle blurted out the truth before she could think. Jimbo was bound to find out soon enough, if he hadn't already. They'd had a civil ceremony at the courthouse, for God's sake. News never traveled slower than the speed of a pinto in Shadow Creek.

The pronouncement was enough to cause Jimbo to tilt his hat back, revealing a large, smooth forehead against which his brows rose with incredulity. "So I heard. I'll admit it was a bit of a surprise when I read about it this morning. Not that Halle hasn't been on the wish list of a long line of Shadow Creek guys. Congratulations!" A gentleman at heart, Jimbo leaned in and gave Halle a kiss on the cheek, then turned to Alastair and clapped him on the shoulder while shaking his hand again. "Congratulations and welcome to Creek County and Shadow Creek, Alastair."

"Thank you." Alastair found his voice before Halle, and she wondered if his teeth appeared clenched because he was angry at her. It was the second time she'd revealed their quickie wedding. Even though he'd said he hadn't expected it to stay secret, Alastair was accustomed to confidential business dealings. He'd learn quickly that nothing in Shadow Creek was a secret for very long.

"What did you mean by you 'read' about it, Jimbo?" Alastair's question was fair.

"It's on *Everything's Blogger in Texas*. They list everything from burglaries to births. That's where you saw it, Jimbo?"

"Yes, read it there about two minutes after you said

'I do.' You two are a good-looking couple. How'd you meet?"

"Mutual acquaintances. Jeremy Kincaid and his wife, Adeline." Alastair's clipped response had the tone of "none of your Texas beeswax, Jimbo."

"Wow, so you're a bud of Jeremy's." Jimbo stuck his thumbs in his gun holster. "There's a classmate who's made it big, for sure."

Halle wasn't about to reveal that Alastair was in fact ten, twenty times richer than Jeremy. It wasn't anyone's business, and even though she trusted Jimbo, she had her child to think of now. Their child. She looked at Alastair and dug deep to offer a sunshiny smile. "We did a trail ride together and the rest is history, isn't it, babe?" Using his earlier Scottish sentiment came naturally. Too easily. She'd worry about that later. Besides, it was probably the shock of the morning. Poor, poor Ernie.

"So, when did you come back to Bluewood?"

"Just now, maybe twenty minutes ago." Alastair spoke with command. Again, she had a sense of this relationship becoming far more than a parenting agreement.

"And you came home to this crap. I am sorry, Halle. Let me go take a look. I'll shoot some photos, collect evidence."

"Have there been any other pranks like this lately?" Halle prayed there had been but couldn't shake the very personal feeling of this. Someone wanted her out of Shadow Creek, Bluewood shut down.

"No, save for some cow-tipping on the dairy farms east of here. Usually the teens leave the longhorns alone. But don't you worry. It usually doesn't get much safer or quieter than Shadow Creek, Halle. You know that." He scratched his forearm. "But that's changed since Livia Colton stirred things up, hasn't it?"

She knew he referred to things like hit and runs that took away her father before his time, before she was ever ready to let go of him. He was too polite to spell it out.

Jimbo walked up to the porch. Halle and Alastair stayed in the small front yard, giving the sheriff space to do his job without distraction.

Alastair faced her squarely. "He's awfully friendly. I take it you were more than school chums?"

Halle looked at Alastair's guarded expression. And laughed. "Please tell me you're not doing some kind of testosterone jig over Jimbo. We were never more than classmates. He comes off as overly affectionate, is all. I didn't date football players." No, she'd always gone for the more intellectual types. The bright, quiet boys who grew up to become brilliant doctors or engineers. Or entrepreneurs. Like Alastair.

"How long has he been in law enforcement?"

"Forever. I think he took criminal justice on his football scholarship to A&M, and he was on the Austin PD for a long while. Here in the States, sheriffs are usually elected and are at the county level. While my address says 'Shadow Creek,' Bluewood is actually outside of the town's limits, in the jurisdiction of Creek County."

"He had to run a political campaign to be sheriff?" The muscles in Alastair's jaw were so taut Halle's fingers itched to see if she could pluck them like a violin.

"Yes, but it's not like any other political position. A lot of times the sheriff runs unopposed, and no one cares much which political party he represents. They just want someone competent in the office. Someone who understands the locals and the conditions of the land out here."

"Hey, did either of you touch this note or the hand-kerchief?" Jimbo held the blood-written note with two latex-gloved fingers, an evidence bag in his other hand.

"We both did, but we were careful to handle them on the edges. I did touch the back of the letter, though, be-fore Alastair reminded me not to." Halle felt stupid that she'd contaminated evidence.

"Okay, no worries but I'll need to get both of your prints before I leave, for comparison."

"He's not getting my fingerprints." Alastair spoke through tight lips.

"He's not going to steal your identity or anything, Alastair. Unless, oh boy." She took a deep gulp of air, chose her words carefully. "You're not doing anything illegal now, or in the past, with this huge business you run, are you?" She knew that it was hard to keep a large corporation like the Clyde Whiskey conglomerate com-pletely clean. She'd read enough suspense novels and kept up with international business news as a hobby. Dreaming that Bluewood might one day become its own huge business.

"I'm not a damned criminal, Halle. So the answer is no, my business isn't dirty. Not in the least. This is about the security measures I've been trying to distill for you in digestible chunks. If my fingerprints get out into a large system like the United States government data-base, someone could hack them and then get into other parts of my identity."

Halle had had enough of Alastair's billionaire worries. "Hey, Jimbo, will you put our prints into a big database?"

"Huh? No, no way. That's against the law and privacy acts. I can only take your prints with your permission and you'll sign a release to allow the Sheriff's Department to use them only for the sake of comparison. Then we destroy them." He sealed the second zipper top plastic bag, the pink handkerchief mocking Halle's sanity. "To be honest, I'd bet my paycheck that we'll only find your prints here. Whoever did this doesn't want to get caught, trust me."

"How can you be certain? Don't mentally ill people do things like this? It could be a cry for help." Alastair's comment sounded good to Halle. And she wanted to believe it—that this wasn't anything real. On her wedding day, of all times.

Jimbo shook his head. "First, they had to know enough about Texas livestock to be able to wrangle this steer out of your paddock without hurting themselves. Second, they butchered the poor guy in cold blood, and if it's their third time doing so, it's a felony in Texas. At the very least they're facing a misdemeanor and stiff fine. Third, they left a threatening note and are trying to impersonate a dead woman with this pink cloth. That's another felony of its own type. I'm going to have to dust the horns for prints, just in case, and send them off to the lab for blood analysis, to make sure it's just cow's blood all over the place. We don't have fancy lab facilities here in Creek County. Have you had any other types of similar, smaller incidents around the ranch lately?" Jimbo directed his query to Halle.

"No, nothing like this." Ever. Which was why her insides were quaking.

Jimbo spoke as he worked. "Is Charlie working today, Halle?"

"He was here earlier, along with one of the part-time hands."

"Have one of them come up here and clean this up."

"I told them to take the rest of today off, on account of the wedding. Besides, I want to bury Ernie properly. He was more than another head of cattle."

"Understood. Which brings me to another ugly question—where's the rest of Ernie?"

Halle hadn't felt even a twinge of nausea since they'd pulled up to the house all hot and bothered, ready to do the horizontal two-step like two lust-struck teens. But when Jimbo reminded her of the dreadful way Ernie had met his demise, she couldn't stop the ubiquitous queasiness.

Her morning sickness had paid an afternoon visit.

Chapter 11

Alastair's anger simmered long and hot as he and Jimbo walked out to the pasture. This was too much for her, between the morning sickness and finding her steer slaughtered.

And despite Halle's protestations to the contrary, Sheriff Jimbo seemed awfully friendly for a simple secondary-school friend. They stopped and stood next to one another in the field just outside of Bluewood's paddock. They'd found the rest of Ernie. He'd been left like shark chum in the middle of the pasture where Halle's other livestock usually grazed.

"Mr. Ford, Halle's dad, used to have this pasture chock-full of cattle." Jimbo snapped photos with his phone, talking as he went.

"If it's up to me, she'll have it full again."

Jimbo paused and gave him a hard look. "I hope you

mean it, Alastair. Halle's good people, and she did right by her daddy. She left a lucrative career in Austin to come home and manage the ranch, to keep the family business going. You don't see a lot of us doing that any longer. She deserves the best."

Alastair remained silent. He wanted to call Jimbo out for posing as a new friend when in reality he was obviously attracted to Halle and cared a great deal for her. Not that Alastair was threatened by that, or felt anything close to jealousy. He hardly knew Halle, certainly not well enough to be jealous, no matter how much he had the serious hots for her.

She's your wife.

"Halle and I are going to turn the ranch around, make whatever changes are needed to return it to its best operating status."

"Glad to hear it." Jimbo shook his head. "Damn it, if this was a group of drunk kids, why did they have to pick Halle's place? Of all the surrounding ranches, they went after Bluewood. And the note was clearly for her eyes only."

"You don't think it's a teen prank, do you?" Alastair prayed Jimbo would dispute his observation, validate his hopes that it was teen mischief, nothing more. That no one was stalking Halle's business the way they were his. Both of them being scrutinized and outright threatened sounded a little too coincidental to him. Both he and Halle, one with a multibillion-dollar industry, one with a barely solvent business that he doubted would make the Shadow Creek Fortune 50, were being targeted.

But by whom?

"The thing is, teens aren't just doing beer and marijuana anymore. We've got a huge heroin epidemic in

America, and right here in Shadow Creek, Texas. That stuff makes folks do crazy things."

"We have the same epidemic in the UK. It's a global issue." Alastair had seen firsthand how many of his corporation's workforces had suffered as one too many employees succumbed to the addiction.

"It's a damned shame, is what it is. Can you believe I had to fight the Creek County Board to approve a budget for Narcan?" Alastair recognized the heroin overdose antidote that Jimbo was talking about. The heroin epidemic in Scotland was a big deal, too. "My deputies and the surrounding police departments have saved no fewer than twenty folks in the last four months with it."

"Sounds like you know how to get things done around here. But what would a heroin or other type of addict be able to do with a dead steer? It's not worth anything, and they didn't take the steer. They slaughtered it. Plus, this seems premeditated. Someone wants Halle to sell the ranch."

Jimbo didn't pretend to not understand Alastair's gauntlet.

"Right. I hear you loud and clear, Alastair. You can bet your last kilt that I'll get to the bottom of this and do what I can to bring the perpetrators to justice. I need you to hear me, too, buddy. Hurt Halle and you'll have the wrath of Shadow Creek on your head. That may not sound like a lot to an international dude like yourself, but trust me, it's not something I'd wish on my least of friends."

"Aye. I've heard you and I'll honor your request." Alastair held out his hand, allowing Jimbo to grasp it. He'd sealed his first deal as a married man. But could he keep it?

The ball of razors in his gut warned him he wasn't going to do anything but hurt Halle, and that was the last thing she needed. She'd been hurt enough, as pointed out by Jimbo. Alastair vowed in that moment to do whatever he had to make sure their relationship stayed on an even keel. So that the divorce wouldn't sting at all. But weren't hurt feelings and shattered dreams intrinsic to a divorce?

Who said Halle's feelings were the only ones at stake?

Halle relished the spray of the cold water onto her hands as she hosed down the front porch and steps. To her relief, the stream from the nozzle was strong enough to remove all the blood. She didn't think she'd be up for scrubbing it on her hands and knees today. Her stomach was empty since she'd tossed her lunch, doing its unique pregnancy hunger-nausea dance. She couldn't stop to eat or drink anything except water until this part of the day was done. Ernie deserved no less.

She'd sent the ranch hands away for the weekend and it was the right choice fiscally. But she'd give a thousand dollars to have this all done and behind her. Better, to have it all be a nightmare she'd awaken from to find Ernie intact and crooning after the females in her neighbor's pasture.

Ernie had been the last remaining steer of her dad's herd. He was a symbol to her of how rich of a gift Chancellor Ford had left her in Bluewood and the animals it provided for.

"You haven't changed yet?" She jumped as a deep voice rolled across the land and reverberated through her center.

"Whoa!" The spray of the nozzle had been loud enough to cover Alastair's steps. Her arm jerked and arced the hose over and around the porch. Alastair got hit with a blast of cold garden water.

He blinked, eyes wide-open and incredulous.

"I'm so sorry, Alastair!" She dropped the hose and went to him. "First our day is ruined by an awful incident and now I've soaked your beautiful suit."

"No matter. It's just a sprinkle." He stood implacably as if he faced water-firing squads on a regular basis. She looked past him to the sheriff's truck.

"Where's Jimbo?"

"He's still finishing up out on the pasture, and then he'll leave. He said to say goodbye. He'll be in touch as soon as he knows anything. And we're to call him at the least little sign of more trouble. He, ah, took Ernie's remains with him. The head."

"I know. He had to. Whatever it takes to catch the jerks who did it." Halle didn't want to spend one more minute on anything so horrible. It was still their wedding day, officially.

She eyed the water dripping down his shoulders and onto his shirt and tie. "I'd say you're soaked. Let's get you into dry clothes." She froze at her words. Did they bring up the same images in Alastair's mind? "I don't mean like when we were camping." Or like she'd felt in the truck only two hours earlier. Her cheeks were hot as was the rest of her, despite the fact she was still in her flimsy dress and the autumn afternoon was sliding into a chilly night.

"No, unfortunately I know you didn't mean it that way." He didn't have to elaborate. What had happened on their foray into the wilds of Texas wouldn't be forgotten by either of them. Not when the result was going to be born in less than six months. And today's make-out session had simply been a release of their mutual wedding jitters.

Her shakiness as she watched him had nothing to do with the possibility that she was developing deeper feelings for her Scotsman.

"There are fresh towels in the linen closet, where I showed you last night. Leave your suit on the guest bed and I'll take care of getting it dry-cleaned. Your shirt and tie, too."

"Not necessary, Halle. Not today." He wiped water off his face and chest. The motion of his highly capable hands on himself made her knees as weak as his kisses did. "I'd say we both could use a shower and time to relax. And get out of these clothes. Since you're the one brewing a baby, you get going first. I'll finish up out here."

She looked down at her dress, flattened and splattered with Ernie's blood. "Yes, I suppose you're right. I promise I won't use up the hot water."

"Don't you have a flash heater?"

She grinned. "No, another big difference between North America and the UK. I loved the flash heaters in Glasgow. I could take as long of a hot shower as I wanted." She referred to the gas heater that fired up on demand and kept a continuous supply of hot water. Unlike the hot water heater in her back room that had a lifespan of fifteen years, tops, and could supply no more than two full showers of fewer than twenty minutes each.

"I'm going to take you back there, Halle, and show you a side of Scotland I daresay you didn't see as an undergraduate."

"Oh, I'm sure there's a lot to see. We were poor students and did everything on the cheap, that's for sure."

She left him there, standing on the tired porch, holding her beat-up green garden hose, his fancy designer label suit in shambles. How far the billionaire had fallen. She grinned again, this time to herself.

While taking his shower, Alastair told himself repeatedly that he wasn't going to lay a hand on Halle tonight. It wouldn't be fair. It'd be taking advantage of her feeling less than one hundred percent. Between the whirlwind wedding, the ghastly specter that had greeted their return, and her ever-present morning sickness, she was off-limits for a roll in bed.

As he dried himself off and stepped into jeans and tugged on a dark cashmere pullover, he reminded himself that Halle had taken everything in stride but she was more than an attractive woman. She was the mother of his unborn child and keeping her safe and feeling secure was paramount. Taking her to bed tonight would risk her waking up in the morning and hating him. Regretting she'd agreed to his marriage proposal.

She's your wife.

He stopped running the comb through his damp hair and looked at his hands—his trembling hands. He wanted her so badly he was all but rutting against the bathroom sink.

Wasn't a sex life supposed to go south after marriage? Granted, their marriage was on paper only: collateral damage from unequaled passion. He was used to moving on quickly with the women he dated, preferring to keep things as casual as possible. It never paid to get too invested in a relationship. He'd learned that with the one other woman he'd ever considered marrying, Heather, who'd dumped him for his flatmate in his early years of running the family business, before he'd helped his father and grandfather take the modest whiskey distillery into the twenty-first century and rake in billions with wise investments. Investments in North Sea oil and Asian tech comprised the bulk of it. And soon, Texas tech, he hoped.

He opened the bathroom door and walked barefoot into the living room, where Halle lay stretched out on the sofa, her cattle dogs on the floor next to her. Millie, the blue-merle-and-white one, raised her head and yipped at Alastair as the other two warily eyed him.

"She's not being mean—she just wants you to be with us."

"I understand. We have several herding dogs on my and my parents' properties." He crouched next to Millie and held out his hand for her to sniff before he petted her. "I see Rhubarb's not as impressed with me."

The reddish dog flicked her ears as if to say, *Take a hike, buddy. The lady's mine.*

Halle laughed and it was all he could do to keep from reaching for her and holding her face in his hands for a long, lingering kiss. A kiss that would lead to more robust activity.

He stood up and nodded at the giant television screen that took up most of the wall at the end of the room. "I take it you watch a lot of telly?"

Halle flicked through channels, her eyes heavy lidded. She had to be exhausted after such a full day. "No, I actually never watched television when I lived in Austin. My life was too full, too busy. If I wasn't working in the office I was entertaining clients at night, or working at home on a project. This monstrosity is a later addition to the house by my dad."

"I'm sorry he wasn't here today, Halle."

"I am, too. At least, I thought I was, but then he wouldn't be very impressed with me marrying for money. But I'm doing it for the ranch, and for his grandchild."

Her words sliced through the air like a lasso wielded by her father would have. No, Alastair didn't think he was good enough for Chancellor Ford's daughter, either. Halle deserved so much more than he'd offered her. More than he was willing to give.

"He'd understand, I'm sure."

"I'm not so sure, but I am grateful he wasn't here to see Ernie's demise. He loved that steer."

"Not as much as he loved you, and wanted you to be happy."

"Maybe." She looked at him. "Please, have a seat. We're in this together for the next year, right? Is there anything you'd like to watch? I'm afraid I don't have all the sports channels that my dad carried—I cut it back to the most basic package that included internet a few months ago."

He could not care less about television programs. "You've been so dedicated to keeping the ranch going, Halle. It will turn around."

She sat up and he saw the pucker of her nipples through her thin, long-sleeved T-shirt. His instant erection was making his hands-off vows almost impossible.

"I don't want it to turn around only because you're capable of pumping an obscene amount of money into it, Alastair. I want to turn it around because of my smart planning and because the guests fall in love with the place. I meant it when I said I wanted to have a lasting legacy for the baby. But in reality I agreed to the marriage more for him or her than for Bluewood." She didn't have to spell it out so bluntly. It wouldn't have mattered who the child's father was.

"Hold that thought." He was going to need something stronger than water to get through the next few hours. "Can I bring you a cup of tea, or a soda?"

"You don't have to wait on me. But since you asked, I'd love some more of the ginger tea that you brought. Help yourself to whatever. There are several bottles of wine I purchased before I knew I was pregnant, and you might find a bottle of my dad's leftover Scotch in there."

Intrigued, Alastair went to the kitchen and scrounged around her cupboards while the tea brewed. "I'm impressed. Your father had quite the taste for Speyside whiskey."

"I have no idea what that means, except that he ordered his single malt from a specialty liquor store in Dallas."

He brought in her tea and his highball glass of a very decent Scottish whiskey, over ice.

"It means he liked the Scotch that is brewed in that part of Scotland. There's Highland, Speyside, the Lowlands, Campbeltown, Islands and Islay. Much like wine regions."

Halle accepted the warm mug of tea with her outstretched hands. "Thank you. My father always had it on the rocks, too. He even used these cold freezer cubes made of stone instead of regular ice so it wouldn't dilute the liquor." She said "liquor" like "licker" and all he heard was "lick her." As in, he wanted to lick her luscious ruby lips and allow himself to sink into her sweetness.

Alastair took a hefty swig of the single malt.

"Iced stones have become quite popular. There are always all kinds of gimmicks with whiskey. Our gift shop at the distillery has a wide assortment of higher-end gadgets, like the stones you mentioned. But as I've said before, it all goes back to the original product. It either tastes good or it doesn't."

"I've never acquired a taste for anything much stronger than a glass of merlot, but I have to admit I do adore the scent of Scotch."

"Mmm. Lots of folks do. You might enjoy it with honey, though that's a bit of a sacrilege to whiskey lovers."

"What do you think?"

Alastair thought he never wanted this evening to end. He and Halle, talking, at peace with one other, the day's monstrosities off the table. He wasn't ready to address the deeper meaning, the more basic needs he'd been missing in his life that had nothing and everything to do with his attraction to Halle.

"I think that all the talk and theory about the 'only' way to do anything, be it drink whiskey or whatever, is hogwash. Life's too short. Enjoy whiskey and anything else however you want to." Oh God. His mind was back on its single track, the deepest groove in his brain at the moment. Enjoying Halle the way he wanted to. Naked and in bed.

"That makes sense to me." She sipped her tea and curled her legs under her. The childlike pose was surprisingly very adult and downright sexy. "My work colleagues, my boss, my friends, all thought I was crazy to leave my job in Austin. They said I was 'too smart' to come back to Shadow Creek, and that giving everything up for Bluewood was a waste." She smoothed the blanket throw that covered her thighs. It was a normal, methodical, absentminded motion but it still made Alastair feel a distinct rush of blood straight to his crotch.

"It was possible, I know. I could have hired out all of the work here and come home on the weekends. Had both worlds." She leveled her amber gaze on him. "But it would have killed me, in the end. I know enough about myself by now to realize I don't do well when I feel torn between two places."

Alastair's stomach did an ugly flip, and he wanted to tell her that she'd be able to live both here and in Scotland. "I get it. When I'm out of town for more than a couple of weeks I need to get back home, recharge. Clyde Whiskey headquarters is in Glasgow, so that gives me reason enough to stay there most of the time."

"Don't you have siblings or people under you who can do the traveling?"

"More and more, yes. But our business has only grown to this point over the last ten years, in a snowball effect. It wasn't big enough for us to pay for all the travel early on. And then, even when we could farm out a lot of the duties, I didn't want to. Some things are best accomplished in person, one-on-one."

"Sounds controlling to me." Halle softened her criticism with a gentle smile. "Said as a recovering control freak."

"Touché. I don't think you're all that recovered, though, are you? I mean, heck, Halle, you're sick as a dog with the pregnancy and still running every aspect of the ranch."

"As you did in the early years of Clyde Whiskey. I'm in the early years, for sure, as it's been like starting over." She stood up, stretched, sat back down. Her pajama material caught on her taut nipples and grabbed her curves in the best places. He got only a glimpse but it was enough to keep his erection in play and remind him of all the ways he desired this woman.

"But your father had a solid business going, didn't he?"

"For a long while, maybe twenty or thirty years, yes. As you know, the various recessions always affected cash flow, as traveling and vacations go out the window when folks are low on funds. And he focused on family vacations that were planned months if not a year in advance, with deposits, full-service menus, a minimum of one week's stay. I want to modernize, bring this into the twenty-first century. You know your Wi-Fi hotspot on your phone? I want that for every client. As much as the trip can be a getaway, not everyone wants that. And then there's an entire industry devoted to travel bloggers and journalists. I'm trying to get in on that, but it's been too expensive."

"Not any longer." Satisfaction rimmed his gut along with the single malt.

"Money is great, Alastair, and I'm not dissing it. That means 'being disrespectful' in American English, by the way." She winked. "It's about more than the dollar or pound. It's the slow drain of clients, and the fact that the needed upgrades to date have wiped out any nest egg from my father."

Alastair suspected she'd gone through her entire savings, too. He understood the dedication to family legacy. More than she might yet realize.

"Bluewood is now part of the Buchanan legacy, Halle. And I treat every business as an equal, no matter its cash flow."

She snorted. "Right. You're telling me Bluewood is in the same class as Clyde Whiskey?"

"Absolutely." He leaned forward. "It's the only way to know I've given each investment vehicle its due share. Trust me, Halle. I've made a fortune this way." And was most probably in threat of losing it, to some unknown stock buyer named SullaXS, but he wasn't going to ever tell her about it. He'd get to the source and stop the cash bleed before it got too bad. He had to. He'd checked his messages before his shower and there weren't any new leads or developments. He didn't expect the respite to last.

Her eyes were sparking with hope as much as she narrowed them in defense. "Bluewood isn't a product like booze, Alastair. Texas isn't Scotland. I know this as much as you, more so. I've spent more time in Scotland than your one stint in the States, I'll bet."

"True. Although you're overlooking a key aspect. Bluewood offers a product that can't be bottled and sent overseas, or put in a distribution network. It offers an experience that changes lives." He didn't have to point out how his time on the range had changed both of their lives, did he?

"*Riiight.* Your point?"

"My point is that once the word gets out, once you utilize social media, or what have you, to have your clients share their experiences, you'll be booked years out." Instead of eking out a minimal existence as he suspected she'd been for the better part of a year since her father had passed away.

She didn't reply and the lines around her mouth deepened. Only now did he notice the shadows under her eyes. He stood up and reached out his hand.

"Time for bed, Halle. It's been a long day."

She allowed him to tug her up, and didn't fight moving into his embrace. He held her gently, knowing that as much as he wanted her he was actually going to be the man of the house tonight and do the gentlemanly thing.

"Alastair, thank you for being so understanding. And about what happened in the truck, after our wedding…"

"Shh." He placed a finger on her lips, her soft, warm, most lovely lips, and kissed her forehead. "We have to learn to be friends first. I'll see you in the morning." He let go and picked up their empty glass and mug.

"Good night, Alastair." Halle didn't turn back as she headed for her room, and Alastair didn't allow himself to think more than was required to rinse out the dishes and put them in the dishwasher.

It was going to be tough to sleep tonight.

Chapter 12

Halle woke before the sun, which wasn't difficult since the autumn days didn't brighten until after 7:00 a.m. After she made a pot of decaf tea for herself, a pot of coffee for Alastair and some steel cut oatmeal for both of them, she waited. For her husband.

"Good morning." Alastair stood in the middle of the kitchen, looking yummy in a fleece pullover and the jeans he'd worn last night.

"Morning. Help yourself to oatmeal and coffee. There's tea, if you'd prefer."

"No, I'm definitely a coffee man when I wake up."

She'd bet her life savings he was a "man" any time of day. *It's just the novelty of having a sexy man in your house, your kitchen.*

Nothing to do with the fact that she'd had the best sex of her life with this man that had resulted in the growing baby in her womb. Not at all.

He slid into the chair opposite her at the table and looked out the window at the corral and pasture beyond. "Lovely view."

Halle followed his gaze. The sun was rising above the rolling hills, shattering the curtain of darkness she'd woken up to and casting the sky with a peach glow that was uniquely South Central Texas. She returned her gaze to Alastair in hopes of soaking in his profile, only to find his eyes on her. Soaking *her* up, as if she were as beautiful as the sunrise.

Silly thought. "I hoped we could go for a ride today."

"Excellent." He dug into the oatmeal like a starving man. "I'll drive. Where do you want to go?"

"No, not in the truck. A horse ride. Maybe out to the first lookout point and back. Nice and easy, on the trail we did together." She'd taken him there on the first day of their fateful camping trip. "You remember the spot, I'm sure."

"Yes. Rattlesnake Gulch, did you call it?"

"It's not a gulch, it's a cliff. And you can run into a rattlesnake anywhere around here."

"Thanks for the reassurance. You're really enticing me to go back out on the trail." He sounded relaxed, reflecting the same humor she felt about the situation. "As much as that sounds inviting, once again, should you be riding while you're pregnant?"

"It's fine since it's something I'm used to. I'm not going to start a new sport like downhill skiing or gymnastics. My doctor told me I can keep up my normal activity level, morning sickness allowing. I'm sure it won't be so comfortable once the baby gets bigger, but right now I haven't felt the baby move, he or she is still too small. My belly feels like I'm bloated from eating too many doughnuts, nothing more."

"I'll bet you've lost weight, with the nausea."

"Again, I am so sorry about yesterday's events."

"It's not yours to apologize for. Think it as our first married problem. I'd say we handled it well."

And like the married couple they weren't, she and Alastair enjoyed a leisurely breakfast together. As if it were something they'd done a thousand times before, with a lifetime more in front of them.

Not the reality of only having a year to establish the legacy they both wanted for their child. Halle's stomach soured at the thought of never being associated with Alastair again, except as the mother of his child. Maybe her Scotsman was becoming more important in her life than she was willing to accept. Because it meant she was in a place of risking it all.

She led them out a different way than before, so that Alastair could see another trail.

"I can tell Buster missed you. He's not pranced like that since you rode him last." She kept Elvis even with Buster so that conversing was easy.

"He just knows that I won't take any funny business from him, is all." He flicked a quick look at Elvis. "What happened to Buttercup?"

"She's a reliable gal for long trail rides. But for a quick day jaunt, Elvis is my man, aren't you, sweetheart?" She patted the gelding's neck.

"He elicits more warmth from you than your groom."

"Hardly. You're too quick to put yourself down, you know. There's a nice, sensitive man under the corporate-shark skin, isn't there?"

"I never thought so but I have to admit—" he maneuvered Buster around an outcropping of sharp stones "—you seem to bring out a side of myself I'm not as familiar with."

Halle let that sit.

"It's new territory for both of us, I think. Unless you have other children you haven't mentioned?"

"Absolutely not. I've never been engaged before, either."

"I should have asked before I committed to a year of marriage. You must think I'm the most naive business person ever."

"I think you're the bravest woman I've ever met. When you meet my mother and grandmother, you'll realize what a compliment that is."

They were coming to the copse of trees he remembered. "We're near the lookout, aren't we?"

"In about a half mile, yes. We'll stop there and take our time with lunch. I'll lead, as the path is going to narrow to allow only one of us at a time."

"After you, Mrs. Buchanan."

She met his gaze and felt the instant bolt of attraction, the following rush of warmth in her most sensitive parts, and the sense of rightness in her heart that had nothing to do with her physical attraction to Alastair. And everything to do with the possessive way he said "Mrs. Buchanan."

Before she could say something stupid or fall off of Elvis because of her wandering hormones, she clicked her tongue and tugged the reins to the left. Elvis knew the route as well as Halle and carried them effortlessly over the mud-packed trail. They trotted under low-lying branches, down and up several ditches. The pace was good enough to be invigorating but steady enough to pose no risk to Halle or the baby.

"Hang on—we're almost there!" she shouted over her shoulder, giving Alastair a heads-up about the last turn that dipped low and then rose steeply to where the ground plateaued into the lookout spot.

Elvis's squeal warned her a split second before her mount reared. He wasn't on his hind legs to help them climb up the steep slope in front of them, but to turn and bolt. Halle saw the flash of a snake, the length of trip wire, a lethal flash of pink. She fought to stay mounted, to bring Elvis to heed. She'd been riding since she was a tot and had been thrown, tossed and tumbled from a horse before. She also knew how to hang on short of her mount rolling.

But this time it wasn't about her—it was about keeping her baby safe. A semi controlled fall to ground four or five feet below her was preferable to being crushed by Elvis or worse, thrown. She forced her body to relax as she prepared for her inevitable landing on the hard ground. Then she let go of the reins.

"Halle!"

Alastair's shout reached her as she fell through the several feet to the ground, the horror of how much worse the moment could have been caught in a sadistic slow-motion defense mechanism in her primal brain. Her feet hit dirt first and she rolled to her rump, the contact jarring through her entire skeleton before she bounced up and landed again, this time on her left shoulder. She lay on her side in a fetal position, struggling to catch her breath. The mud was cold under her fingers, the scent of pine needles sharp and reassuring. Halle could smell and feel and didn't think she'd been badly injured. Her shoulder might complain for a while. The baby was safe, which was all that mattered. She was certain she'd not done her midsection any harm, and the fall hadn't been that rough.

A warm hand on her shoulder. "Halle."

"I'm good." She lay still, wiggled her toes and fingers, then her legs and arms, before she sat up. "I've had worse."

"What happened?"

She motioned toward the trail, five feet away. "I saw a rattler, and I think there's a trip wire down there. I saw a length of cable wire right across the main trail, about twelve inches above the ground. There was a pink handkerchief on one end of it. It had to have been put there on purpose."

Alastair let loose a short but incredibly powerful epithet that she'd never heard before. "Where does it hurt?"

"My pride, mostly. It was a calculated risk." God, if she'd landed differently…even this shake-up could have hurt the baby. "I allowed myself to slide off on purpose, in case Elvis bolted. The jostling of a hard throw or worse, if he'd fallen on me, would have been too much for the baby. Trust me, I'm okay. But I think I'd better have my doctor check me over. Just to make sure."

The furrows on Alastair's brow were deep, his mouth pressed in a harsh line. His expression contradicted the warmth that radiated from the depths of his eyes. "I'm calling in a helicopter."

"Oh no, that's absolutely not necessary. Honestly, Alastair, if I start cramping or bleeding, I'll tell you. But it was just a tough tumble. The baby's still small enough that I'm sure he or she is well protected." She meant it, too. She didn't feel there'd be more than surface bruises, maybe a sore butt as her bottom had taken the brunt of the fall. "Let's take a slow ride back, then I promise I'll go to the doctor's."

"We'll have medical personnel waiting at the house for you. I insist." He'd already pulled out his phone and was talking to someone. It took her a moment to realize it was Jimbo.

"Alastair, please." She placed her hand on his forearm.

He held up his hand in the international signal for "stop" and kept talking to Jimbo, relaying where they were. "You can ping my phone's location, can't you? If we're not back within the hour, or if we need an air ambulance, I don't want to have to waste time."

Jimbo must have calmed Alastair because he hung up in short order and looked at her with the same grim expression but a shadow of relief fell over his eyes, too. "We can ride back. If you have any hint of feeling unwell, you won't hesitate to tell me, right?"

"Right."

"Jimbo's getting a team of folks together to meet us at the ranch house. And he's coming out with a deputy to collect evidence here."

"That's so not necessary, Alastair—having the folks at the house. But if it makes you feel better, so be it."

"It does." He helped her onto Elvis, although she could have done it herself, and mounted behind her. He led Buster with his reins. They started toward home and she leaned into him, needing his solid warmth.

Alastair fought with his emotions over whether to force Halle to wait for an air ambulance or take her back the short distance to the ranch himself. He believed her when she said she felt fine, just bruised. But the fear that reared as deftly as Elvis had at the trip wire was gripping him by his balls.

He could have lost Halle, the baby.

"Stop, Alastair. I'm right here. The baby's here." She took his left hand off her upper waist and put it on her lower abdomen, where their child grew. "We'll all be okay."

"Thank God."

Because they were walking the mounts so slowly, conversation was easy, and he heard her even though she faced to her front. "It's not two coincidences, Alastair."

"No, I'm afraid it probably isn't."

"There's something you're holding back. What is it? Have you seen something odd that you haven't mentioned?"

Damn it, she'd noticed his distraction and he hated to lie to her. But he wasn't worrying her, not until he was conclusively certain someone was trying to wipe Clyde Whiskey out.

"Nothing that I can be sure of, Halle. Right now I'd say both our emotions are all over the place. And to be brutally honest, I'm freaking out a little bit over all of this. If anything happened to you or the baby, I'd never forgive myself." He shook his head. "Damn it, I was right there next to you and I couldn't do a dang thing to save you."

"You didn't have to. There was nothing to save, Alastair—I had it. Elvis knew exactly how to land so that I'd be safe. I train my horses to be able to survive just about any situation imaginable. To Elvis, this was another practiced rattlesnake exercise."

"Don't lie, Halle, just to make me feel better. Elvis knows it was real, just as Buster does. They don't miss one iota of our emotions. And I know you of all people know that."

He felt her sigh, how she leaned into him, her back curved in a soft C as he sat straight and led them all back to the house. To home.

Because wherever they were together, it was home to him.

"This is reminding you of that awful woman again, and your father's accident, isn't it?" He had to ask her.

"Yes, yes, it is. Except I have you to lean on now."

Her sentiment was a balm to his battered heart, and reminded him of why it'd been so scary to see her fall off the horse. And allowed him enough space from his fear to wonder if SullaXS was the third instance of trouble brewing against them. He'd find out as soon as he heard from his staff, or better, returned to Glasgow. No person or thing would dare harm Halle or the baby. Not while he was her husband.

Halle was becoming more precious to him than anything else in his life.

The reminder of Livia Colton brought back chilling memories that even the woman's death couldn't erase and Halle settled against Alastair's body again as they rode home.

Unable to change her new husband's mind about the need for emergency medical care, Halle decided to focus on determining the extent of her injuries as they rode. Unbeknownst to her at the time she'd skinned her knee and the blood was seeping through her torn jeans. At least Alastair hadn't noticed it yet. She'd tell the paramedics that met them at the house and let them decide if she needed stitches. There was no sense in upsetting Alastair more than he was already.

Rattled didn't come close to describing Alastair's demeanor. Halle found that while she enjoyed his complete attention when he'd made love to her she didn't enjoy it as much when he was acting as if she were mortally wounded.

"We are getting out of this godforsaken place." He maneuvered Elvis around some tricky rock outcroppings, in between hedges of sagebrush. Halle waited until they cleared it to speak.

"You don't just mean this trail, or Bluewood, do you?" She waved her hand around as they slowly rode back to the ranch. Even she had to admit that two malicious acts this close together stood a good chance of being related. First Ernie and now Elvis and almost her—and the baby.

He nuzzled the top of her head and his hands on the reins in front of her were strong. "No. We need to get away for a bit, and you need to see where I live. Where our child will spend a good portion of his or her time."

Halle wanted to blame the bile that rose in her throat on her morning sickness or on the nefarious setup that had spooked Elvis, but the tumult in her stomach was from neither. "What do you mean by 'a good portion'?"

She sensed his sea-blue eyes checking every inch that was visible to him, as if she'd disappear at any moment. When his arm tightened around her waist, she looked up sideways at him. Raw vulnerability and fear were reflected in his eyes. "I'm sorry, Halle, I don't mean to imply I'd ever decide on my own where the baby will spend their time. That's a decision we'll make jointly."

"It won't work to do the split custody thing, you know, where the child lives half the time with me and half with you. We live too far apart and it would be awful for school, once they're old enough." She spoke more sternly than she felt. Someone had to shake Alastair out of his worry.

His enigmatic expression returned. "We'll work it out. And there's a lot of time in between now and when we have to make any of those decisions."

"I'll never agree to boarding school." She blurted the fear she'd ignored, thinking the baby would grow up in the States with her, seeing Alastair during school breaks. How foolish had she been? She looked at her husband again and tried not to panic. She'd married a very powerful man who could turn circles around her with his financial status alone. Plus, he was the most intelligent man she'd ever met, as well as the most attractive.

Why had she allowed him to convince her that she was on the same playing field as him?

Because you are.

"Who said anything about boarding school?" He halted Elvis and leaned forward to better see her.

"You're in shock, I think. No one is going to take your child from you, Halle. We're partners in the parenting of this baby."

As she searched his gaze she desperately wanted to believe him, but she knew how birth and death could irrevocably change a person. "You have no idea how much you'll love the baby once it's here. How much you'll want to spend every minute with them."

Amusement sparked in his gaze. "No, it's impossible to know now, isn't it? But I have an inkling." He leaned down and planted a firm kiss on her lips. It wasn't a seduction or even romantic move. It was reverent in nature. "I promise you that we're in this together, Halle."

She believed him. Which was scarier than any trip wire.

"I want to get back to the house." She couldn't trust herself to say any more. Wanting to sob with relief that she and the baby were okay warred with her defense mechanisms that were on high alert. Alastair was right; she was worked up over the fall. "It must be my body's natural reaction to a threat to me and the baby."

Alastair nodded. "You still okay? Any cramps?" He looked her over and his gaze stopped on her knee. "What the hell is that?"

"I scraped it coming off the horse. It's probably like a road rash. It doesn't hurt," she lied, because it stung like hell but that was from the scab forming against the denim. Or so she told herself.

"Come on. We'll get back as quickly as we can and get you checked out. Then we're packing for Scotland." Her Scottish husband didn't wait for a reply but instead sat straight and jerked the reins, his powerful thighs issuing a quick squeeze to Elvis's sides. Halle was grateful for the chance to relax her expression, not needing to feel his constant gaze sweeping her face for the least little change.

And she owed him a response, even though he'd demanded she go to Scotland with him. "Maybe a trip to your home in Glasgow is a good idea. For a short while."

"Thank you." His response was soft, a glimpse into the tender lover he'd been on the trail.

Still, the entire way back to the ranch, she swore she

felt two laser beams boring through the top of her head. Alastair was a man who took his responsibilities seriously, like the baron of industry he was.

Chapter 13

Halle looked out the corporate jet window at the blanket of rolling green beneath them. It was amazing what a little—no, make that a *lot*—of money could do. It could take her from her struggling ranch in Shadow Creek, Texas, to Glasgow, Scotland, in just under ten hours. No long airport lines and minimal security was the life of a billionaire like Alastair.

She turned from the window to study him in the late morning light. His short hair was tousled from how many times he'd run his fingers through it. Casual in jeans, white T-shirt and one of his endless supply of cashmere pullovers, the T-shirt contrasting sharply with the charcoal gray of the wool. Smudges of exhaustion emphasized the length of his sooty eyelashes. Lashes that when he was awake framed the stormy gray eyes she'd grown too accustomed to. Thank goodness he was sleeping—she needed a bit of a break from Alastair's ruthless scrutiny. They'd left last night after the EMTs and her midwife checked her over. Jimbo had taken a report and promised to keep Alastair appraised of the situation. She'd slept most of the flight but she didn't think Alastair had dozed off until the past hour or so.

Judging from the landscape and the digital map read-out in the very comfortable, posh cabin, she figured they were over the western part of Scotland and would be landing within the hour. Maybe Alastair was one of those people who slept during a landing. The changes in cabin pressure while descending used to put her father to sleep, too.

Chancellor Ford would have a lot to say about the mess she'd made of her life. The horrible financial state of Bluewood, the physical state of the ranch, getting involved with a guest. Not only catching a roll in the hay with said guest but finding herself pregnant with his baby. Their baby.

But he'd be proud of her courage, and the stubbornness she'd inherited from him. And he'd adore Alastair.

That thought came out of nowhere, startling her with its conviction.

So she'd agreed to a marriage of convenience—so what? It was more like a marriage of financial convenience but she refused to go there. Beating herself up over the failures of Bluewood was one thing, but she and Alastair had used protection when they'd had their fun. It could have happened to anyone. Babies were always a risk with sex.

"Stop staring at me, Halle." He didn't open his eyes as she jumped in surprise.

"Geez, let me know you're awake next time." How

the heck did this man tick? Did he have X-ray vision through his lids?

"I keep telling you that you have nothing to fear from me. I only have your and the baby's best interests at heart. Honestly." His eyes opened and he rubbed them.

"Why do you think I'm still thinking about that?"

"Because I'm getting to know you." He yawned.

"What time did you go to sleep?"

"As the sun came up."

Since they'd flown into the rising sun, so to speak, that meant he'd caught about three to four hours and not the measly amount she'd suspected. Still, it wasn't enough. "Do you always sleep so little?"

He yawned again, stretched. "No. I need a good night's sleep like anyone else, and I'm not a martyr about it. I relish going to bed earlier and getting up with the sun. But the last few weeks, especially these past several days, have been stressful, wouldn't you agree? Or do you frequently find beheaded steer on your front porch after a run into Shadow Creek?"

She couldn't help it, she laughed. Alastair's dry humor was something she was learning to enjoy more each day. Instead of being the dry silliness she thought Scottish humor was in college, Alastair's wit provided a sense of comfort to her. Her father had had a similar sense of mirth.

"No, I've never found a dead animal or even parts after being in town. Of course, there are the leftovers from the hawks' and owls' prey, but the turkey vultures usually take care of that. It's quite the efficient ecosystem when you think about it."

"Hmm. I don't want to think about it anymore right now. If I do, I'll force the plane back around and not stop looking until I find the person or group who did that to your beloved Ernie. As it is, I trust your sheriff Jimbo to take care of it."

"He's not my sheriff." Alastair wasn't jealous of Jimbo, or any other man where she was concerned. But territoriality was another matter. Still one that she didn't want to waste time on. "What do you plan for our stay in Glasgow?"

Sharp eyes on her. A blink. "I thought you'd enjoy resting at my parents' estate. It can get lonely at my place in the city."

"Your parents'? Are you kidding me, Alastair? I'm showing up as your new wife. Don't you think they'll have some questions as to how and why we met and married so quickly? And once they find out about the baby, there will be a lot more questions." She wasn't going to spell it out for him but she was certain his family would look at her as an opportunist.

"We'll stay in my house on the property just outside of Glasgow. My folks and grandmother each have their own separate houses, as I mentioned earlier." At her silence he leaned forward, his eagerness to calm her apparent. "My parents are human beings, Halle. And my grandmother is the one you should be concerned about approval from, anyway. But don't worry, she'll give you her special blessing as soon as she meets you. Besides, the baby will end a lot of speculation."

"Great." She pictured a tiny, wrinkled woman emerging from a yurt, her walking stick topped with a glowing orb. "Maybe she'll cast a spell on me."

He waved his hand in front of him. "She's not like that. Not really." His funny little grin didn't reassure her. "Gram just happens to be very protective of the Buchanan clan and the Clyde Whiskey legacy."

"That's fair. She's been there since it began, right?"

"No, that was my great-grandparents. But she was raised by them, at their knee as they perfected the Clyde recipe."

"And here comes the knocked-up American, breaking up the Scots lineage."

"You can have fun looking over the family archives. And she'll be delighted about a great-grandchild. She's been praying that I'd marry for forever."

She was going to be disappointed when she realized the marriage was meant for only a year.

"Do you intend to tell anyone that we've agreed to only a year together?" She'd meant to play it cool, sound sophisticated and detached. Instead, her voice cracked.

"No."

Okay, then. She dropped it.

"How long do you plan on staying in Scotland? With me?"

"A week or two. I'd prefer to keep you here for the duration of your pregnancy, away from the danger at your ranch, but I know you'll never agree."

"You're correct about me not wanting to stay here for the next six months. And my ranch isn't the problem, Alastair. It's all about some misguided teens pulling pranks. The only real danger at Bluewood is the broken fence and maintenance issues I haven't been able to afford to fix. Ernie's demise and the trip wire were deliberate, but the snake could have been a coincidence." She didn't have to feel the dip in her belly to know that she didn't believe any of the crimes were by chance. Someone was trying to scare her away from Bluewood, to sell.

If she knew of someone or a corporation that wanted to buy her land, that would help, maybe lend a few clues. But Bluewood had never been approached by buyers, even when the lands around her father's had been sold off to the highest bidder during the burst of the real estate bubble almost a decade ago.

Alastair looked out the plane window as if bored. "I've done market research and while acres upon acres of Shadow Creek were sold to investors a little less than a decade ago, none of the original plans were followed through."

"I hope you didn't pay someone to tell you that, Alastair. I know my hometown and the area as well as anyone. Originally the land around our property was slated to be the site of a high-end suburban neighborhood. McMansions but with larger lots, more of a miniranch feel. One of the lots was sold to a luxury condominium developer, too. But nothing happened. Whoever bought the land has sat on it. I recall it changed hands a few times since, but only as investments. No building permits were ever filed."

"Did you know that all of the land around your ranch, save for Jeremy's, is owned by the same developer?"

"No, I didn't know that particularly." And why hadn't she? She prided herself on keeping up with all business dealings in Shadow Creek and surrounding areas. "I'm surprised Jeremy hasn't mentioned that to me."

Alastair was looking at his phone, tapping away. "I doubt he knew. The most recent purchase was two weeks ago."

By his frown she knew Alastair thought more about the land ownership's significance than he revealed. "Spit it out, Alastair. What do you really think?"

His laser steel gaze pinned her to the spot. "I think someone's trying to own as much of the land around you in order to choke off your business. Add on Ernie's slaughter, and the trap on the trail, and…" He trailed off and she watched as it looked like he was trying to gather his composure. Alastair, strong as an ox, one hundred percent Scottish and probably a descendant of Viking warriors, looked on the verge of either a huge angry outburst or tears. When he finally opened his eyes and looked at her, a zing of awareness braided with a thread of complete connection hit her in her chest and continued throughout her midsection. "I was afraid you'd been killed out there, Halle. I know you're made of strong stuff and I trust your horsemanship. But when someone sets a deliberately vile trap like that it's hard to fight it. I never want to feel that sense of impending doom again."

"Maybe your concern is misplaced. I'm sure you thought you felt that way, but your concern was for your child." Her doctor had assured her everything was fine after the fall.

"I'm not always a man of absolutes, Halle, but one thing I'm certain of is that I know my feelings. If I tell you I was afraid you were going to be seriously injured or worse, believe me. If you'd seen how you looked, crumpled in a heap on the ground, with that rattler only yards away from you… I didn't know if you'd been bitten or not. I figured if the fall didn't kill you the snake-bite would."

"I'm thinking that's what our criminal was counting on. Your travel isn't a secret, as you've mentioned. Our marriage was instant news on *Everything's Blogger in Texas*. Anyone could have seen us at the courthouse and then in the diner after the ceremony. Has it occurred to you that someone is stalking *you*, Alastair? You're a billionaire and you've been moving around in more common, regular-folks areas. It makes you an easy target."

"If they wanted me they would come after me. And the pink handkerchiefs indicate it was someone local, don't they? Someone who knows about Livia Colton's history? Because she used to leave pink handkerchiefs in places as her trademark." He'd obviously paid attention to every part of the cow's head investigation. "There's still no denying, however, that now that we're married, you're as much a target as me."

And their baby would become a prime target for a kidnapping once born. Shivers of apprehension raced up and down her spine and she shivered. Alastair leaned over from the leather reclining seat that matched hers and covered her with his blanket. "Take this. We'll be landing within the next thirty minutes."

Indeed the plane was slowly descending, the tiny white dots of sheep on the endless green below turning into cotton-ball-sized puffs. "Are we landing at Glasgow Airport, or let me guess—you have a private landing strip on your property?"

Alastair laughed. "No, no landing strip. I do have a helipad, though we won't be taking the helicopter today. I thought you'd be tired enough of flying. We'll land at Glasgow and I'll drive us home. It'll be about an hour longer."

"No driver?"

"Do you want a driver?"

"No." She preferred being in a car alone with Alastair. No matter how confused her feelings toward him were, she was certain of one thing: Halle felt the safest she'd been since her father had died—as long as she was with Alastair.

This made no sense, since incredibly awful things had occurred with him present. But she didn't blame Ernie's death on Alastair any more than she did her needing to jump from Elvis.

Someone was coming after Bluewood Ranch and was willing to do whatever it took to get their way. Even if it meant raising the stakes from livestock to human life.

Alastair worked while Halle got settled and rested a bit once they arrived at the family estate. He'd had to fight the urge to kiss her, make her his in every way, when they'd arrived. Something about seeing her in his home made his need for her all the greater.

He noticed yet another security sale, again to SullaXS, and he immediately called his securities officer. Their conversation was brief but the somber effect lasting. All signs pointed to a hostile takeover attempt. He'd survived them before, and he would again.

"Alastair?"

He'd been so immersed in his work that he hadn't heard her come up to the office door. He immediately stood up and walked around the desk.

"You're still awake."

She blushed, and he wanted to make her do that with his lovemaking.

"I can't sleep. I'm too excited to be here."

"We can't have that. Let's show you around." The depressing state of his business would still be there when he got back. And then he'd tackle it.

Alastair was absolutely delighted to see the sparkle in Halle's eyes as he toured the house and grounds with her. It kept his mind off his stocks, and the increasing concern of his security team that someone related to SullaXS was behind not only the buyout but the warnings at Bluewood, as well.

"I have a very nice, spacious loft flat in Glasgow, and another in Edinburgh, but I prefer to spend my weekends here. I drive but the train is easy to use, too. It's no more than an hour into Glasgow proper." He opened the double French doors onto the terraced back slate patio. "All of the land you can see is ours, well past that house." He pointed to what looked like a small cottage on the far horizon.

"Ours? As in yours and your parents'?" She assumed it all was Buchanan land, all part of his family fortune.

"As in yours and mine." He grabbed her hand. "I meant it when I said this marriage was going to be all in, financially. It's for the baby, Halle. The year timeline we've agreed upon is for your reassurance that I won't hold you to anything you don't want." He watched her expression closely but tried his best to appear casual, as much as one could be when discussing their situation.

"Please, Alastair. I didn't sign up for all of this." She arced her arm in a semicircle, enclosing his land. "Our agreement was that you'd give me the funds needed to get Bluewood going. But I can't accept that, Alastair. For me, it's a loan from you. I'm going to pay you back with interest. It'll be a good investment for you, I promise."

"Yes." He'd never take any money back from her but he wasn't going to argue with her. Not now, not today. He had one chance to be a newlywed.

"I'd love to go for a longer walk—is that allowed?" Her grin was deep enough to bring out her dimples but he heard the trepidation underneath her attempted levity.

"It's completely safe, yes." How much to tell her? "Once it became clear that our financial success was like catnip to criminals of all ilk, I had state-of-the-art security measures installed."

"By 'all ilk' do you mean kidnappers, thieves, or worse?"

"Yes. Primarily the former." He started walking, indicating she join him by raising his hand before letting it fall back to his side. She hadn't shown any indication of wanting to hold his hand and he didn't want to push her. Nor tempt himself.

"You must have the equivalent of the crown jewels here somewhere, I assume."

"Not at all. We Buchanans live a fairly simple life, all told. Yes, we are richly blessed with financial security beyond our wildest dreams. Yes, we have land and big homes, fancy cars. But I was raised with a very practical sensibility. Don't buy more than you need, give more than you think you can away to charity, give back with your time and talent, too. You'll see when you meet Gram. She's no-nonsense, a living vestige of Scottish frugality."

"Frugality is something we all could use more of. That's another reason I wasn't unhappy to leave Austin. At times it got to be too much about what I'd wear to my next proposal meeting, at my presentations. It's important to look good but it does get ridiculous after a while." Funny how she agreed with so much of his outlook on life. It would be wonderful for the baby.

"We're skirting around the real issue, though, aren't we, Halle? Do you feel safe at Bluewood?"

"Right now? No. It's been unsettling, to say the least. But this distance you're giving us from the awful events—it's good. I'm hoping that with some time and rest, and hopefully less morning sickness, I'll get a better perspective on it. I still can't accept that someone is that eager to see me sell that they'd go to criminal lengths to threaten me." He saw the shiver go through her and wrapped his arm around her shoulders.

"When it comes to money there's no limit what some people will do."

Chapter 14

Alastair's comment was so starkly frank that Halle stopped midstride and faced him. The wind was blowing in from the west, ruffling his already mussed hair. She had to consciously keep her hand from reaching up and smoothing it, cupping his jaw and letting him know he could relax around her.

"Do you mean to sound so grim or is your guardian-protector energy still on overdrive from Shadow Creek?"

His eyes reflected turbulent emotions. "This has nothing to do with feeling protective of you or the baby. There is that, yes, but I didn't accrue the equivalent of one and a half billion dollars in just under a decade without witnessing the best and the worst of human nature."

"The worst had to be really bad if you're so certain you're a constant target."

"I didn't say constant. Not in the physical sense. Since

we installed the security perimeter and employed a team of guards 24/7, we've only had one or two breach attempts. One was a group of tourists, a ladies' wedding party looking for selfies with a bachelor billionaire."

"Did you oblige them?"

He gave a short laugh. "I was in Thailand at the time, working out a restaurant deal. So, no, they never did get their selfie portraits but they did get a quick ride to the local constable and a lecture on proper legal behavior during wedding celebrations."

They started walking again. "And the other physical breach?"

He was silent for several paces and didn't answer until they'd come to a soft rise that afforded a spectacular view of the Scottish countryside as it undulated westward.

"It was a solo criminal, operating with a larger ring of terrorists."

"Terrorists?"

"Yes. Their plan was to hit Scotland in three different places—Edinburgh and Glasgow proper, and my estate. They were stopped at the border, the airport and before they infiltrated my property."

"That's, that's just terrible." Her nausea was back. What on earth had she gotten herself into? What had she brought her baby into? "You said you were bringing me here for safety and now all I want to do is go back to Bluewood."

"The point is that we're not safe anywhere, no matter who we are, right? Life is vexingly precarious and can be taken away at any moment."

Halle only needed to walk another step to be reminded of that. Her backside was incredibly sore from her fall. "Yes." She didn't want to stay on such dark ground but she had to know everything. "What about other breaches?"

"The usual expected in the twenty-first century. Computer systems lockdowns, hacking, the occasional attempt at a hostile takeover of Clyde Whiskey."

"Has anyone ever come close to buying you out?"

"Not yet." He didn't look at her and she wanted to press him. He was holding something back.

"Enough of this. How are you feeling, Halle? I have a sense that you're hurting more than you're letting on." His concern was genuine and she felt the warmth of their budding friendship. The sexual attraction had been immediate and showed no sign of ever burning out, but the deeper part of their relationship had finally gained traction. She wanted to hang on to it, cherish the refuge from the storm her life had become.

"I'm good, I'll be fine before you know it. Yes, I feel each and every step in my backside, but that's a good thing, right? My body absorbed the shock that could have harmed the baby."

"Thank God you're in good shape and were able to allow yourself to fall as smartly as you did."

"I wouldn't call it 'smartly.' Usually, when I've been thrown or fallen from a mount before, there's a split second of warning before the horse misbehaves, and in that time the years of experience and riding lessons come into play. It's still all instinctual but there's room to live, or more practically, not get as many broken bones."

"But the other day?"

She shook her head. "It was all too fast. The snake, the trip wire, Elvis's freak-out. He's the most steady mount I've ever had, and I've had five in my lifetime. My dad kept horses and I learned to ride them all, no matter the size or age or experience. I like to think I have a connection with horses. Yesterday Elvis and I were definitely disconnected."

"Is it fair to put it on yourself, or even your mount? There's no way to anticipate such a brutal, unexpected incident." His mouth's trademark grim line was back.

"I'm not blaming myself for the accident, but I am wondering if I could have been more in touch with Elvis. I was a bit distracted at the time."

"You mean by me showing up and demanding you marry me?"

"That, and the wedding, and Ernie." And her lust for the man walking next to her.

"Careful, Halle. You're starting to sound like a married woman already. Blaming me, your husband, for something out of our control."

"I'm not blaming you. It's the circumstance." They both laughed.

"To be honest, I blame myself for agreeing to go on the ride in the first place. Every concern I had about a pregnant woman riding came to fruition." His honesty took her breath away. He was right—he was getting to know her better.

"No, it didn't. I'm fine and so is our baby."

They walked in silence for the next twenty minutes or so and Halle wondered if she'd angered Alastair with her dismissive comment. As they neared what had looked like a small building from afar, the place Alastair had referred to as a "cottage," his countenance brightened. "And now, you get to see who really is the center of Clyde Whiskey."

He held out his hand and while her own reached instinctively for his, she wondered if it was such a good idea. Holding Alastair's hand felt so right; doing more of it would make it an awfully difficult habit to break.

They walked up to the front door, painted a bright cheery yellow. Before Alastair's free hand reached the Loch Ness Monster brass door knocker, the door creaked open and a wisp of a woman stood before them, her grin beaming as widely as her arms were open. A ridiculously huge Aran cable-knit sweater nearly swallowed her bird-like frame, and she wore muddied Wellies as if she'd just come in from the garden.

"Alastair! Where have you been? Come here, boy." She had to be half of Alastair's height as her head barely reached his chest. The smacking sound of her kiss on his cheek brought tears to Halle's eyes. Pure, unadulterated family love. Or in the Buchanan case, clan love.

"And who is this fair lass?"

"Gram, this is my wife, Halle. Halle, meet Jean Buchanan."

"Wife, eh?" Halle was enveloped in a warm wooly hug that if she hadn't seen how tiny Gram was, she would have sworn it was from a yeti. The woman had incredible arm and hand strength. She smelled of fresh wool, roses and sugar. "So pleased to meet you, Halle. Welcome to the family." She pulled back and looked her directly in the face, her nose only millimeters from Halle's. Deep, gray eyes, no doubt the source of Alastair's, assessed her. Gram's hands moved from Halle's cheeks to her shoulders and the woman nodded. "You'll do."

As quickly as she'd hugged them, Gram disappeared into the country house, calling over her shoulder. "Come on in. Keep the draft out and take a seat in front of the fire. Rain's moving in—my hips are singing to me."

"Is she always this lively?" Halle whispered to Alastair.

"Oh, no. She's usually way worse." Alastair's wink was casual, comic. It was clear he adored his Gram. The cozy cottage, Gram's warm greeting, the way Alastair's fingers twined in hers—all seemed so familiar. Too familiar. She could get used to this, and that was more dangerous to her than any trip wire or rattlesnake. What bothered her most was that instead of feeling homey and at ease, she wanted to crawl out of her own skin. Because her skin was on fire with her lust for Alastair. Her desire was spiking as if he'd hauled her up against him and kissed her senseless.

As if they were a real couple.

For now, they were a real couple, at least for the Buchanan family. And tea with Alastair's grandmother added to the sense of normalcy. A way for Gram to meet the mother of her future great-grandchild.

"What do your parents think of your beautiful bride?" Jean stirred two heaping spoons of white sugar into her Earl Grey, the tiny teaspoon clinking against what Halle was certain was century-old porcelain. It was easy to see the genes his Gram had passed on to Alastair, and yet the nonagenarian in front of her was decidedly feminine and soft where her grandson was all guy, rugged, sexy guy.

"Ah, we haven't been home yet."

"It's only a quarter mile up the path, Alastair." Jean's words admonished but her tone was clear. She was thrilled that he'd brought Halle to her first. As a kind of family benediction. "Do they know you two got married, Alastair?"

"That would be a negative, Gram."

Jean put her cup down onto a matching gilt edge saucer with tiny peonies painted around the edge.

She laughed, a weathered tinkle. "You are a schemer like the rest of the clan, Alastair." Harsh words that only emphasized Jean's obvious love for her family. "Tell me, Halle. Are you afraid to meet Alastair's parents? Your new in-laws?"

Halle blinked at Jean's quick change of focus. "Er—I wasn't. I'm not. Well, maybe I'm a little nervous. Are you both telling me I need to be concerned with their reaction? I'd assumed Alastair had already informed the entire family about our...situation. Until we were flying over the pond."

Jean's eyes widened briefly before the wise woman concerned herself with a plate of baked goods. "Here, have a biscuit. I didn't make them but the bakery in town is as good as if I had."

"I love cookies. Thank you." Halle chose a round shortbread with white icing and a portion of a mara-schino cherry on top.

"That's an Empire biscuit. I have a recipe for you if you'd like."

"I'd love it. I lived here one year, as a junior in col-lege. I've never been able to find shortbread as delicious as I had then. I can't say I'm much of a baker, though."

"You'll learn. My grandmother would save for months to be able to purchase the sugar she'd need to make her Empire biscuits, and sometimes she'd have to save for the flour, too. We always had plenty of butter." Jean leaned forward confidentially. "We had our own dairy farm. I still keep a cow and some chickens. I'll show you later."

"Gram means we pay someone to keep their livestock on our land."

"I'll have you know I can still do all of the chores. But if I did everything, the younger generations wouldn't learn anything, would they?" Jean reminded Halle of Aunt Betsy, the woman who'd been her only female role model after her mother had died.

"No one does it as well as you, Gram."

"Speak to me, Alastair. There is something going on with the business, isn't there?"

"Nothing for you to be concerned about, Gram. You're retired, remember?"

"I'll have you know I'm a sitting board member. If there's something I should know before next week's meeting, just spit it out."

Something wrong with Alastair's dynasty? "Was that why you had to have your phone with you the entire time you were on the trail?"

He shot her a guilty look that gave Halle pause. "What is it?"

Alastair shook his head. "Nothing." He turned his attention on Jean. "Yes, I've had a few concerns over some of our IPOs being traded. Some seem to be going to the same obscure corporation. But I have a handle on it." He leaned over and clasped Jean's hand. "We have it all under control, Gram."

Halle wanted to close her eyes and believe it was true, but she knew Alastair well enough to know that she'd seen the same odd expression on his face before—when he'd been worried she could lose the baby after falling off Elvis.

"You don't fool me any more than when you lied about clogging the tub drain when you were four so that your boats would float!" Jean shook her finger at Alastair and to Halle's delight he actually blushed.

And continued to avoid the question. "There's never

been any beating around the bush with you, Gram." He kissed the wrinkled hand with affection.

Halle allowed the ugly reality that Alastair's business could be in trouble take root. They might not be a real husband and wife with all the love and romance, but they were partners in raising their child, and that meant she had an interest in what was going on with Clyde Whiskey. She waited until his loving interlude with his Gram passed before she grilled him. As soon as Jean left the room to boil more water, she faced her new husband.

"What exactly is going on, Alastair?"

Alastair had to fight to keep a grimace off his face. First Gram and now Halle were onto his ruse. Not that he was being deceitful, exactly. He wanted to keep his business concerns intact without alarming the family. Even if the public portion of his business got bought out, he'd been careful to put away a significant portion of earnings each year. Enough to take care of his parents and Gram. He'd always figured he and his siblings could handle taking care of themselves. But now he was a father, a husband, with his own family to support. Being able to hold on to the family's fifty-one percent of the shares in the company would be very difficult if whomever SullaXS was bought up the public shares. It made the threat of significant financial losses all the more frightening.

Halle put her hand on his arm. "You're keeping something from me. What's going on?"

"This isn't the place to talk about it. Later."

"Here we go." Gram brought in her electric kettle and poured water into the dainty cups before adding more of the strong brew from the teapot. "Surely you have time for one more cup. You'll need the brace of it for when you tell your parents."

"What's the worst they can do?" Halle had a hard time believing the parents who'd raised Alastair would be anything but honest and accepting. Eventually.

"They can freeze us out, for a bit." Alastair tried to inflect a casual note into his reply but feared he was failing miserably. It didn't escape him that Halle was very much an equal to the other women in his life. Gram and Mum. Though Gram could be a tough mother-in-law to his mum, his mum gave back every bit that Jean dished out. Halle was fitting into the Buchanan clan all too easily.

"Freeze you out? Do you mean 'ghost' us?"

"Hell no. It's Scotland and no one turns family away. People have come here for centuries to get married, you know." Jean clucked away as she sipped her brew.

"Gram, Gretna Green hardly draws a parallel with our family dynamics."

"My parents didn't approve of me marrying a Buchanan. But they came around, as soon as I had your father." Sharp eyes that reflected the same intelligence Alastair demonstrated.

"In that case, it shouldn't be a problem." Alastair placed both arms on his thighs as he leaned toward Jean. "Halle and I got married on the quick for the best of reasons."

Jean looked from him to Halle and back again. Her eyes flooded. "Don't be teasing an old woman, Alastair. It's not good for my health!"

He shook his head and smiled. "I'm not teasing, Gram. Halle's pregnant. The baby is due late spring."

"Will you have it here? All of the Buchanans have been born right here on this land."

"Gram, that's not true and you know it. I was born in the hospital in Glasgow."

"Okay, but close enough. What say you, Halle?"

His bride's cheeks flushed peachy pink. Leave it to Gram to fluster Halle. Probably the only person who could unsettle her. Even a throw from a horse had done little to rattle her. "I say I'm comfortable with my medical team in Shadow Creek. If there are any complications, Austin has a world-renowned children's hospital."

"I do understand wanting the same doctor the whole time." Jean nodded. "So Alastair will have him flown out here."

"My doctor is a woman, as is my midwife, and that won't be necessary." Halle had the look he'd learned not to cross. She meant to return to Shadow Creek and her sanctuary at Bluewood as soon as possible.

As soon as he caught the bastards who were committing crimes on her property, she'd go back. His grandmother continued to stare at him and the hair on his nape prickled. Gram might be ninety-plus but she was sharper than most people his age.

"Gram, we have months to figure this all out. The most important thing is that you have a great-grandchild on the way, and I expect you'll be needing to start knitting up a blanket for him or her."

"Are you going to find out the sex?"

Halle looked at him. Alastair was at a loss. "Um, I don't know. Halle?"

"We need to discuss it. I'd like to be surprised, to give me something to push for."

"Oh, dearie, you won't need a reason to push by the time your term is up!" Gram actually cackled, and Alastair wished for once that she'd use a mental filter before she let go the one-liners she was famous for. He didn't want to believe that the reminder of the physical ordeal Halle was going to have to endure for their baby was making him nervous. He didn't do nervousness. Anticipation, eagerness, yes.

"So I've been told." He watched Halle take Gram's comment in stride. Still, she didn't need to be rattled so soon after the two shockers back at Bluewood.

"Thank you for having us, Gram. I hate to scoot out so soon but Halle and I need to rest up before we have dinner with Mum and Dad."

"So you'll be going to their place now?"

"No, I thought it'd be easier to have a quiet meal with them at my house a little later this evening." He looked at Halle. "Our home."

"Good luck to you both. You'll need it."

Chapter 15

Halle stretched under the hand-knit throw she'd found atop her bed when Alastair had left her alone to nap. He'd said he had work to do and would take a rest when he had a chance. Dinner wasn't until eight o'clock, very late to Halle's Texan sensibility but very usual for Scotland. And a godsend to her jet lag. As entertaining as Gram was, it had been hard to keep from yawning through the tea.

She looked at the view through the windows that surrounded the large bed and was met with little more than darkness. With winter approaching, the sun had set almost as soon as she and Alastair had returned from their time with Gram.

Halle liked Gram. Jean Buchanan was her kind of woman: tough, ribald and as sweet as the peonies that decorated the Buchanan family heirloom tea service. But more than all of that, it was the sense that Gram's strength came from a deep love for her family that made Halle feel she'd found a kindred spirit.

A soft rap on the bedroom door, and then she heard a soft "Halle?"

"Come in." She scrambled off the bed before he walked in.

Gone was the casual wear Alastair had on earlier. He looked as if he'd walked off the *Everything's Blogger in Texas*'s eligible bachelor page in a pale button-down shirt, dark tie, charcoal blazer and jeans. All he was missing was his new cowboy boots.

"I didn't realize we were dressing for dinner. You said all I needed to pack was casual clothes." She went to the cushioned bench at the foot of the bed and unzipped her suitcase as she spoke. "I'll need a few more minutes to change and freshen up."

"Halle." His scent reached her before he did and her knees reacted like the jelly traitors they were. She allowed him to turn her around, his hands warm and reassuring on her shoulders.

"My parents are not the ogres Gram was trying to make them out to be. Even if they were, you're my wife, the mother of my child. It's my choice whom I marry. I picked you."

"Under duress."

"Really? In this day and age, do you believe I had the least sense of obligation to marry you for appearance's sake? Other than the baby's security?" She looked into his eyes, his lids at half-mast and his pupils large in the well-lit room.

Alastair traced her cheekbone with a trembling finger. He felt the pull, too. The constant awareness of their mutual chemistry. "I want you, Halle. Keeping you safe is my first priority, but damn it, I can't stop thinking about how we are together. I want to be with you again."

"Why are those two things mutually exclusive? We're not in Texas—there aren't any teens pulling awful pranks here, are there?"

His self-control was admirable as he remained still, the only concession to his inner conflict the way his hands were gripped at his side. "There are bad people everywhere, Halle. I'm not going to allow anyone to hurt you or the baby."

"You have security here, right?"

"I have a security team, actually."

"Then let them do their job, Alastair. Is there something else? Are you worried about hurting the baby? Because giving in to our, um, physical wants won't put the baby at risk." Was that her voice, so blatantly full of want for him?

He closed his eyes for a moment, his nostrils flaring. When he opened them, she didn't doubt the fire in them, the sparks were for her. "I don't want to lead you on, Halle. If we give in to our physical cravings, it might make it a lot harder to separate in a year."

"Alastair." She tried to think, not merely stare at his sensuous lips. It was a losing battle. "I can't tell if it's you and me, or just me and my crazy pregnancy hormones. But all I can think about is how good it feels when we're together. It can't hurt to enjoy ourselves, can it?" She reached her arms up and pulled his face down to hers. And showed him what she couldn't express in mere words.

Alastair's response was immediate. His impatience at flirty kisses was clear as he thrust his tongue past her lips, his mouth hot and greedy. He pulled her hips to his and Halle moaned at the exquisite sensations the contact shot through her. She grasped at his hair, keeping her mouth on his, needing Alastair as close against her as possible. She wanted him, had to have what only he could give her. He lifted his mouth from hers and she let out a high-pitched protest.

Where was her usual no-nonsense self? The one who'd never risk her heart like this?

"We have thirty minutes before my parents arrive." He slid his hands up under her long-sleeved blouse and unclasped her bra with expert technique. "I don't think this is a good idea, but where you're concerned my judgment seems to fly the coop." His hands moved to her breasts, hot and warm as his tongue found her left nipple. "I wanted to take our time if we did this again, Halle."

"You have taken your time. Too much, in fact." They were both short of breath and Halle was done talking. She undid his tie and belt in record speed, then turned and pushed him onto the bed. When she reached for the waistband of his underwear, he stopped her with his hands. "No, Halle. It's all or nothing. You get undressed, too."

"I am. No more talking." She yanked his underwear off. His need for her underscored her own for him.

She made quick work of the rest of her clothing. As soon as her skirt hit the floor Alastair helped her peel off her tights and in one move he tugged her atop the bed, under him. His erection jutted against her thigh, saying what he couldn't verbally express. He wanted her as badly as she did him. They were powerless over the attraction that blazed between them. Their time on the trail hadn't been a fluke, or due to the circumstance of having just met.

What they shared was as raw as it was real.

"Now, Alastair." She tilted her hips, her needy ache for him unbearable.

"Look at me, Halle."

This wasn't courtship or the seal of a wedding vow but as she met his hot gaze she acknowledged she'd never wanted a man like this—to the point of insisting he make love to her, regardless of any doubts he had about the aftereffects. His eyes were communicating his total focus on her. When he thrust into her, it was all she'd craved and more.

She met him push for push, thrust for thrust, with no inhibitions. A hard, breathtaking orgasm rocked her. Halle cried out a moment before Alastair's rough curse of release filled her ear, the spicy edge of his brogue underscoring the waves of pure sensation that reverberated through her.

His mouth left a hot kiss on her temple before he rolled to his side and looked at her. Alastair kept his arm around her waist, as if afraid she'd scoot off the bed as soon as he let go.

"That was the best predinner cocktail I've ever had." His skin crinkled around his eyes and the sparks that had only moments before been sexual were of a more amused nature.

She reached up and tugged on a strand of his hair. "I love your hair. The curls are perfect. Maybe our girl or boy will have them, too." It was safer to talk about each other's physical merits. To stay out of the mire of emotions that she sank deeper into with every day of her pregnancy. As they spent more days together.

"Mmm. I'm hoping he or she inherits your beauty." He seemed tense again. Were his parents going to be that awful about their marriage? The baby? "We need to get dressed. This is why I didn't want to do this again until we were able to enjoy a more leisurely time with each other."

"Nothing with you is leisurely." She slid out from under his arm and onto the floor, searching for her clothes. "Besides, if it were leisurely it wouldn't have been so hot, right? We're physically compatible but don't worry—I'm not taking it as anything more than that." Words that rang false but with a meaning her heart had to hold on to.

Alastair didn't answer her as he got dressed and Halle took the silence for what it was.

Consent.

Alastair's staff had been busy while she and he made love in her bedroom. The dining table was set with sparkling crystal glasses. Candles were lit in an elaborate candelabra she thought might be a family heirloom, as it was simple in design but looked like solid silver. A huge fire in the oversize hearth made the welcoming drinks cozy instead of stiff.

The fact that Alastair's parents were open and engaging didn't hurt, either. They sat in the comfortable easy chairs in front of the hearth. Halle drank in the sight of Renée and James, Alastair's parents, holding hands as they spoke to her.

"Halle, it's a delight to meet you. Alastair didn't tell us we were having a guest until a couple of hours ago. I'm afraid Jim and I were both in the city all day, so I'm glad we're here tonight. You'll have to come over to our place tomorrow for a proper Scottish feast." Renée Buchanan had hair the same light brown shade as Alastair's but longer. Halle liked how the woman was so obviously unguarded and frank. But of course she didn't know who Halle was, not yet.

"How was the flight over?" Jim, Alastair's father, spoke to her as if she jetted to Scotland regularly. His tall frame and arresting good looks were shockingly similar to Alastair's. Even their gestures were mirrors of one another, as Jim relaxed back into his chair the same way Alastair did. Easy yet composed. Always aware of his surroundings.

"Wonderful, actually. I've never been on a private jet before." Too late she realized she should have kept her mouth shut.

"Not because you couldn't have in your previous job, I'm sure." Alastair's body heat warmed her left side as he stood near her, his eyes on his parents as he spoke. "Halle had a huge accounting job in Austin but gave it up for the business her father started. A tour company that gives visitors a uniquely Western experience."

"Cattle drive included." She sipped at her ginger ale and wondered when the Buchanans would figure out she wasn't in fact a teetotaler but was pregnant. "We own several horses and plenty of livestock to give our clients an authentic Texas ranch experience."

"How lovely!" Renée looked intrigued.

"Sorry, no sheep yet, Mum." Alastair teased his mother and turned to Halle. "Mum is crazy for sheep."

"Merino and Corriedale, to be exact."

Alastair rolled his eyes. "Yes, Mum. But they're all sheep to the non-fiber-freak world." Alastair's irreverence of his mother's obvious passion for wool was hilarious. Halle giggled. Three sets of Buchanan eyes were immediately on her and she gulped, wishing her soda drink was spiked with the family's whiskey.

"I'm not laughing at either one of you. My own mother passed away when I was young and I've always wished for the kind of relationship you share. And you, too, Mr. Buchanan." Jim raised his glass to her in salute, his gesture expressing that being the quiet one of the bunch was his typical role.

They all laughed. "Thank you for your kind words, Halle. So, did your father raise you?" Jim Buchanan was smooth and where his son had gotten his charm from, no doubt.

"Yes."

Alastair's hand went from the small of her back to her hip as he firmly wrapped his arm around her. "Halle's father was killed in a tragic auto accident less than a year ago."

The Buchanan family's outpouring of concern and sympathy overwhelmed Halle. They'd never even met her father, and barely knew her.

"It's okay, really. Nothing I would have ever wanted to happen but I'm lucky I was able to come back home and keep the family business going." She inwardly cringed at what a mess it was. But it was going to get better; it had to. Wasn't that what marrying Alastair was all about?

"Where is your home, Halle?" Renée's unapologetic curiosity was refreshing.

"Shadow Creek, Texas, a town outside of Austin." At their blank looks she continued. "About an hour from Dallas, in the center of the state."

"Oh, I've been to Dallas!" Renée beamed. "I went for a wool convention."

"Mum really wants to fancy herself an expert knitter and fiber authority, but until she's done with cutting skulls open it's not happening." Alastair filled Halle in.

Halle knew that Renée Buchanan was a neurosurgeon from what she'd found on the internet about the Buchanans. She'd been looking for information on Alastair, but he and his family seemed to hold the UK's, if not the world's, fascination. To be so willing to continue in public service as a surgeon, when her husband and son had made a fortune, made Renée a type of modern-day saint in Glasgow.

"You'll have to excuse my family, Halle. They like to talk about me in the third person."

Before Halle reassured her new mother-in-law that she had nothing to worry about, Alastair caught everyone's attention.

"Mum and Dad, I have something important to tell you." He put his arm around Halle's shoulders and she appreciated the warmth. There was a good chance they were about to receive a frosty reaction.

"Halle and I were married when I was in Texas."

Complete silence, followed by a raucous round of "Cheers!" and slaps on Alastair's back. Everyone gave Halle a hug or kiss on her cheek.

All eyes were back on Halle and Alastair. Halle looked at him, and she knew he was going to tell them why they'd married so quickly. Her hand reflexively went to her abdomen.

"Oh my gosh, you're preggers!" Renée jumped up and down, her hands clasped in front of her. "I told you!" She looked at her husband, who in turn stared at Alastair before his gaze moved to Halle.

Renée composed herself like lightning and stepped forward, grasping Alastair's hands. "You could have told us, sweetheart. We would have pulled out all the stops for you both." She turned to Halle. "This is awkward for all of us, I'm sure, but please know I'm beyond thrilled. I've longed for Alastair to find someone special and settle down. Right, Jim?"

"Yes. Of course! Welcome to the family, Halle!" Jim stepped forward and kissed her on each cheek, then shook Alastair's hand.

Halle fought to keep the grimace off her face from the guilt Renée's loving response elicited. She had no intention of moving to Glasgow. The surprising jolt of pain to her heart caught her off guard. Would she be as disappointed as Alastair's family when their marriage agreement ended?

Chapter 16

After dropping the "hey, we're married and by the way Halle's pregnant" bomb on the Buchanans, the family gave them room to be the newlyweds they all thought they were. Alastair claimed he didn't have to be back in his Glasgow office for a few days and they used the time to explore Scotland with day trips, always returning to the estate at night.

Halle enjoyed the relaxed routine she and Alastair fell into. Together. They shared the same room and hours of spectacular sex by a silent agreement. Sleeping in, coffee for him and the usual decaf tea for her in bed first thing, followed by a bracing walk through the meadows and woods that made up his family estate. Afterward they'd wander through a small village, where she'd find precious ornaments to take back for her tree in Texas.

"It's incredible how your family owns land the size

of a county in the States." They were traversing her favorite band of woods that had a variety of trees whose leaves had mostly dropped, the fauna well into the start of its winter dormancy. "I do miss the trees back home but these are okay, I guess."

"You guess, eh?" He gave her a lingering kiss and Halle pulled back.

"What's wrong?"

"Nothing. I mean, this time together has been good—don't get me wrong—but aren't you worried about us getting too close, emotionally? We have to keep the endgame in mind." She was so afraid that giving in to the sexual nature of their relationship was leading her to heartbreak.

"Geez, Halle, you sound like a secondary school sweetheart ready to break up with the boy at boarding school."

She laughed. "What I'm trying to say, because it's important, is that this is all pretend. Except for the part about giving our baby a secure future and unquestionable identity as your child."

He started walking again, not meeting her eyes. "We're two adults. There's nothing wrong with enjoying our time together. It doesn't always have to be weighed against the inevitable end."

"This has to be the exception." Her heart couldn't take getting so used to Alastair's incredible body, his hands, the way he made her feel, only to have it ripped away in a year, if not sooner. "It's going to end—we agreed on a year. You're the one who insisted it be in the contracts."

A fleeting shadow of guilt crossed his face. What was he hiding?

"Let's take it day by day, shall we? We're here for a

few more nights before we have to return to the States. Although with the recent criminal mischief at Bluewood I do believe it'd be smart to cancel your holiday tour groups."

She shook her head. "No way, no how. The Thanksgiving-through-Christmas family excursions are some of my most lucrative. Charlie, my ranch hand, can't do it all on his own like he is now. Even if I hired extra hands, no one has his experience, or mine." And she loved cooking the big meals for the guests. Instead of overnights on the trail, they did daylong rides and returned at night to enjoy fully prepared home cooked feasts. She had a housekeeper and cook who helped her through that part, making family recipes that Halle had grown up with. Her aunt came, too.

"What are you going to do if another trip wire throws you off a horse this time? If Elvis or Buttercup bolts, leaving you to ride with a client the rest of the way home? Or if a guest gets injured?"

"I don't deal in what-ifs except for the safety of my clients or the ranch. And while I need to be prepared for any kind of incident, I'm hoping that having the security cameras installed while we're gone will make a difference. They'll serve as a deterrent." She was lying to him, because her gut didn't buy it. Whoever had been sick enough to slaughter Ernie in cold blood, leaving his head on her doorstep, wouldn't stop at any security measures. And if it had been the same person who'd tried to get her thrown and possibly maim Elvis, they were dealing with a monster. Someone who relished evil and bringing it upon innocents. Wickedly so.

"We'll get through it. The question I have is, what would you like me to do on the rides? I don't want to be just another rider for you to worry about."

"You're not going on my trail rides, not as a guide or my protector. You've got your own gazillion-dollar industry to run, remember?"

He ignored her reply. "I am not allowing you to go out on the trail alone. Period."

"I won't be alone. I'll have my guests, and I can take a ranch hand along to help with the heavy lifting, literally and figuratively. With the investment you've generously offered, I can afford it. It'll make for a much nicer experience not only for the paying guests but for me, too. I'll be free to focus on keeping the guests entertained."

"How so? Besides the fact that you won't be tired?" They were nearing the end of their walk. She had to be careful or she'd start thinking of Alastair's modernized farmhouse as home. There was only one home for her: Bluewood Ranch. At least, it had been, until Alastair came into her life. She wondered if she'd ever again feel settled if he weren't around.

"With another rider I can carry more food, more supplies. We can offer hot beverages, because he can bring either a small propane burner for a pot of water, or even a portable hot water urn we can use. And if I have that extra pair of hands to do the menial tasks, I'll spend more time giving the guests history and nature classes." She sighed, pushing her hair out of her face. The Scottish winds in November were brutal compared to the milder climate of central Texas. "There's so much equipment that I can consider purchasing now. Bluewood has a decent chance to reach its full potential. I can't thank you enough for helping me make this dream come true, Alastair."

"It's mutual, Halle. You've made the dreams I didn't

even know I had come true by agreeing to have our child."

"A little after-the-fact, though." She laughed.

"You said yes."

Alastair held the back door open for her and as she entered the warm house and prepared for her shower, she wondered how she was going to be able to tell her heart no when it came to Alastair. She had a mere year to figure it out. A year that it was easy to believe was going to be as relaxed and joyful as this brief respite from the danger shadowing her life in Shadow Creek.

Someone was after Bluewood, and in her gut she knew that wasn't all. They were after her. The baby.

The protection of Alastair's family estate wasn't enough to keep cold chills from racing over her spine like the Scottish gales scouring the countryside.

Halle ran a wide-toothed tortoise comb through her wet hair and relished the warmth of the thick terry robe she'd put on after a long, steamy shower. It was hard not to imagine Alastair joining her under the falling water, but since they'd just made love an hour earlier he'd gone to work in his home office. They were staying in what she now realized was actually the fourth property on the estate—this house was much smaller than his parents' but fully modernized and incredibly comfortable. Luxurious, even. He'd also given her plenty of space. Since they'd made love in that urgent, desperate way he'd continued to stay with her at night, and mornings had become their choice time for intimacy. Their lovemaking was slow and earth-shattering. He'd told her he didn't want to disrupt her sleep, that the baby needed rest, too. She suspected he'd been up working at night, staying ahead of the markets as they opened around the world across global time zones.

Ready to face the day, she left the bedroom and walked in stockinged feet down the long hall toward the living room and small home office where Alastair spent most of his time.

She sensed he was near but she found no one in the living room. The lights were on in his office along with three huge computer screens but he was nowhere in sight. The mug of tea on his desk blotter was still steaming, so he'd be back soon. Halle poured herself a cup of hot water from the kettle he kept on the sideboard and dropped in a bag of decaf English breakfast blend. Jean Buchanan would chide her for not making a pot of loose leaf, no doubt. Alastair's grandmother was a tea purist and Halle had noted she didn't have tea bags in her house. She held the warm mug as the tea steeped and began to make sense of the endless spreadsheets and stock tickers that crept across the systems displays. The first screen was easy—an overview of all open markets, beginning with Hong Kong, where it was actually the following morning already. The stock numbers didn't interest her overall but one square in the display did, the IPO part of Alastair's business.

Her stomach sank at the arrow that indicated the stock's value was dropping. Worse was the comparison to last week's and last month's values, also in the same standout box. She'd worked with financial figures long enough to be able to accurately interpret the figures on Alastair's display.

Something was horribly wrong with Clyde Whiskey.

She forced her gaze off the first screen to the middle, which she surmised was Alastair's digital to-do list. The man was incredible—did he really accomplish this much in one day? Task after task, many of which included video conferences and livestreaming with employees on the other side of the globe. No wonder he was tired. How did Alastair ever get ahead if all he did was have a list as long as her arm?

She preferred to write out her monthly plans, and of course kept Bluewood's business calendar online. But usually she wrote her daily goals on a sticky note and put it on the refrigerator. When she got back from a trail ride or taking care of the animals, she'd evaluate what she'd accomplished.

She shook her head. Even in the face of his business being in trouble, all she could think about was Alastair's well-being. What she needed to be focused on was her baby's future.

Moving her attention to the third screen, she noted that it listed the buyers of his company's stock. Most of the amounts appeared negligible bought by other companies she didn't recognize.

Until she got to the middle of the spreadsheet's first column, and the letters SullaXS were highlighted in red, standing out like ugly warning signs. As she inspected the spreadsheet further, it was clear that SullaXS had purchased nearly all of the stock publicly available for Clyde Whiskey.

How could this be? Alastair was too smart to allow another entity to buy out all of his public holdings, wasn't he?

"Ah. How was your shower?" His voice sounded like he was pleased to find her. Halle put her cup of tea down on his desk.

"Who the hell is SullaXS, Alastair?"

* * *

Alastair hated the look of complete betrayal on Halle's face. He'd wanted to keep her from any more pain after the ordeal in Texas, and yet she appeared more vulnerable standing in his home office outside of Glasgow than she had after falling from Elvis and lying so still on the Texas soil.

"Halle, I can explain." At least, he thought he could. Up until the part where a dead woman was buying up his company.

"How many relationships have ended with those words?" She ran her fingers through her damp hair. "Please tell me this is a nightmare I'm about to wake from. You never mentioned this. But I knew better—this is what you've been avoiding telling me."

Her anger was justified but didn't hurt any less. "I saw no need to upset you until I knew more facts."

"Why? Why would your business upset me, Alastair? You know I don't care about your worth. I do care about being misled and treated like a child who can't handle the truth." The tears that shone in her chocolate eyes were from her wrath, he suspected.

He took in one deep breath, let it out in an explosion of frustration. "Someone's been after my stocks since I went to Texas. It's become an all-out war since we married. Apparently the website *Everything's Blogger in Texas* isn't the only one interested in our personal merger."

Halle paled and he reached for her but she shrugged away. He felt like the lowest of reptiles.

"I'm sorry, Halle. I should have told you right away. I have to let you know I think this could be connected to the nasty events at Bluewood. Someone has it in for us."

Her eyes blazed. "I know it has to be my hormones,

our sudden marriage, the almost-fall, Ernie, but if I didn't know Livia Colton was dead I'd swear she was behind this." She shook her head. "I'm crazy, aren't I?"

"No, just the target of some very sick person or group. And we're in this together, Halle."

"God, Alastair. The last time I checked, Livia Colton was presumed dead. Killed when her car went into a raging river. Her body was washed away. She's *dead*." Terror punctuated every syllable of Halle's rage. "Oh my God. Please, tell me that there's no freaking way that evil woman could still be alive!"

"I wish I could tell you that for certain." He went to her and tried to touch her, hug her, embrace her—anything to comfort her. Halle backed away, holding up her arms to ward him off.

"No, don't touch me." She paced the office hardwood floor, her bare feet small and pale against the century-old planks. "I need to think about this, Alastair. I've comforted myself with the fact that the murderer of my father, the one person on the planet who took him away from me, is dead. That there's no chance she could ever come back to hurt me or anyone I love." Halle crouched on the edge of the office sofa and looked out over the small pond where his swans were making circles in the otherwise still water. Her profile was so achingly beautiful with the romantic backdrop, in direct opposition to the tortured heart she was wrestling with. Alastair was helpless to do anything but wait for her to open up. And pray she didn't decide to fly back to Texas that minute.

"Losing a father is hard for anyone, at any time. My dad was the only parent I had. I'd looked forward to sharing so much more of my life with him. To make him proud. The big stuff like career success, maybe marriage and bringing him his first grandchild. But just as important, the little things that can't be quantified. The Sunday dinners. Friday pizza nights at my condo in Austin or back at Bluewood. Long rides to check out the state of the land, to talk to each other without any distractions. To just *be*." She turned her amber gaze on him. Tears glistened but his Halle didn't allow one to fall. She still didn't trust him enough to let go totally with him. And now he wondered if she ever would. "Livia Colton took all of that away from me, Alastair."

"Halle, I've been monitoring this situation since before we met. It's not like a hostile takeover attempt doesn't ever happen—I've survived three. But this one is different, more calculated. First they tried to buy stocks on the sly, under various assumed names, at times when no one would pay much attention. My data experts were able to trace the names back to a single account. In Texas."

"I find it hard to believe there's any time you aren't paying attention. You follow every bit of your business and I'm sure you pay people to do so when you can't. Your phone is part of the reason you ended up in the darn river!"

"True. But I have a special interest in this because it feels more personal. They're not coming after my company, or the whiskey part of the business. They're coming after me. The stock name you see here, on the spreadsheet?" He walked over to the monitor and pointed at SullaXS. "It's the name for a front organization. I believe the same person is behind up to eleven different false names, or business fronts, who have attempted a takeover in the past four months. And when I had my operations team and security officer run the stats, there is only one common thread to all of the pseudo corporations, SullaXS, and it's directly linked to Livia Colton. I won't bore you with all the technical details, but trust me, her name is on this."

"But she's dead, Alastair. Please, please tell me she didn't survive that plunge into the river."

They stared at one another and his heart was in shreds from the anguish in her eyes. Pain he'd put there by leaving his damned display up and running while she was in the house. He hadn't wanted to share anything with her until he'd figured out what she was already coming around to.

"I wish I could tell you she didn't live, Halle. The slivers of pain you've shared with me about how tough losing your father was make me want to lie to you to make you feel better. But I can't."

"Cut the crap, Alastair. You've lied by omission."

"I couldn't say anything until I knew for sure." He took a step closer to the sofa where she sat. "Stranger things have happened. People devise ways to disappear, fake their deaths all the time. It's a moneymaker for anyone with a large insurance policy or inheritance, depending upon who the funds are set up to go to."

Halle narrowed her eyes. "Her kids had divorced themselves from Livia and her evil ways years ago. They wanted nothing to do with her or her money."

"That matches what I and my security team dug up. She wasn't a nice person, to say the least." And if she were still alive, he'd be the first one to want her in jail for life. He risked sitting next to Halle and to his relief she didn't move over. "I didn't want to tell you about this because it's so troubling, and you don't need it right now."

Her eyes were clear, flecked with sunlight. "We may not be a real married couple, Alastair, but we're partners. If your business or reputation is on the line, so is my baby's future. You're absolutely certain that this person is trying to buy you out?"

He nodded. "Yes. While I—we can't rule out that Livia Colton is still alive, I highly doubt it. All of the police reports indicate no one could have survived being washed away by the river. By the time the early responders arrived her car was upturned and the two surviving agents with her had escaped it. Whoever is behind this isn't an amateur, and it's someone with substantial resources."

"Then you can find this person? It's a man, right?"

"That's what's so hard about all of this. I haven't been able to narrow it down to one person yet, due to the privacy laws in the States."

"It says a lot if even you can't find out who's causing all of this trouble." Her color was returning, the reassuring soft peach hue on her high cheekbones. "It would almost be worth it to see her alive and watch her go to a federal penitentiary for good this time. To one she'd never be able to escape from. You know she was a prison escapee, right?"

"Yes. The internet is full of reports not only on Livia Colton's rap sheet, but how she got herself out of prison. No one likes to see a criminal who's supposed to be doing time escape."

"No." Halle offered him a shaky smile. "I'm sorry I went off the handle. I should trust you more."

"No, you shouldn't. I mean, of course you can trust me, but we've only spent a grand total of what, maybe two weeks together? And while bringing you here to meet my family is one way to show you that my intentions are sincere, there's no reason for you to believe that. It takes time, Halle."

She looked at him. They were inches apart on the sofa, her warmth a balm to his anxiety over the potential buy-out. "My father said that he knew the minute he saw my mother that she was the one. Trust was a part of that."

He cupped her face in his hands. "Gram says the same about Grandpop. They had over fifty years together. Nothing to sneeze at."

"And we only have to last a year. At least we have okay chemistry."

"Okay?" He caressed her bottom lip with his thumb. Making love to her right now would be callous, and he knew that their incredible sex every day this past week might come with dark consequences, but he was tired of living by the rules. It hadn't kept a hostile bidder from moving in on his stocks, and it hadn't kept him happy these past several years.

She lifted her lips to his and teased him with a provoc-ative whisper of a kiss. "Maybe a little more than okay."

He groaned and deepened the kiss, needing her heat to drive away the cold truth of their agreement. Proof that she still reacted to him in a positive way—and yes, damn it, that she trusted him. If not with her life and heart yet, at least with her body.

Chapter 17

The next day, Halle accompanied Alastair to the family headquarters in Glasgow. "Halle, this is Jane, my executive assistant. She's the person responsible for how smoothly everything runs here at headquarters."

"Nice to meet you." Halle extended her hand to the petite redhead.

"Likewise. I'll leave you both to it, unless you need anything else, Alastair?"

"Not for now. Thanks." Alastair looked at Halle as Jane left for her desk. "What do you think?"

"This is incredible." Halle looked at a priceless Édouard Manet in the lobby of Clyde Whiskey and grinned. "I thought you'd have something more Scottish on the walls, or at least something to do with Clyde Whiskey."

"Gram found that at an auction almost fifty years ago. She used all of her savings at the time, which wasn't a whole hell of a lot compared to what we've accrued to date. If the company goes belly-up, this is our combined nest egg."

It was more than a nest egg, more than a life's earnings for most working class folks, but Halle didn't call him out on it. Nothing about Alastair had ever suggested that he took his financial status or power for granted. He didn't even fuss about what he ordered off menus, or indulge in what he termed "fancy" coffees like cappuccinos and lattes. He was an English breakfast tea man. Clear and strong.

"And here's where I spend a lot of my time when I'm in town." He ushered her out of the reception area and into a modest office that was located adjacent to a smaller office, where Jane sat at her desk.

Alastair's office was blindingly modern and masculine in its decor. Gleaming glass desk, contemporary shelving, state-of-the-art computers. But nothing over-the-top. He tilted his head, ever so slightly. "You look surprised."

"I thought you'd have a whiskey keg in here somewhere."

"It's a barrel, and there is a more rustic desk at the distillery. The original that my great-great-grandfather used, and every owner until me. When I decided to branch out with global investments, it was time to buy an office space in the city, closer to an international airport."

He motioned at a chair and she sat down while he took his seat behind the extra-long desk. "I'd love to take you out to the distillery. We could spend an entire day, stay the night in a local bed-and-breakfast or an inn to enjoy the local ambience."

"You're telling me that you stay in a regular place without your secret security posse?"

"I don't have a security detail except for when I'm traveling abroad. I have body guards, yes, because I don't want to put my family through the unnecessary hell of a kidnapping and the ransom negotiations."

She didn't like the idea of Alastair or any of his family in danger. "As much as you've said *my* security needs have changed, so have yours. You're going to be a father."

His eyes sparked with awareness. "As if I could forget." She had a feeling he wasn't just talking about the baby as his glance lingered over her body. A body that she felt was growing more curves each day.

"Don't you think you need to ramp up the security here? If I'd been alone I feel like I would have been able to walk right in off the street." She wandered around the room, needing a distraction from the sexy dance her hormones were doing.

"There's more security here than meets the eye. We have state-of-the-art technology. We don't keep anything valuable here save for my backup files, which are stored on servers in remote locations."

"So that's your backup?" Her firm in Austin had had duplicate and even triplicates.

"The cloud, or my version of it, with multiple iterations."

It was her turn to stare at him. "I suppose there's 'your' version of everything."

"There's always been a Buchanan way of doing business. We pride ourselves on quality over quantity, forethought over crisis. Unfortunately, in a business our size, it often feels as though we're reinventing the wheel with each new iteration of technology. I have to ensure no one else can copy our security plans, not exactly, anyway. All of our computer software programs are proprietary, of course, from our website and social media to our financial records to the centuries-old whiskey recipe. If we used any software 'off the shelf' we'd be fools."

"I understand, and not just because I worked for a large corporation before coming back to Bluewood. At my small level, I'm competing against every other ranch that's trying to stay alive these days. I make sure I'm aware of what my competition is doing, but stay with what works best for my business."

"I hope you never regret what you've done to ensure the ranch survives." Alastair's guarded posture indicated he might be worried that she'd come after him later. After the baby was born, after she'd put Bluewood back up on its feet. After they'd divorced.

"I can't regret anything that will provide for my— our—baby. That's a given. As for actually getting married instead of a simple business negotiation?" She waited, made sure he was looking at her. "No, I can't regret that, either. You were right. Our child deserves more."

Jane rushed into the office, her previously professional demeanor shattered with flushed cheeks. "I'm sorry, Alastair, but there's a security alert on your estate property that needs your attention."

"At home?" Alastair didn't question Jane's interruption, and alarm clenched Halle's stomach. The nausea that had been at bay reared and she sat down.

She remained quiet as Alastair's fingers flew over his keyboard, Jane at his side, speaking quietly.

"There, in the second quadrant, third camera." Jane pointed to the grainy image that Alastair had brought up

on the center display. The other two screens were filled
with video feeds of what Halle recognized as the family estate. She spotted her favorite woods and the view
that expanded out over the western hills.

Her stomach lurched when she saw the intruder. A
man, dressed in dark clothing, scaling the perimeter wall
that surrounded Alastair's parents' home.

"Did the local authorities get him?"

"They did, but then he was released. He was found
by your grandmother after he'd entered. The security
guards were right behind him, but not before he spoke
to her while she was in her garden. He asked her if you
were around to speak to. The guards escorted him off
the property and took him to the station. He told the constable that he was hiking and had wandered in."

"What was his name?"

Jane looked at her electronic tablet. "Samuel MacGuire. Irish passport."

"That sounds familiar." Alastair frowned and he
clacked on his keys again. Halle was enthralled by how
intense, how focused he was. She'd only seen him like
this when she'd been in danger, or in bed.

"There it is. Get the authorities on the line. That's one
of the pseudonyms for the corporations who have been
purchasing my stocks in huge numbers." His eyes were
on Halle and she leaned in over his desk.

"He wouldn't have been stupid enough to use his own
name?" Halle's mind raced. "But no one knows who
Livia Colton meant to leave her cash to or where it went.
Do you think this is him? Or worse, someone representing her, if she's somehow survived?"

Alastair nodded. "We may have located our bad guy,
and maybe even Livia Colton's heir."

* * *

It had been the closest he'd come to failure since working for his boss. When the idiot who called himself the local constable had interrogated him he'd been sure he'd earned a one-way ticket to a Scottish jail. Fortunately the source he'd utilized for his passport and associated fake IDs had done his job and he'd been released.

Now to tell the boss.

"This better be good to risk exposure from overseas." The words weren't as harsh as his boss's tone, which was deadly calm.

"Don't pay attention to any reports you see or read. We're still good to go with our big picture plan."

"What the hell does that mean? Now what have you screwed up?"

"Nothing—I didn't get into the house as planned but I came close enough to shake them up." Briefly, and in as few words as possible, he outlined what had happened, emphasizing that he'd gotten past some of the best technology on the market today. He reluctantly admitted his arrest but made sure his boss understood he'd been let go without any charges filed, all under his assumed identity. They were safe; the plan was intact.

"I'm in a commercial jet on the tarmac of Dublin airport, new passport. We're headed for the runway and takeoff in five minutes." He looked around at his fellow passengers in coach. The boss wasn't big on spending for luxury travel.

"Try not to screw up anything else before you get back to Shadow Creek."

"You don't have to worry. This was a one-time error." And it wasn't his fault, not really. He'd been given the wrong details on Buchanan's security setup. What a waste of money the guy he'd bribed in Glasgow had been. No matter. He'd sent the informant to the bottom of a deep loch, unavailable to corroborate any other witnesses to his bungled break-in attempt. One thing he prided himself on was no loose ends.

"I'll decide what I'm going to worry about. Just remember that you work for me. There is no 'we' in this. Your next mistake is your last." The line went dead and he powered his phone off as the flight attendant walked by. He didn't need any more trouble, that was for sure.

His boss was always in a pissed-off mood, so he was used to being treated like a speck of dirt. Fine, for now. What he was about to do to Halle Ford Buchanan and her unborn kid would erase any bad impressions his boss had of him. And make them both rich enough to disappear for the rest of their lives—together, because he was going to make sure there was no other way for it to go off.

"Blanket?" A young attendant who looked like she'd love a tumble held out the plastic-wrapped amenity.

"There's other ways to stay warm." Her eyes narrowed at his comment and he made sure to give her his most charming smile as he accepted the cheap afghan. She moved on without further comment and he couldn't take the grin off his face. Once he had the money he wanted, no woman, young or old, would refuse him.

"I'm sorry, Alastair. He had a legit passport and we had no reason to keep him any longer. He seemed pleasant enough, though I know that's no comfort when he was in your Gram's cabbage patch."

"No, it's not." He wanted to be angry with Kip Nelson but his childhood friend and university classmate was sincere. "It's not your fault, Kip. You had no idea about the surveillance footage. None of us did—even my security detail missed it the first go-round."

"That's a little concerning, as that indicates he may have insider information or be highly technically trained. He may have frozen the feeds in your security office on-site."

"Not impossible but definitely improbable." Alastair knew his security detail and the system they used. It was nearly foolproof.

Kip let out a long sigh. "Times have changed, Alastair. It takes an experienced criminal mere seconds to do something like this."

"Why was he on my property?"

"Why not? To prove he could do it, to show off to friends or even the world if he intends to put it out there on social media. Or the worst option..." Kip obviously didn't want to have to say it.

"It was a practice run."

"Yes. But as I told you when you first called in, he's well on his way to Ireland, as his passport cleared customs not an hour after he left here. Anything changed with you since we did our yearly walk-through?" Kip's eyes were on Alastair. He looked relaxed but Alastair knew the man and understood every nuance of his demeanor was being recorded.

"I've recently married. And...and my wife is pregnant. But it's all private, for now. We haven't made any official announcements." He didn't deserve to feel as thrilled, as excited about the declaration as he was. He wasn't a real husband to Halle. Certainly he wasn't protecting her the way he felt a real husband should.

"Congratulations! That's wonderful. Truly."

"But?"

"You know the 'but.' The bull's-eye on your family just increased twofold. Exponentially, really, since your child will be a kidnapper's dream."

Alastair's insides couldn't be more torn up than if Kip had sucker punched him. "If I could rethink my earnings, my company—"

"Hey now, none of that, man. You've earned your resources fair and square." Kip reflected the local pride in the Buchanan rags-to-riches story. A downtrodden old whiskey distillery, due to foreclose, had been turned around by Alastair to provide thousands of jobs for the economy. "There are always going to be bad folks out there, Alastair. It's inevitable. Trust us to do our job. We'll keep the area safe for you. You keep your security detail up-to-date on the latest tools of the trade, okay?"

"Will do." He and Kip caught up on a few more family details before Alastair stood to go home. To Halle. He'd sent her back to the estate with his driver earlier, after Kip had told him the intruder was out of the country. Fear wound around his throat and closed tightly. Everyone thought Livia Colton was dead, but he'd seen evidence to the contrary. How could he be certain that this man posing as Samuel MacGuire would stay in Ireland? Was this truly MacGuire, or an imposter?

And had "MacGuire" ever been to Shadow Creek, Texas?

Chapter 18

"We're flying back to Shadow Creek tomorrow." Alastair made the pronouncement minutes after he returned home from the police station. Alarm shot through Halle. Not at the prospect of going home, but at Alastair's grim demeanor. He was a man possessed.

"I thought we were going to stay here for a full week? It's about the break-in, isn't it?"

He ignored her as he made them a pot of ginger tea. "You look green around the gills, Halle."

"Answer my questions, and maybe I won't feel so sick."

"Is it the morning sickness again?" She felt a warm, strong hand on hers as she stared out his home office window. The rolling green of Scotland didn't look a bit like the Texas hills but it offered her the same comfort. And disbelief that someone had tried to intrude upon this serenity.

"A bit, but also vertigo. I'm prone to it. The doctor mentioned it could be part of the pregnancy sickness." Alastair's decision to take them back to Shadow Creek so quickly wasn't helping. She leaned back on the leather swivel chair, staring at the horizon in an effort to settle her stomach.

"Here." The scent of Alastair's aftershave mingled with the smell of the ginger beverage and she closed her eyes as she grasped the porcelain mug.

"Thank you. You seem to be doting on me an awful lot. Shouldn't I be the one doing this, to keep my billionaire husband?" Her eyes sought his as she took her first sip and the fleeting hurt that crossed his features before he resumed his in-charge attitude stunned her.

"Of course you should be doted on. You're almost four months pregnant. It's time for you to stop caring for everyone else and take care of yourself."

"Alastair, I'm sorry. I didn't mean to suggest I'd roped you into this arrangement." She winced at the rodeo pun.

"I don't enter into any contract unless I want to, Halle. Never doubt that marrying you was exactly what I wanted."

For the baby.

She forced her gaze away from him and allowed the soothing tea to work its magic. "How did I live without ginger tea before now?"

He was silent and she didn't, couldn't, meet his gaze. And see the turmoil in his.

"We're going back to Texas because you're right. You need your routine, and it's important that you're settled and ready for the baby to arrive where it will spend most of its time."

"Glad you figured that out." Was he going to time her showers, too?

"Halle, you will still be running the ranch—but at a more steady pace. I expect you to use the funds available to the business to hire more hands and at least one personal assistant." He'd given her access to the money via a joint account effective the day they were married.

"Says the billionaire with one assistant." Darn it, there was her focus on his financial status again. She'd promised herself she'd ensure he understood she was attracted to him, not his bank account. And she'd dropped the *b*-word twice in the last few minutes.

"I have one EA here, yes, but there is an entire staff of one hundred working in Glasgow. And at each satellite office of Clyde Whiskey, depending upon what the business model in that area is." He leaned back in the chair opposite her, swiveling to enjoy the view, too. "For example, in London, we have an entire office suite with a staff of fifty. Indonesia, the same. Hong Kong only requires a staff of five and they all telecommute—to this office. I, or one of my department heads, visit once per quarter."

"That's a lot of travel for your company." For him. Would he ever be able to let go of his obvious need to travel? She felt foolish, thinking their baby would make him want to spend more time at home, either here or in Texas. As if she wished he'd want to stop jetting around in order to spend more time with her.

"You're looking pale again. Would crackers or soda water help?"

"No, it's not my stomach this time." She paused, unsure of how much to reveal. Sharing her emotional vulnerability with Alastair was more intimate than their no-limits sex. "It's a bit overwhelming, isn't it?"

"The security breaches?"

"No, I'm not even thinking of that right now. I mean how we're going to manage this year of a fake marriage, learn to parent, then negotiate a divorce that oh, by the way, will include a custody agreement satisfactory to both of us. And through all of that, keep our baby safe and healthy."

"Why don't we focus on today, Halle?"

"Today's not good enough." She stood up and placed her mug on the sideboard. "We have to plan for the future, Alastair. You're right. Going back to Texas is the best plan."

She walked to the door and paused. "I'm going to pack. I'll be ready whenever you need me to be." No more getting off course due to her feelings for Alastair.

As she walked back to the room they shared, it hit her that it wasn't only her hormones that were affected by her contract husband. Her heart was irrevocably changed.

He watched her go and it was all he could do not to throw his mug at the wall. The last person he ever wanted to upset was Halle. And it wasn't only because she was carrying his child. It was more. Their agreement had become far more than a marriage of convenience. Even if he hadn't been able to make love to her as much as he wanted, his feelings for her had deepened, grown into a full-blown commitment. With Halle Ford, nothing less was possible.

He grabbed his keyboard and refreshed his screens. It might take hours to add to what his security team had gotten on MacGuire. While he was at it he ordered their flight back to the States.

He brought up his videophone link. Jeremy answered on the first ring. "Hi. How's it going? How's Halle doing?"

"Lousy and she's still queasy. I'm taking her back to Texas. She needs her own surroundings."

"That's fair, and we miss her. I'm a little stunned that you move so quickly. And impressed. No matter what the local blog is reporting."

"What is *Everything's Blogger in Texas* saying?" His mention of the blog started his blood boiling.

Jeremy's face scrunched up on the pixelated screen "You haven't read it?"

"I haven't looked at it yet but I'm aware of the local website."

"I'm surprised your EA didn't let you know." Jeremy liked to tease Alastair about his staff, as Alastair did to Jeremy. They were good friends who knew one another well before either of them could afford such a luxury.

"Spit it out, Jeremy."

"Let's see." Jeremy stared at the screen, obviously opening another screen. "Britain's most eligible billionaire is off the market, married to Shadow Creek native Halle Ford, in a ceremony so hush-hush it leaves reason to believe a Scottish baby is on the way."

Heat rushed to his head. He did not want Halle to know about this. She deserved to keep whatever privacy and peace she could. "Anything else?"

"Let's see…they mentioned that you were wed in the courthouse of Shadow Creek, Texas, last week."

"Damn it!" Security for Halle was becoming increasingly difficult. "That was never private, but I thought it might take them a little longer to get so worked up over it."

Jeremy's eyes pierced his through the computer screen. "You'll deal with it, man. Call ahead, send a security detail out there to fence in her house. Wire that place for sound—you know what I mean. Let me do whatever I can to help."

"Thanks, Jeremy. And I've already done most of that. I do appreciate your direction, though." He'd ordered full wiring of Bluewood before they'd left.

Jeremy grinned. "Anytime. Halle didn't have a problem with you adding the security to her property?"

He grimaced. "I haven't told her yet."

"Are you kidding me? Halle's not an acquisition, you know. She's your wife, the mother of your future child, and no matter how deeply certain you are that your way is the right way, you must allow her to participate in your decisions. Trust me on this." Jeremy's voice rang with experience.

He ran his hand over his face. "I don't know what I'd do if she didn't agree to the security measures. She's wound up about the costs involved in saving her business. If she finds out I dropped hundreds of thousands of dollars on security alone, she'll have my balls in a sling."

"I hear you."

He filled Jeremy in on the break-in and what he knew about Samuel MacGuire so far.

"You think it's an alias, and the jerk's probably on his way here as we speak." Jeremy was the best at putting together seemingly disparate pieces of information. It's why he relied on him for business advice. He was killer in a boardroom.

"Yes, I do." And it made him seethe with the need to take the bastard down.

"But you're still coming back, with Halle? Where you think this criminal is headed?" Jeremy whistled. "I'm not surprised. You've never been one to back down from a fight. Give us a call if you want Halle to stay here, if it gets ugly."

"I will. I know it doesn't make total sense, except I know in my gut that this is best for Halle." And it might be the best chance he had to show her that he wasn't in it solely because she was pregnant with his child. Not any longer. It was more.

But would Halle ever agree to giving their contract relationship a chance to be more?

Within thirty-six hours Alastair and Halle were back at Bluewood, their time in Scotland a memory. Halle was impressed at how just like her, Alastair didn't let any grass grow under his feet when it came to business concerns.

"Halle, this is William Anthony." Alastair motioned to the man who'd accompanied him into the house. William Anthony had come at the suggestion of her friend River Colton, a US Marine Corps combat veteran who worked with William in the military. William also did contract work for Adeline's PI firm in Shadow Creek. The other man held his cowboy hat in his left hand, and his shoulders had to be nearly as wide as he was tall. He'd make a perfect bodyguard, physically at least.

"Ma'am. I go by Will." He held out a hand large enough to span the oak beams that ran the width of the front room. Halle shook his hand, holding back a smile when she saw how her hand was engulfed in her new bodyguard's right hand.

"Nice to meet you. River speaks so highly of you."

"We served two tours together. River's good people." Upon closer inspection Will's face was chiseled as if from granite, and his dark brown eyes sparked with attentiveness. Yes, he'd be the perfect one to protect them.

"Yes, he certainly is." She gestured toward Alastair. "I'm not sure how much Alastair has told you but I'm hoping your work here won't get too complicated. I expect we'll only need you if I'm going to leave the ranch."

"Will will be with you at all times that I'm not present, Halle. We've already discussed this." Alastair's gaze was laser sharp as he looked at her. He didn't want her to broach a fight, not in front of Will. So she wouldn't.

"That's fine. I'll need you to accompany me on the trail rides, which are scheduled weeks in advance." She walked over to her desk and pulled off a sheaf of papers, which she handed to Will. "The top sheet is the tour schedule from now until when the baby's due. I won't be riding the last month or so, and we don't have any rides scheduled until at least three months after the baby is born." She waited while Will looked over the spreadsheet. Alastair's frustration with her radiated off him in waves, and she risked a glance at him. He wasn't thrilled about her riding at all while pregnant, and she understood his overprotective instincts. But instead of a glare she found nothing but appreciation and respect in his eyes. She smiled, the comfort of Alastair's acceptance of her role as head of the ranch palpable. They'd surveyed the ranch's new security system together as soon as they'd arrived yesterday afternoon. Maybe they would work this out beyond her wildest dreams. If it didn't crush her heart in the process.

"I take it each trail ride is different." Will brought her back from the depths of Alastair's gaze.

"Um, yes. I customize them to each group. The only repeats are when we have a family or business that wants the exact same experience, which is rare. It keeps things fresher for us, as well as a better experience for each group."

Will nodded. "I like it. Is there anything I need to know about before we leave on our next ride?"

"I'll be briefing you on that. But why don't we have lunch first?" Alastair guided Will from the office and Halle lingered behind.

"I'll meet you both in a bit. I've got some phone calls I have to make first."

"Don't be long." The warmth of Alastair's smile made it clear that he didn't want her at lunch with them for business reasons. He enjoyed her company as much as she did his.

Could she do this? Could she trust Alastair with her ranch, her baby, her life?

"Yes, that'll be perfect, Mr. Slater. We look forward to hosting you." Halle clicked off from her conversation with the client arriving tomorrow and stretched her arms over her head. Since they'd been back at Bluewood, her nausea had subsided enough for her to be able to square away the details for the next six tours, which included hiring more help. Since they'd brought Will on board she hoped Alastair would be more comfortable with her going out on the trail if he was unable to join her due to his work.

And she had to make up the cash flow that Alastair's money had afforded her. She was going to repay Alastair for the funding he was putting into the ranch, plus interest. She couldn't wait to see the expression on his face when she pulled it off. Alastair wasn't the only entrepreneur in the family.

Family. A word that once frightened her seemed closer, more attainable than ever since her father died.

Familiar steps sounded on the hallway outside the office and she ignored the thought that Alastair wouldn't always be here. That all of this would end in a little over a year, if not sooner. After the birth and as the baby grew, she expected Alastair would spend more time back in Scotland and around the world.

"Fancy a chat?" Alastair entered the room, and any anxieties she had over their it-was-business-but-is-it-more relationship vanished. Dressed in a cowboy's work shirt and American blue jeans he looked every bit the Bluewood ranch hand. A very sexy one. And his eyes feasted on her in a way no ranch hand's ever had.

"Sure. Why don't we go sit on the porch? It's unusually warm for November and we need to grab it while we can. A cold front is heading in by tomorrow."

She rose from behind the desk and as she did, felt a distinct fluttering motion low in her abdomen. As if a small fish were in her belly, knocking at its sides.

"Oh!" Halle reflexively put her hand over the spot and stared in wonder at Alastair.

Concern made the frown lines around his mouth deep, his forehead wrought with tense wrinkles. "What's wrong?"

"Nothing's wrong. Here, give me your hand." He held

out his large hand and she placed it under her shirt, just below the edge of her jeans waistband. "Now shh, wait."

Alastair's eyes were downcast, and Halle fought to stay still, praying the movement occurred again. She stared at the rugged brush of a day's beard on Alastair's jaw, and thought about the way the cleft in his chin felt under her tongue. He was already a wonderful father. Her physical and emotional attraction to him were no longer separate entities, if they'd ever been.

The baby kicked, this time more strongly. The rat-a-tat-tat movement made her grin. Alastair's eyes flew open, meeting her gaze with unadulterated joy. "That's our baby?"

She laughed, tears streaming down her cheeks. "Yes. Unless a school of guppies has taken up inside my belly."

"Is that what it feels like?"

"At first. But this time, it's as if he or she knows it's you." Knows it was their father. Her husband. Regret welled and she took a step back. Alastair's hand fell to his side and he looked at her.

"What is it?"

"Nothing. Dang pregnancy hormones have me all over the map." She swiped at her cheeks, willing the tears to stop but they didn't heed her wish. "I'm not sad, I'm happy. It's the delight at feeling the baby move for the first time." She sniffed.

"You sure don't look very happy." The concern was back on his expression, wiping away the shared joy of only moments before. He took a step toward her, closing the distance between them to inches. Halle backed up until she hit the wall of the small office. With her desk blocking her side, and Alastair in front of her, she had nowhere to go. Nowhere to look. But up at his face.

His dear, sexy face. With his impossibly blue-gray eyes, intent on her. Simmering with what echoed in her heart.

"Halle. Stop keeping it all bottled up. This is why I'm here, what I'm here to do. I'm walking down this road with you as you have our baby."

She nodded. "I know."

"But?"

She swiped at her face again, but he waved her hands away and wiped her cheeks himself. His fingers were soft and gentle on her skin, his breath a comfort as he spoke, so close. "Tell me what's really bothering you." He pressed his forehead against hers.

"It's silly, stupid, typical of me. I can't help but sometimes think what it would be like if you weren't you, you know, part of Clyde Whiskey, and we'd just met here, and then had the baby, and—"

Alastair's mouth was on hers, his hands moving from her face to her waist, her hips. His lips begged her to stop thinking and to give in to her feelings. She tried to fight it, tried to do the honorable thing as she shoved at his chest.

"No, not like this. I want to, but…"

He nibbled on her earlobe, then gently turned her head so that he could land a very precise love bite on her neck, right where it met her shoulder. Shivers of need racked her and she held on to his shoulders so she wouldn't sink to the floor with want.

"Make love to me just like this, Halle. As we are right now, right here. Just me and you. Nothing, no one but us."

His pelvis pressed against hers as he bent his knees and his erection teased her hot center. "Oh, oh, Alastair."

She breathed his name into his mouth as she covered it with her own, no longer caring what their future held.

Today was beautiful in and of itself.

Halle's Dragon

By Wednesday she was late again for the seventh time that week, but what could she do?

Chapter 19

Clear, blue November skies reflected the winter sun so strongly that Halle needed her sunglasses even in the shadowed part of the slow walk on her mount. She stopped Elvis to look around. Alastair didn't like her riding alone, but she had her phone with her in case anything happened, and Will hung back on Buster, giving her space to feel alone but also the reassurance that she wasn't. She wasn't taking any unusual risks. Since her baby bump was turning into a definite basketball she knew her riding days were limited, as was her alone time. She'd hoped to ride until the end of her pregnancy but found herself thinking maybe she'd stop sooner. The baby's health was too important to risk. But she'd miss this solitude. Halle thrived on the mental space being alone gave her.

The trees were bare and while the temperature was

very mild, almost balmy thanks to a southerly wind, the woods and fields that led home all looked quintessentially late autumn.

Next week was Thanksgiving, and then came Christmas. The holidays at Bluewood. Festive gatherings with Dad were over and her heart still pinched at it. Her baby kicked and rolled over as if reminding her that she had a new family to focus on. A new reason to celebrate the holidays.

Her phone alerted and she pulled it out of her jacket pocket. It sounded the unique ding again, one she'd set up to let her know if her internet search found anything new on Clyde Whiskey. Since they'd left Scotland almost three weeks ago Alastair had conducted a board meeting via video conference and nothing had come up. Halle had started to believe that what he'd said was true. That there were no more ties to the heirs of Livia Colton's estate.

The alert proved her wrong. Clyde Whiskey was again in a cyber stock war, with the main aggressor being none other than the same buyer that Alastair promised he'd divested himself of. The group of buyers he'd connected to Livia Colton's probable benefactor had disappeared and now only one entity was buying out his IPO.

SullaXS.

He hadn't mentioned this new attempt at a buyout to her, after promising to keep her informed and appraised of the situation. They were supposed to be partners in all of this; he'd promised. A horrible twist in her gut that had nothing to do with morning sickness, pregnancy or nerves had her clutching the horn of her saddle as she struggled to stay calm and keep herself from getting the baby riled up.

Betrayal. It could be her hormones, she knew. Or was

she finally listening to the small voice she should have stuck with from the start of their relationship?

How desperate had she been when she realized she was pregnant? She knew she shouldn't trust a man who, despite billions of dollars, impregnated her the very first time they were together. A man who continued to seduce her right to the altar and since.

No more. Halle was a Ford, and Alastair was on her Texas turf. In her neck of the woods, men kept their word or were held accountable.

Time for a reckoning.

"You're fired, Jameson. As is your entire staff. Clear out." Alastair disconnected the video conference with Glasgow and immediately contacted his security divisions in London and Hong Kong to ensure the entire body of the investment department were removed from Clyde Whiskey. He'd locked their access to the company systems before he made the axe-landing call, following the same protocol he'd used since growing Clyde Whiskey to its current size.

A size that was cut by two-thirds, according to the stock markets. He answered a call from his lawyer, working out the details of gaining his stock back from the shell corporation.

His lead attorney had ugly news, but promised to keep fighting for the company. Of course he did; his entire life's savings, and his family's, depended upon it.

A loud slam followed by hurried footsteps had him standing and moving toward the office door. But not before Halle beat him to it, standing in the home office in front of him.

"Why didn't you tell me?" Wild hair, a breathless accusation.

"Tell you what?" Just in case she didn't know yet, he'd have her sit down first.

"Just stop it with the gallant Scotsman BS! You lied about telling me of any further connection to a person tied to Livia Colton. The woman who murdered my father!" Her hands were on her hips, her cheeks had spots as big as cottage roses and her eyes were narrowed. On him.

"Do you tell me every detail of every trail tour you've planned? And the news just broke. I had to talk to my securities people. I fired the entire Glasgow staff just now."

"You did?" She paused. "This is different than my trail tour business, Alastair. A lot."

"I thought you were tending to the horses."

"I was riding."

"By yourself?"

"Don't look so put out about it. I wasn't alone—Will was with me. I know my business, which is riding horses. And I believed that you're an expert at yours."

"If you believe that, then you have to trust me that I know what I'm doing." It grated that she wasn't giving him the benefit of the doubt, after all they'd been through.

"How can I trust you, Alastair? How? You manipulated me into marrying you, promised to help me get Bluewood back on its feet. And I told you explicitly why I can't have anything to do with anyone who was in cahoots with Livia Colton. She killed my father, Alastair. What part of that don't you get?"

"Halle, I'm trying to catch this person at their own game."

She yanked off her worn leather gloves and ran her fingers through her tousled hair. Her eyes sparked and he wished it were with desire. Because no matter how much hate she threw at him, he wanted her more than ever. "Alastair, there are many ways to capture a criminal. I don't think this is the way you want to do this. I know it isn't. I told you how evil and self-serving she was. Anyone who did business with her when she was alive would be just as bad. Worse. You know the Midas touch myth? Well, around Shadow Creek, it was the Livia Colton Touch, except hers turned everything to death. She was a living, breathing witch with poison in her blood."

"You have to trust me, Halle. I have the best people on the planet working this. I've tightened the noose on this criminal."

"Really, Alastair?" She let out a brief gasp of snide laughter. "How freaking stupid do you think I am? Do you think all I know about is how to dress a horse, run a trail tour, balance the books?" She took her phone out of her pocket and after a few taps started reading.

"From today's *Financial Times*:

"Alastair Buchanan's brilliance loses some of its luster as he executes the equivalent of Tchaikovsky's swan dance with an anonymous buyer known only as SullaXS. The assumed corporation has links to a former troublemaker of Shadow Creek, Texas, an area outside of Austin, Texas. Livia Colton, presumed dead after driving drunk and causing an accident that left a local man dead, may have survived, judging by her anonymous representative's actions. If she's still alive, Livia

Colton is benefitting from dipping into the Clyde Whiskey fortune, to the tune of two-thirds of the company's holdings. It is pretty clear that while not public yet, the identity of the buyer will be confirmed when Alastair Buchanan signs a merger with SullaXS. Why else would such a brilliant captain of industry allow an unknown to gobble up 68 percent of his company's shares? Until now the Buchanan family has held on to at least fifty percent of Clyde Whiskey shares, but faces an almost definite takeover."

She turned the screen of the phone around so that he could see it. "Hard to deny it now, isn't it?"

"Damn it, Halle, this is just some crackpot reporter thinking he's got it all figured out. You'll see, as soon as it works out, that SullaXS has nothing. I'll get my holdings back, and they'll be in jail." He couldn't tell her everything, not yet. Not until the bastards who'd helped sell stock to this loser were arrested.

"Oh, Alastair. You don't get it." Disappointment crept in on the edges of her furious expression. "Even if you're telling the truth, which I have no way of knowing, you didn't involve me in this decision. I don't give an armadillo's behind about your business, except when it came to this person who's obviously become part of your company. How do I know if you've been honest about the security breaches? Were those manufactured events to get me back here? Did you think that if I was back at Bluewood I'd not have the time or inclination to pay attention to what you were doing, against my best wishes? We agreed to be partners, to raise our child together." She bowed her head for a moment before raising it to look him square in the eye. "It's over, Alastair. If we can't even be partners in business, I don't see how we're going to raise a child together."

She turned and he reached for her but she slipped away too quickly and was out the front door of the house as he closed the gap between them and stopped on the porch. Her leg swung up and over Elvis as she got on her gelding and turned back to him one last time.

"Where's Will?" He heard the desperation in his voice.

"I sent him home. I'm not going anywhere. But you are." She looked so regal astride Elvis, the soft rounding of her belly accentuating her femininity.

"Please, Halle. Let me help you stable Elvis. We can talk this out."

"Get out. You have thirty minutes." She turned Elvis toward the paddock and dug in her heels.

"Wait!" He ran toward her and as the dirt raised puffs from Elvis's hooves he realized how futile chasing her was. A wave of relief washed over him when Halle guided Elvis into the paddock and began to circle him, keeping a slow and sedate pace. He knew her insides were fuming and she no doubt wanted to run Elvis long and hard, but Halle was a mother who'd protect her unborn child at any cost. At least she was safe in the fenced area. Hopefully she'd reconsider as she cooled Elvis. He'd never seen her so angry, though.

He needed to do something for her that proved he wasn't ever going to do anything to hurt her or their child. The problem was that he didn't want to admit what he knew was the one thing that would make Halle see that he was not a man who'd ever harm her.

He'd only started to accept it himself. He was in love with Halle Ford.

* * *

How stupid could they be? As he watched the bitch circle the paddock with that pretty boy horse, he couldn't believe that Buchanan would leave her alone and go back into the house. The security guards were posted at their usual places and sure, cameras were all over the property. But she'd waved off that sack of rocks bodyguard, and nothing was left to stop him from going in and taking her. The horse would be easy to take out, but he wouldn't have the pleasure of seeing it die as he had the steer. That had been messy but real fun. It reminded him of when he was a boy and just learning how to kill animals in the most exciting ways. Long and slow was his preferred method, but the horse might have to be put down quick, so that he could nab the prize for his boss. Halle Ford's land was his target, along with her husband's company, but he had to be sure to keep her alive long enough to get what he wanted. And that baby she was carrying. Most of it was out in the press and on the internet but he'd caught all he'd needed by capturing her wireless signals and reading her emails. Listening to her phone calls was over, though, thanks to that bastard Buchanan. He'd shut down all open communication on Bluewood. Every phone call was encrypted, so he couldn't even monitor her day-to-day business calls.

No matter. He'd get her, and when he and his employer were done they'd both be all the richer, living the good life on a beach far away. Halle Ford would be dead, and Buchanan would run back to Scotland with his tail between his pale-as-a-rattler's-belly legs.

Halle wanted to shout, scream and sob her way to peace of mind. As Elvis cooled down she tried to allow his gait to soothe her, to take away the angst her row with Alastair stirred up.

Alastair. He was the mysterious stranger who'd appeared on her ranch less than five months ago, but now was the father of her child and her husband. *Her husband.*

She thought of her father's recollections of her mother and their relationship. He'd said it had been so stormy at times, so crazy, but they'd always made up and made sure to go to bed each night at peace with one another.

Halle didn't want peace. She wanted justice. Justice for Ernie's terrible slaughter, most likely killed by the same man who'd stalked her to Scotland. Justice for the risk her unborn child had been exposed to. But most of all, justice for her father's untimely, criminal death. As she'd learned almost a year ago there was no justice, no vengeance possible, when the father she'd loved and idolized so much had been killed by a woman who was now dead.

Was she?

The lingering doubts over Livia Colton being alive were making her crazy. If only her body had been found, this wouldn't be an issue. Of course, the fact that she might be alive and causing Alastair all this trouble would still need to be dealt with.

Elvis let out a snort as his lungs sucked in oxygen for his tired muscles, and she joined him as she tried in vain to practice the slow and steady breathing she'd read about for childbirth. She and Alastair were due to start the classes next week. She'd forgone the opportunity for Lamaze when she'd read about the Bradley method, as she was more of an internal-thought-process gal. She couldn't see herself screaming with each labor spasm, gasping for breath. But the idea of breathing like she'd done in her yoga practice when she'd lived in Austin had appealed to her. No matter how crazy her workload at the marketing agency had been, the long, sweaty sessions in the darkened, candlelit studio had eased her stress and given her hope.

She halted Elvis with a solid backward pull on the reins and dismounted. Softly leading him to the barn, she murmured to the intelligent animal, stroking his skin.

"You get it, don't you, sweet boy?" His neck was so smooth and the muscles rippled under her hands as he strained to reach back to her with his muzzle.

"Here you go, sweetie." She kissed him just above his nostrils and was rewarded with his hot, grass-sweet breath blowing against her chilled cheeks, warming her soul. Elvis knew her. And accepted her, unconditionally.

It was a gentle reminder of what she felt for Alastair. They shared a raw, primal bond and it wasn't because of the baby. Or because of the incendiary sexual chemistry that she knew would have been explored for a long time to come if she hadn't just blown everything with her dang temper. Hadn't her father always cautioned that she'd one day pay for her tantrums, her quickness to harshly judge those she cared for?

After she'd walked him enough to finish his cooldown, Elvis whinnied and nudged her shoulder with his head. Not enough to knock her over but enough to get her attention.

"What, boy? Do you feel it, too? Yeah, I'm a big hot mess." She wrapped her arms around the gelding's neck, wishing she were five years old and it was Chancellor Ford she was hugging, that her father could tell her how to fix things with Alastair. That her problems were small enough to be consoled by a horse. "Let's get you

into your stable." She might have to ask Charlie to finish
with the brushing and feeding of Elvis as she had a strong
desire to get back to the house and talk to Alastair. No
matter how awful they'd both been to each other. If she
took long enough to figure out why, she'd have to accept
that she was in love with Alastair. Somehow during the
past months he'd gone from being the Scottish billionaire who wanted a private tour of Bluewood Ranch to
her baby's father, to her husband, to the man she loved
more than life itself.

The same amount of time it'd taken her to destroy
their relationship. "Oh, Elvis, what am I going to do?"
Apologizing might be a first step. As soon as she had
Elvis settled for the night.

Lost in her self-created misery, she didn't hear the
footsteps until they were upon her. At Elvis's insisting
nudge she whirled around to face the interloper. Her heart
prayed it was Alastair as her intuition and brain told her
otherwise.

"Don't move and you won't get hurt." The grizzled
man in a too-new cowboy hat stood in front of her, half
a foot shorter than her, but broad and muscular. Like a
thug.

"Brannigan James? What the hell do you think you're
doing?"

"Ah, so you remember me. I didn't think the princess
would recall all the work I did around here. Work that's
gone to pot, I see. You'll never be half the rancher your
daddy was. But then again, he was stupid enough to get
himself killed, now, wasn't he?"

The spiritual equivalent of bile made her vision go
hazy around the edges and she ignored the gun the bas-

tard pointed at her. "I have to put my horse away. Then we'll talk."

"Make it fast or I'll kill your horse. We don't want your new husband coming out here, do we? I'd hate to hurt his pretty Scottish face."

She put Elvis in his stall and started to brush him down. Her legs shook but her hands were steady, soothing the horse with practiced movements. *Keep him talking.*

"What do you think you're going to get by pointing that gun at me? You realize there are security cameras and guards all over Bluewood. You've already tripped an alarm, I'm sure."

"Shut the hell up. I take care of anyone and anything that gets in my way. If you want to live and keep your baby safe, you'll put that horse up quick and come with me. I don't want to hurt you but I will. It's time the Fords paid for the slander they've caused the Coltons. Your hubby's going to pay, too, for thinking he can come to Shadow Creek and take it over."

As she listened to his rants and raves, she grabbed a small crowbar that hung on the wall and shoved it into her boot, masking her motion with brushing Elvis's hindquarters, out of Brannigan's direct line of sight. The slow-witted crook thought *she* was the idiot?

"The Coltons? They're all my friends." A chill of frightening proportion raced up and down her spine as she faced the wall, away from the gun that could rip its lethal bullet through her with no warning. The only Colton who believed she or her father had harmed their name was dead. Washed away in a flash flood while her father's bloodstains marred the Shadow Creek road.

Halle acknowledged the ugliest of possibilities. That it wasn't her pregnancy hormones or her revenge fantasies. Livia Colton might still be alive.

Chapter 20

Alastair forced himself to remain in the house at his laptop, fighting every instinct to go out to the barn and talk to Halle while she finished walking and stabled Elvis. He'd known her long enough to know when she needed space.

An unwelcome alarm sounded from his phone and over the house system he'd had installed as soon as they arrived back in Texas. The guard from the ranch entry point came up on the laptop.

"What's happened?" He stood, taking the laptop with him to where his jacket hung.

"Boss, the security camera in sector three was disabled five minutes ago, and the camera in the stable has been either turned off or covered with something."

"And you're telling me this now? Where are the

guards?" He shoved into his boots, grabbed his gloves from his jacket pocket.

"We didn't confirm it until ten seconds ago. I've got five officers fanning out over the ranch from the paddock out to the trails, and two headed for the stable."

Halle.

"I'm headed to the stable."

"Sir, it's not your job."

"My wife is there!"

Alastair didn't waste time explaining. He grabbed the rifle Halle had agreed he could keep by the front door. He slowly crept onto the porch, his focus on the stables.

Then he spotted the barn structure lit up inside like the Fourth of July, its bright overhead lights spilling their warmth into the late fall darkness. With no evidence of people moving about inside or out, his heart slammed into overdrive. He ran for the barn, instinct pushing him to get there, get to Halle.

He wanted to scream out her name, to shout so that she'd know he was coming. But if she'd met with a threat he'd have to stay quiet or lose any chance of helping Halle. And their baby.

Not now.

His gut told him it was bad and as always, his instinct proved correct. When he got to the open barn door, he peered around the corner and saw a man in black jeans, shirt and black vest. It could have been a ranch hand but they wore regular blue jeans and didn't carry the weapon he saw in this man's hand. Halle's voice carried to him and he froze.

"My husband will never let you get away with this. Do you think he really cares enough about me to hand over any money to you?"

"I'm betting he'll hand over money for his kid."

"Our marriage is a sham. He won't pay you."

Alastair would have to analyze how he felt about Halle's convincing statement that their marriage wasn't real. Right now he had to save her life. He crept along the stable stalls, hoping none of the horses acknowledged his presence. As the man and Halle spoke, he used the cover of their voices to walk without detection. Sweat dripped down his face and it had nothing to do with the warmth of the barn.

Halle. He would do anything he had to for her. He had to. Only two more steps—

The man looked over his shoulder but kept his gun trained on the stall where Halle kept Elvis.

Alastair didn't hesitate.

"Stop right there and drop your weapon." He aimed straight for the man's head.

The man spewed a rough string of epithets that ended with "shoot and I'll pull my trigger." Before Alastair could respond, the man dove into the stall. Alastair ran up and came upon a scene he'd never wish on his worst enemy.

"Lower your weapon or I'll put a bullet in her brain, Buchanan." The man who looked exactly like the photo of Samuel MacGuire, the criminal who'd trespassed on his Glasgow estate, had one arm around Halle's neck as his other hand held the barrel of his gun against Halle's temple. Halle stared at Alastair, her eyes pleading with him.

What did she want him to do?

"What do you want?"

"Lower your weapon now." A hard jerk on Halle's neck had Halle's feet coming off the ground, the hay sticking to the undersides of her boots. Halle's tortured cry was involuntary and it took every ounce of Alastair's self-control to lower the weapon instead of charging into the stall and strangling the assailant. It would end with a bullet in at least one of them, if not both him and Halle.

"Here." Alastair held out the rifle before he let it drop onto the cement floor. "I'll give you whatever you want. Let her go first and then we can talk this over, man-to-man."

"Screw that. I'm the one making the rules here. You're going to give me what I ask for, all right. Turn around and walk back out of this barn."

"There are going to be dozens of SWAT teams swarming all over here within five minutes. You're not going to win. Right now you've got trespassing and possible stalking on your crime tally—don't add attempted kidnapping to it. Do the right thing and let her go."

"Get out of here! Now, or I shoot!" The man was demented but Alastair didn't have a choice. Halle's eyes begged him to do as the man said.

No way in hell was he leaving Halle. But he could pretend to. "I'm going. Just tell me who you are, who you work for." Alastair held his hands up as if in surrender, and took a step back.

"Brannigan. His name is Brannigan." Halle's response was met with another hard yank with the arm around her neck and her feet again came off the ground. If not for the cold steel barrel dug into her temple, Alastair would kill this man.

"Yes, that's my name. More important is who I work for, though. You both think it's a ghost. You all thought Livia was gone. You were wrong." As he spoke he half pulled, half dragged Halle toward the back barn door.

Alastair prayed his team had men there, but it might take another few minutes. Damn it, why was Texas so big? He vowed to fire his entire physical security team when this was over. To start completely over.

Because it had to end with Halle and the baby alive.

"Leave her here. Last chance."

"Never." With that Brannigan disappeared through the door, Halle with him.

Alastair grabbed his rifle off the floor and bolted for the door. He edged around the jamb, crouched low. To his horror he saw Brannigan shove Halle into the back of an old Buick from the driver's side.

"Stop!" He ran like hell toward the car but it was too far and he realized Brannigan had kept the engine running as the wheels immediately spun into the Texas night. Stopping short to aim and fire at the tires, Alastair got off three shots before he heard shouting and a vehicle pulled up alongside him.

"Alastair, get in." Sheriff Jimbo had the passenger side of his vehicle open, siren lights flashing.

Once in Jimbo's vehicle Alastair buckled his seat belt and held on to the dash. Jimbo gave chase to Brannigan, at least five hundred yards ahead of them. Alastair measured the distance by the length of the fence. "Can you go any faster?" Fear tore at his gut.

"Sure, if you want me to break an axel or blow a tire on these rocks. Hang on," Jimbo yelled as the sound of the engine grew louder along with their speed.

"Do you think he'll hurt her?"

"If he survives this car chase, naw. Halle knows him—she'll talk some fear into him, stop him. He wants money for his boss."

"You know who his boss is?"

"I have a good idea. Where the hell is your body-guard? Didn't you hire Will Anthony?"

Alastair didn't want to answer Jimbo, didn't want to focus on anything but closing the distance between them and Halle. The car ahead of them was bumping and making jerky swerves that he knew had to be painful for Halle's bladder. And the baby—

"If you get closer I can aim out my window." He lifted the hunting rifle and hit the button to roll down his window.

"Not so fast, buckaroo."

"Trust me, I'm as good a shot as you." He could shoot with the best Texas had to offer.

"I'm sure you are, but what are we going to do if you take out Brannigan or the vehicle and it's out of control? It's too risky for Halle and the baby. We've got to slow them down and stop him."

Alastair lowered his weapon. God, he was right. What was he thinking?

He was thinking that the woman he loved was in danger and he would do whatever it took to keep her alive.

"You're making a big mistake." Halle yelled over the roar of the old Buick's engine as Brannigan floored it over the bumpy terrain. Each impact jolted through her skeleton like a lightning strike. She prayed that their baby was safe in the watery world of her womb.

Their baby. Hers and Alastair's. Why hadn't she caved and told him she loved him? Why had she let her wounded pride get in the way? The man she knew had integrity and would never intentionally do business of any kind with a woman like Livia Colton, dead or alive.

Livia might have lived to cause this kind of torture to Halle, the baby and Alastair while her father had died.

She wouldn't allow it to keep her from doing what she needed to do to save her life.

"I'm about to pee all over your nice seats back here if you don't slow the heck down!" She held on to the back of Brannigan's plush velour upholstered seat as he navigated another bump that had them soaring through the air for all of three seconds before the ancient frame crashed onto the Texas terrain.

"Shut the hell up back there and git your hands off my seat!" Brannigan's beady eyes were visible in the rear-view mirror but he didn't take his eyes off the road. Halle had used the seat belt automatically, needing to protect the baby. If she thought that choking Brannigan from behind would help, she'd do it in an armadillo's heartbeat. But at these speeds, the car would most definitely end up crushed against either a tree, boulder or fence. And so would the baby.

Fear welled up again and she shoved it back. Her baby's life depended on her keeping her wits. She looked back through the window and was reassured, albeit infinitesimally, that the sheriff's vehicle was right up on them. The lights flashed blue and red and the sound of the siren was deafening.

"I'm. Going. To. Pee." She screamed and prayed that the thirty-year-old boat of a car, a collector's item obviously precious to Brannigan, meant enough to him for him to stop. "Stop now."

"That won't get me what I need."

"I promise we'll give you the money. I can make Alastair do that—he wants people to think he's a big, brave cowboy."

Beady eyes left the road for a split second to war with hers in the mirror.

It was enough of a lapse for him to miss the sharp rocks she felt the car lunge over, and what she thought was a gunshot coming from behind them. She turned to look behind them right before a huge explosion sounded from the left rear.

Thank you, God.

Brannigan had blown a tire. As the car spun on the dirt, it was sprayed with rocks and debris. A sharp *crack* against the passenger window preceded the complete splintering of the glass. Pebbles of the shattered safety glass scattered over her, but didn't feel any different than heavy rainfall on her skin. She instinctively covered her belly with her arms. "Stop! Just stop! You can't keep going."

"Shut the hell up!" Brannigan's profile was as wild as a cornered boar's, his teeth biting his lower lip in a snarl as he continued driving. The car lurched in horrendous, jarring jolts and she knew they had to be driving on a bare tire rim.

Her worst fear had come true. Brannigan wasn't going to stop even if it meant he'd never get the ransom he sought—because she and her baby would be dead.

"Damn it! Why won't he stop?" Alastair aimed the rifle again as Jimbo pulled up alongside their target, the big Buick still making good speed over the rough terrain. Only a car built like a tank could withstand driving on a bare rim. Sparks flew each time the rim hit a rock and Alastair knew the ride was rougher than hell for Halle.

"He will. The trail widens up ahead, and he's going to stick to the left to keep us from pulling up and taking out the rear left tire. But I'll head him off. Hold steady until you know you have a clear shot."

Alastair said nothing. He didn't need Jimbo telling him what he needed to do.

"Sheriff, we've got two units on scene. Please direct us where to send them." Voices crackled on the radio.

"Have the ATV circle the back way, on the old horse trail. Send the other unit back to the ranch house to clear it. Then wait for Buchanan's security detail to check in."

Alastair heard Jimbo talk as if from a great distance. It was as if he lived in a tunnel of horror. All he saw, all he felt, was Halle in the crippled car ahead of them, driven by a madman.

"Floor it!" His words came out of a primal place as he willed Jimbo to draw even with the Buick before the road narrowed. When he'd lose his one last chance to save his family.

As the wind chafed his cheeks and made him squint his eyes, tears pouring down, he aimed the rifle at the tire and prayed Brannigan's car wouldn't spin out of control. He knew without a shadow of a doubt that he'd do anything for his family.

Halle and the baby were the only family that mattered to him now. And he'd die without them.

Chapter 21

"Bastards think they've got me, they've got another thing coming." Apparently crazed with his need to escape with Halle, Brannigan was unreachable. She'd got him to spill his story when he wouldn't let her go, had figured out who he worked for. Had braced herself to see if his boss was indeed the ghost of Livia Colton. She didn't believe it was Livia's ghost any longer. It had to be Livia. Halle hadn't come this far to give up now, no matter how much the odds were against her. She'd never give up, not while the baby she and Alastair had made grew inside her. A solid kick to her abdomen that she felt through her hands, over her belly, made her cry out. It was as if the baby was saying, *We're a team, Mom. No one hurts our family.*

Brannigan might be a hardcore thug but he wasn't the brightest—not when he'd trusted her in the back seat.

She'd managed to get the long iron crowbar out of her boot, but there hadn't been an opening for her to use it yet. They were upon the part of the trail that was going to narrow, with high walls on either side, carved out by a long-ago creek or river. There was no way the vehicle chasing them would be able to take out another tire.

She had a split second to act.

Halle acted with gut instinct and all the courage her daddy had shown her as a child. She lifted the slim crow bar over Brannigan's head and pulled it down, into his throat. Her fingers felt a sickening *crunch* and by Brannigan's roar, she'd busted his nose.

"What the—" He broke into a coughing spasm, his foot momentarily off the accelerator. But his hands were off the wheel, too, as he fought to get the tool off his neck. Halle pulled tighter, pushing against the back of his seat with her feet. While he struggled against the iron she leaned between the two huge front seats and grabbed the pistol he'd used against her. An unexpected calm came over her and she leaned into it.

"Steer us straight through here, then pull over on the left, where the next pasture opens up."

"You think I'm going to listen to you, girlie?"

"You don't have a choice. What do you think your boss will do to you if you don't report back with the ransom?"

"It's not me she'll be after. It's you."

She. God, was it Livia?

"Pull over. It's your only chance. If Alastair is the one to take you out, you'll never see a penny."

Miraculously, he listened to her. The Buick swung into a large doughnut, spewing gravel against the bottom and sides of the body. Halle held on to the front seats for dear life, her seat belt undone so that she could get Brannigan to do her bidding and stop the car.

As soon as the car stopped, she opened her passenger door and dove out, using her arms to pull herself away from the vehicle, away from Brannigan. Bright headlights blinded her and she raised her arm to protect her eyes. Only then did she realize how close the sheriff's car was. Too close.

"Damn it!" Jimbo slammed the breaks and maneuvered the wheel as Alastair had seen it done thousands of times on the big screen. But in the movies it was all pretend. The woman lying on the ground directly in the path of their speeding, careening vehicle wasn't acting.

"Halle!" The scream came out of his chest like the primal roar it was. As soon as Jimbo had the four-wheeler stopped they were both out of the car, advancing toward Halle. A huge obstacle on his chest stopped Alastair in his tracks. He looked down at Jimbo's huge hand and then at the sheriff. "Let me go."

"No. Wait. We don't know what Brannigan's got in that car."

"It's going to explode!"

"No, we don't know that." Jimbo held his finger to his lips and motioned for Alastair to follow him, rifle in hand.

As they approached the car, Brannigan jumped out of the car and lifted Halle up against him. Alastair's eyes fought to adjust between the high beams Jimbo's vehicle shone into the darkness and the moonlight that revealed the acres and acres of pastureland all around them. All he focused on was how the bastard held her, and the fact that she was looking at Alastair. She wasn't unconscious;

she was faking for Brannigan's sake as she hung limply against him, his arm again around her throat.

"It's time to deal, Buchanan." Brannigan's voice, rough but steady, called from their left.

"What do you want? It's been you buying up the shares, hasn't it?" Alastair had to keep him talking until he or Jimbo saved Halle.

"Took you long enough to figure that out. It's how Livia and I were getting her money into legitimate stock. Then we're going to sell it all so fast you'll never have a chance to recoup your losses."

"Why?"

"Why? Because Livia's been treated like dirt long enough in this town. I'm the one who can save her and help her get her life back. The life she deserves. It was a lot of fun talking to your grandmother. I hope you've put in some better security by now." Alastair was dimly aware that Brannigan had basically just confessed to all he'd done, but all he saw was Halle. She was still alive and he intended to keep her that way. Halle was everything.

"Stay behind the car." Jimbo's order was firm and unflinching. As was Alastair's direct disobedience of it. He stayed a few steps back, creeping along in the darkness not lit up by Jimbo's truck.

"It's the County Sheriff, Brannigan. We've got you surrounded. Come on out and we can all go home nice and easy like."

"Not until I strike my deal with Buchanan."

"There is no deal, Brannigan. You gave up your negotiating rights when you kidnapped Halle Ford."

"She came willingly. Didn't you, sweetheart?" A gasp followed by Halle's unmistakable cry of pain jolted through Alastair. Brannigan would know she wasn't knocked out.

"Let her go and we'll deal." Alastair ran past Jimbo, ignoring the other man's attempt to grab his arm. "You want to help Livia and you go free, you talk to me. I won't talk until you let Halle go."

"How stupid do you think I am?"

As Alastair continued toward the voice, the same image from the barn came into view. Brannigan had Halle around the neck, a knife to her throat. Brannigan's arm bunched up her shirt, baring her round belly. The small baby bump glowed in the moonlight.

Alastair couldn't read Halle's expression, couldn't see what she was thinking. Until Brannigan jerked at Jimbo's voice.

"Listen to him, Brannigan. Let her go or you'll have nothing to deal with."

"Do you think I care?" Brannigan sneered and tugged on Halle again. This time she didn't make a sound. Alastair fought back panic that he was cutting off her air. And the baby's oxygen, too.

Alastair's hands ached to be around Brannigan's throat. He watched the coward talk, made eye contact with Halle. She could read his thoughts, he knew it.

You're safe, babe. I've got you and the baby.

"You all think you can talk your way out of this." Brannigan snarled. "Look at you, Jimbo, all full of yourself in that scout uniform. If you were doing your job right I wouldn't be able to get around the county the way I do. While you were all conducting criminal investigations, I was helping to plan my boss's next move. I'm making myself a millionaire. Do you think I'll give any of that up for you? Do you think it would pain me to knife Halle Ford and leave her here?" He used his knee to hit Halle's leg, making her stumble as he held her neck tight. She coughed.

Alastair raised his rifle and took aim.

"Go ahead and pull the trigger, Buchanan. I'll move her so that you hit her just right."

He looked at Halle's eyes. What did she want him to do?

"Hang on, Alastair. Halle knows what to do." Jimbo's quiet murmur reached him and he prayed the sheriff was right.

Halle allowed the vile creature holding the knife against her throat to keep talking as she consciously forced her limbs, her body, to relax. It was a risk, as the knife's blade could easily slip into her skin if Brannigan lost control. But he was too wrapped up in his argument with Alastair and Jimbo, which was to her advantage. She caught the frightened yet determined energy in Alastair's eyes and made sure he was staring at her when she winked. She knew Jimbo understood what she was going to do.

Exactly what he'd taught in community workshops every spring since he'd been deputized.

As Brannigan shouted at Alastair, she pulled on his forearm with all her might, bit into his wrist and landed a solid heel dig to his instep. His grip on her loosened and the knife hung loosely from his hand. She used the millisecond to knock the knife away and drove her free elbow into his solar plexus. When he doubled over, she turned and kneed him in the groin. The beefy thug who was Brannigan teetered on his boots and Halle shoved his shoulder to hasten his topple.

She didn't wait to see him hit the dirt but instead turned toward the men and ran straight for Alastair, who was already there, already scooping her up in his arms, his fingers through her hair, holding her to him.

Chapter 22

The next few hours were a blur to Halle. She witnessed Brannigan James placed in handcuffs and into the back of the sheriff's car while EMTs tended to her scrapes and insisted she go to the ER. Alastair's worried expression punctuated it all. He never left her side, even when the EMTs put her in the air ambulance as a precaution.

She watched her husband's face as the flashing lights on the ground grew tiny and the helo's lights emphasized the grooves around his mouth, the grim set of his shoulders. Halle squeezed his hand, as he'd not let go of hers since she'd wrapped her arms around him after escaping Brannigan.

"Hey." Her voice was too soft for Alastair to hear over the din of the rotors. She slid a quick glance to the EMT, who was tending to her IV of saline solution. They'd told her it was a precaution, more for the baby than her.

Their baby. He or she appeared to be okay. They had to be.

"Hey, Buchanan." She spoke up this time, and was rewarded with the glint of his eyes, the initial warmth that flamed bright before something darker dimmed it. "Want to tell me what you're thinking about?"

He looked out the window before returning his gaze to hers. "There's nothing to say. You're alive, the baby's safe, that's all that matters." Alastair spoke like a robot, as if the lines were part of a script.

What about us? Will we be okay? She wanted to ask him but it wasn't fair to do so when there was only one answer that would work for her.

"We saved ourselves with your help, Alastair."

"You had no help from me. None at all."

"Is that what's bothering you? That you weren't able to take out Brannigan with a single shot? That would have been insane, Alastair. You could have hurt the baby doing that."

"Don't you think I know that?"

She moved her free hand to stroke the top of his as he held her other hand but was brought up short by the IV line.

"Please keep your arm here for now. Once we're at the hospital, you'll have a regular line and usual mobility." The EMT was young, but her voice was backed by professional training and experience.

"I understand." Halle looked at Alastair, willed him to meet her gaze. But his eyes remained resolutely on the bright lights of Austin as they flew in toward the hospital's landing pad. Her billionaire Scotsman was upset and wouldn't let her inside his thoughts. If he wouldn't give her a glimpse of what was going on in that brilliant mind of his, how was she ever going to break into his heart?

"Here we go. Hang on, just a few more secs." The EMT spoke as the chopper touched down with the barest of bumps. It was certainly smoother than the ride in Brannigan's old car had been.

"And we're home." The pilot spoke over his shoulder as he powered down the blades and Halle was whisked off and lifted onto a full hospital bed atop the roof. She knew it was probably the best view of Austin anywhere but Alastair was all that mattered to her.

"You'll stay with me, right?" She tugged on his sleeve.

"Of course."

True to his word, he walked alongside the gurney and into the elevator. Harsh fluorescent lighting only emphasized the obvious distress he was under, written in every line on his face. His dear, dear face.

She had to get through to him.

"Everything looks great with you, Mrs. Buchanan. All that remains is to do an ultrasound of the baby." The attending physician snapped her electronic tablet closed. "They'll be coming to take you to Radiology within a few minutes."

"Thank you. I was due for one next week, anyhow."

Attendants came and unlocked the brakes on her bed. As they wheeled her gurney into the ultrasound room, Alastair let go of her hand and stood aside. She'd hoped to get him to agree to find out the sex with her. As soon as the orderlies left them alone Halle turned to him. "Should we find out if it's a boy or girl? I told your Gram I'd wait to find out, but now I'm so excited to know."

"It's up to you." His clipped tone broke something inside of her.

"Damn it, Alastair, it's up to you, too. We're a family." She reached for him and he held her hand. Whatever he was going to say had to wait as the ultrasound technician entered.

"Evening, folks. Let me get my machine warmed up and as soon as we have an image I'll call the doctor in." The tech busied herself with the equipment and Halle watched Alastair, waited for him to respond.

"You'll feel the cold, slippery gel now." A squirt of the ultrasound paddle fluid was spread over her growing belly and Halle blinked back tears. Fine. She'd been on her own long enough. If Alastair wanted this arrangement to go back to strictly business, she'd do it.

"Here we go." The tech moved the paddle around on Halle's belly, which put pressure on her full bladder. She grimaced.

"Are you okay?" Alastair was right there, his hand again grasping hers, his face near enough to kiss.

"Fine. I just have to pee."

The tech smiled. "Sorry about that. A full bladder allows us to see the baby more clearly." She glided the paddle to a spot and then enlarged the screen. "See that? That's the heartbeat." She pointed, and then explained the various organs that Halle could only make out as shadows and shapes. "We're ready for the doctor in room three." The tech spoke into a mic attached to her smock.

"Do you want to know the sex?"

Halle sucked in a breath and took the biggest risk yet. She looked at Alastair. "Do we?"

"Why not?" He had his CEO game face on, staring at the screen.

"Here we go. Here are the legs," the tech droned on. Halle would look at the photos later. Right now the best show in the house was her husband's face. As they waited for the baby's sex to be revealed, his demeanor morphed from steely to tough, inquisitive to interested, and then, miraculously, to awe.

"Oh my God." His voice was husky, all masks dropped. But that wasn't what had Halle transfixed. It was the tear that wound its way down his cheek, over his chiseled jaw, and dripped onto their joined hands. "It's our baby, Halle."

"Yes."

He tore his eyes from the baby's image and looked at her. "Will you ever forgive me? Will you give me a second chance?"

"Forgive you? For not shooting at us and risking everything? There's nothing to forgive. You saved us. But I won't forgive you if you walk away from this."

"I could never leave you." His lips met hers in a tender, sweet caress that meant more than any legal documents or even their wedding vows. "I love you, Halle. You're not getting rid of me."

"It's mutual, Alastair."

A cough as the tech cleared her throat. "Um, would you like to know if it's a boy or a girl?"

They both startled, then laughed.

"It's up to my wife, but I'd sure like to know. Unless you still need incentive to make it through labor." North Sea blue eyes on her, lit with the same hope she felt blossoming in her heart.

"Are we sure we want to know?" Her voice came out as a whisper.

"Absolutely." He kissed her, and she wished they were alone. Except they did need an answer.

Tears ran down Halle's cheeks. Tears of joy, of the hope that burst open her heart as she'd never experienced.

Hope for the future. A future with Alastair.

"Here." Alastair placed a paper cup of tea in her hands the minute Halle exited the sheriff's conference room. It had been a long two weeks but she'd made her last statements, signed all the paperwork needed for the county DA to put Brannigan away for good. She sniffed the steaming liquid.

"What kind is this?"

"Lemon ginger. They have a surprisingly large assortment of herbal teas. And yes, I checked for any unsafe-for-pregnancy ingredients. And no, there weren't any." Alastair took the plastic bucket seat next to hers and put his arm around her shoulders as she sipped, her mouth dry after giving her report to the investigators. "How are you holding up?"

"Besides the Frankenstein bandages?" She referred to the butterfly wrappings that dotted her throat where Brannigan's knife had dug. "I'm good." Halle allowed herself to lean into Alastair. His strength, warmth and promise of tomorrow. Not that she needed that—oh, who was she kidding? She snorted.

"What's so funny?" He nestled his chin atop her head, pulling her closer.

"I thought the way we got together, then married, was unique, not to mention quick. But what's been incredible is how we've finally come together as a team and as husband and wife. When you think about it, a lot has happened over the past couple of months."

"Try the last two weeks." He'd already apologized and she wasn't going back to how poorly they'd both behaved.

"Why don't we do something a little different? As soon as we can, I'd like to have our closest friends and family over for a sex announcement party."

"Okay, you're losing me here—I think they know we've already had sex, Halle."

She fake-punched his shoulder. "You always have sex on the brain. No, a sex reveal party. Where we all find out the gender of the baby."

"Is it okay if my family comes?"

"Of course, but that's an awfully long way to come for a small get-together."

"They won't mind."

"You know what? With Christmas in two weeks, it will be a perfect time to do it. Can you have them come for the long weekend? Do they like roast beef or ham? Or is anyone vegan, gluten-free? Wait—where will we put them all?" Gram was down-to-earth enough, as were Alastair's parents, but still, she didn't think they'd fancy bunking it in the barn. They'd have to stay at a hotel in Austin when they visited.

"About that. I wanted to wait until we solved all of the drama, which apparently we have." He looked guilty.

"What is it?"

"I never want you to think I didn't tell you what's going on, ever again. My lawyers have assured me that SullaXS is directly linked to Brannigan and Livia Colton, and that they're going to have to relinquish the shares they gobbled up. The district attorney is forcing Brannigan's hand in exchange for a plea bargain against Livia Colton. My lawyers are weighing in and part of his plea bargain will be to sell the shares back to me. Once we catch Livia Colton."

"That's great news! And she will be caught." Halle kissed him but he still had a closed look on his face. As if he was afraid to tell her something else. "What is it, Alastair?"

"I took the liberty to hire an architect." At her widened eyes he held up his hands. "Don't worry—she's local and familiar with the kind of house you like."

"A new house? This is the only house I need."

"Of course it is. But as our family grows, I thought you might prefer something with modern conveniences. Especially when you come back from a trail ride."

"Go on."

"We can keep the ranch house as it is, and it can still be the center of your business. Or it can be converted to guest quarters. It's your call."

"You're right. I can't talk about this now." She spoke as Jimbo walked up and stood in front of them.

"The boss is happy with your statements, so you're both free to go."

"What about Brannigan?"

Jimbo's features were stamped with exhaustion. "He's going to be behind bars for a long while if I and the county judge have anything to do with it." He wiped his face with his huge hand. "We're close on the trail of Livia, too. I don't want you to worry about your safety anymore, Halle."

"How can she not when that crazy woman is still on the loose?" Alastair's voice was steady but the lethal note wasn't lost on Jimbo.

"I hear you, Alastair, and believe me, we're going to have her in custody sooner than later. Halle's not the only one with needed resolution from the crimes committed by Livia Colton."

Halle put her hand on Alastair's forearm. "He's right. She's hurt a lot of people in Shadow Creek."

"It stops now, Jimbo. Whatever assistance you need from me and my security detail, you've got it." Her Scotsman looked prepared to fight.

Jimbo nodded before letting a Texas-sized grin split his features. "We're always happy to accept donations for new equipment. We're hoping to start our own K-9 unit. As it is now, we rely on the K-9 in Austin."

"Don't waste any time, do you, Sheriff?" Alastair stood up and held out his hand to Jimbo. "I can't thank you enough for all you've done. The other night could have ended so differently without you and I'll never forget it."

Halle watched in fascination as her big, strong Scotsman spoke with such emotional intensity to another man.

Jimbo clasped Alastair's shoulder. "We're family around here, Alastair. You may be called on to do it for someone else in the future."

"Right." The men shook and Jimbo offered Halle a quick wave before he left.

Alastair held his hand out.

"Let's go home."

Halle gratefully placed her hand in his and allowed him to tug her to her feet. They left the sheriff's office arm in arm.

Just for today she wasn't going to stress about the fact that even though they seemed to have forged their bond in steel, there still remained the question of where Alastair would want her and the baby to live. He knew she wasn't going to give up Bluewood, but he'd said nothing about wanting to settle down in Shadow Creek.

Three weeks later

"Okay, everyone, you've survived your first American Christmas. Now are you ready for the grand reveal?" Alastair spoke as if he'd been to dozens of similar parties in the past, as if this were a matter of course.

The puzzled expressions on his parents' and grandmother's faces proved otherwise. Their friends Jeremy and Adeline, and Maggie and Thorne had shown up, making the event even more special.

"Halle?" Alastair looked to her expectantly.

"Here we go." She faced the small group, happy to see her best friend and her husband as well as Jimbo, a few of the ranch hands, and her aunt. "Please help yourselves to a cupcake, but don't bite into it yet." She walked around the room with a silver platter that she'd placed a doily on. A couple dozen cupcakes were stacked on it, the white creamy frosting in a perfect swirl, sprinkles of blue and pink dusted over them.

"These look too pretty to eat!" Gram was in awe of the perfect minicakes.

"Our bakery is the best. Folks come from Austin to get their wedding cakes made in Shadow Creek."

Halle handed out the cupcakes, all the while aware of Alastair's constant attention on her. He'd become quite the doting father-to-be since his admission that he'd fallen in love with her. Not that she minded.

"Okay, everyone. Now go ahead and bite into your cupcakes as Alastair and I cut the cake." She lifted the crystal-handled cake knife and moved next to Alastair. "Put your hand on mine."

"Are you ready for this?" His voice was cast low for her ears only.

She met his gaze. "Yes."

Alastair looked over his shoulder. "Okay, everyone. One, two, three!"

Together they sliced through frosting and a cake that was identical to the cupcakes, and sliced once again to be able to remove the piece. As the hue of the center of the cake came to light, Halle gasped and Alastair laughed.

"It's a boy!" Gram's shout could be heard all the way to the Rio Grande.

"Congratulations, darling." Alastair kissed her, sealing his love in the most public way since their wedding, which no family had attended. "May I do the honors?"

He meant announcing the name they'd agreed upon. She nodded, too choked up to verbally reply.

"In a few short months you'll all get to meet Ford Buchanan."

He turned back to her as the others exclaimed what a great name it was, incorporating both of their surnames.

"I have one more little surprise for you." His eyes twinkled and his grin was ear to ear.

"What on earth?" She shook her head. This man was constantly surprising her. He pulled out a cardboard mailing tube from under the table, hidden by the tablecloth.

"Everyone, while you're all enjoying the cake, I want you to share in my delight as I give Halle her wedding present from me, even if it's a little late."

"Alastair…"

"Just open it."

She snapped off the cover and pulled out a roll of

paper. Her breath caught as she unrolled the blueprint for a very large, but very *Bluewood*-style ranch house.

"Alastair." He was turning her into a regular leaky spigot. She brushed at her tears. "This is too much."

"I told you we're going to need a larger family house. One with guest rooms for my relatives to visit. And I need a place to declare residency so that I can become a US citizen."

She stared at him. His lips were moving and the crowd was applauding but she wasn't computing it all.

"You're staying here? In Shadow Creek? You have homes all over the planet and you want to make Bluewood your home?"

He gently took the scroll from her trembling hands and handed it to his father, who started to ooh and aah over the plans. His arms went around her growing waist and he pulled her in close.

"Bluewood is your home, Halle, and it will be the baby's, too. And since home for me is wherever you are, it's a done deal. If you'll have me."

"Forever."

* * * * *

If you enjoyed this suspenseful story,
don't miss the previous installments in the
COLTONS OF SHADOW CREEK *series:*

MISSION: COLTON JUSTICE by Jennifer Morey
CAPTURING A COLTON by C.J. Miller
THE COLTON MARINE by Lisa Childs
COLD CASE COLTON by Addison Fox
PREGNANT BY THE COLTON COWBOY
by Lara Lacombe
COLTON UNDERCOVER by Marie Ferrarella
COLTON'S SECRET SON by Carla Cassidy

All available now from
Mills & Boon Romantic Suspense!

And don't miss Geri Krotow's thrilling
SILVER VALLEY P.D. *romances:*

SECRET AGENT UNDER FIRE
HER SECRET CHRISTMAS AGENT
WEDDING TAKEDOWN
HER CHRISTMAS PROTECTOR

Available now from
Mills & Boon Romantic Suspense.

MILLS & BOON®

INTRIGUE
Romantic Suspense

A SEDUCTIVE COMBINATION OF DANGER AND DESIRE

A sneak peek at next month's titles...

In stores from 16th November 2017:

- **Always a Lawman** – Delores Fossen *and* **Redemption at Hawk's Landing** – Rita Herron
- **Military Grade Mistletoe** – Julie Miller *and* **Protector's Instinct** – Janie Crouch
- **Ms Demeanor** – Danica Winters *and* **The Deputy's Witness** – Tyler Anne Snell

Romantic Suspense

- **Special Agent Cowboy** – Regan Black *and* **The Marine's Christmas Case** – Lara Lacombe
- **Wyoming Undercover** – Karen Whiddon

Just can't wait?
Buy our books online before they hit the shops!
www.millsandboon.co.uk

Also available as eBooks.